25¢

Also by Edie Claire

Never Buried
Never Sorry

NEVER PREACH
PAST NOON

A Leigh Koslow Mystery

Edie Claire

A SIGNET BOOK

SIGNET
Published by New American Library, a division of
Penguin Putnam Inc., 375 Hudson Street,
New York, New York 10014, U.S.A.
Penguin Books Ltd, 27 Wrights Lane,
London W8 5TZ, England
Penguin Books Australia Ltd, Ringwood,
Victoria, Australia
Penguin Books Canada Ltd, 10 Alcorn Avenue,
Toronto, Ontario, Canada M4V 3B2
Penguin Books (N.Z.) Ltd, 182–190 Wairau Road,
Auckland 10, New Zealand

Penguin Books Ltd, Registered Offices:
Harmondsworth, Middlesex, England

First published by Signet, an imprint of New American Library,
a division of Penguin Putnam Inc.

First Printing, October 2000
10 9 8 7 6 5 4 3 2 1

For my parents, Jack and Pat,
who gave me my love of mysteries,
and who want you to know that
they are *not* like Randall and Frances
(except, of course, for my mom
and the clean-freak thing).

ACKNOWLEDGMENTS

First off, I would like to thank my editor, Joe Pittman, who is not only a fabulous editor, but an all-around great guy. I also owe continued thanks to Siri Jeffrey for her priceless wisdom of police procedure, and to Joe Jeffrey for his expertise in fraud investigation. Other individuals who selflessly lent their knowledge include Lawrence Caliguiri, M.D., Jan Barber, R.N., M.S.N., Ann Kinzler, Earl Marsh, and Tom Interval. And last but certainly not least, a special acknowledgment goes out to Reger's Asteroid Destiny, April 1987–July 1999, who will live on forever as the spirit of Mao Tse. I miss you, Aster.

Chapter 1

Deciding not to replace her recently deceased answering machine had seemed like a good idea at the time. Leigh Koslow was busy enough at her fledgling advertising agency without coming home to a message light that blinked like a neon sign in Vegas. Especially when half the calls were from some eager soul whose mission in life was to convince her that her fourth-floor apartment needed vinyl siding.

But the call-back-later plan had its disadvantages. One significant one, Leigh thought to herself as she buried her head under her pillow, was being awakened at midnight by an incessantly ringing phone.

Six rings. Seven rings. It was probably a wrong number. Who would be calling her this late on a Thursday night? Eight rings. But then again, it might not be a wrong number. It could be an emergency.

She forced herself upright and stumbled into the living room, where her telephone sat vibrating on a cheap end table. She shook her head and attempted to clear her throat. "Hello?"

There was a short pause on the other end, then a woman's voice, unfamiliar and uncertain. "Hello. Is this Leigh Koslow?"

Leigh's heart skipped a beat. So much for the wrong-number theory. "Yes, what is it?" she asked anxiously.

"This is Gretchen Cawley at Passavant Hospital.

We've had a patient brought into our E.R. who asked us to call you. Her name is Elizabeth Cogley."

Leigh swallowed, then took a deep breath. She sank down on one end of the couch, her legs shaking. "That's my aunt. Is she OK?"

Another pause. "Her condition is listed as fair," the woman said encouragingly. "I'm sure there's no reason for alarm, but it would be helpful if she had a family member here. Can you come down?"

"Of course," Leigh answered automatically. "What happened?"

"I'm sorry, but I don't know any details. You'll have to ask her yourself when you get here. All right?"

Suddenly feeling very cold, Leigh hung up the phone, ripped off the overlong T-shirt she'd been sleeping in, and pulled on a sweatshirt and jeans. She felt hideous, but knew she wouldn't be the first person to show up at Passavant with messy hair and bags under her eyes. She grabbed her wallet and coat, locked her apartment door, and started down the stairs.

When she got to the second floor, a strong impulse pulled her toward Warren Harmon's door. She wanted to tell him about Bess, to see if he could go with her. But she fought the urge. They were still just old pals, after all—he was under no obligation to help out with her family crises. She bit her lip and made her feet stay on a downward course. Work had been so crazy lately she'd neglected him even as a friend, and waking him up at midnight was no way to make up for it. She couldn't afford to tax his ordinarily abundant good nature, or things would never work out like she wanted.

The drive up McKnight Road was dark and cold, but the pavement was clear of snow, and there were hardly any other cars out. Such fantasy conditions on that hectic corridor would ordinarily excite any local, but Leigh couldn't be cheered. What on earth had happened to Bess? And what did "fair condition" mean, anyway?

Her fears did not abate when the E.R. desk informed her that her aunt had been admitted to the intermediate-care unit. Too antsy to wait for an elevator, Leigh located a stairwell and hastily climbed to the third floor. It was eerily quiet, and she could hear her heart pounding in her ears as she opened the door to the intermediate-care waiting area.

The small lobby was separated from the patient area by thick glass windows, through which she could see the woman she sought in a bed by the far wall. Bess Cogley, Leigh's mother's older sister and the self-proclaimed black sheep of the Morton clan, sat propped up on a series of pillows, her body consuming a large majority of the slim hospital bed. Despite the oxygen cannula in her nose and the various wires attached under her hospital gown, Bess looked much like her usual flamboyant self, and Leigh breathed a deep sigh of relief.

"Can I help you?" asked a nurse who had opened an adjoining window.

"I got a call about my aunt, Elizabeth Cogley," Leigh replied, still watching Bess. The older woman's modified beehive was intact, as always, and her cheeks were their usually ruddy hue, but her face seemed dirty. One heavily bandaged foot was propped up on a stack of extra pillows, and she seemed to be coughing. "I was told she needed a family member to come down. Can I see her?"

"One moment," the nurse answered.

Leigh took another deep breath. Bess didn't seem badly hurt. What could have happened? A car accident, maybe? Her attention wavered enough to notice that a man was standing near her aunt's bedside—a man who didn't look like a hospital employee. A new boyfriend, perhaps? Leigh watched the couple closely. The man was very attentive, and seemed to be speaking to Bess earnestly. Bess, oddly, was avoiding his eyes.

The nurse interrupted the scene, and the man nodded as if preparing to leave. Leigh watched as he placed a hand gently over one of Bess's hands. The patient just smiled stiffly and gave a cursory nod, and the man walked away. Leigh's brow furrowed. Perhaps he was more of an old boyfriend.

She watched as the man made his way back into the waiting area, then lifted a pair of dazzling green eyes to meet hers. His whole face lit up instantly, as if he'd been waiting his entire life for just such a moment. It was probably the same greeting he gave everybody, Leigh thought sensibly, but it certainly packed a wallop. He smiled and extended his hand, then retracted it quickly. It was covered with white bandages and, from the way he was holding it, seemed tender. He chuckled slightly and extended the other hand, smiling warmly. "I'm so sorry, but we'll have to do this backward. Do you mind?"

Leigh shook her head and extended her left hand, shaking his awkwardly. "I'm Reginald Humphrey, Bess's pastor friend. You must be her niece."

"Leigh Koslow," she offered. "It's nice to meet you. Thanks for coming." She studied the man carefully, wondering how he had gotten to Bess before she had. Was he a hospital chaplain? Last she heard, Bess didn't have a pastor. Not since the tiny Presbyterian church by her house had fallen on hard times and gone defunct.

"I'm afraid I have to get busy finding myself a place to stay, but you tell Bess I'll come see her again tomorrow. She's a plucky woman, your aunt!"

The pastor's eyes twinkled as he spoke. He was on the short side for a man, missing Leigh's own height by at least an inch. But he had a presence that was difficult to quantify. His face was weathered and lightly freckled, topped with a precisely trimmed crown of carrot-colored hair, and his light green eyes had an unusually piercing quality that gave the impression he could see into her soul. Yet despite his confident introduction, his clothes were rumpled, his face and neck were smudged with grime, and he smelled like a chimney sweep. "Plucky?" Leigh repeated, distracted. "Oh, yes, plucky. That's Bess for you."

Leigh stole a glance at her aunt, who was watching them from the bed, eyes anxious. An unsettling feeling brewed in Leigh's stomach—the feeling that Bess's anxiety was related more to this man than to her medical problems. "If you'll excuse me," she said politely, "I need to see her now."

"Of course you do," Humphrey said pleasantly. He reached for her left hand again, but this time he held it firmly. "If you need anything, you call me. Promise?"

Leigh smiled and nodded. Magnetic. That's what Reginald Humphrey was—and unnaturally so. She withdrew her hand, gave a small wave goodbye, and followed the nurse into the ward.

"Your aunt's a lucky woman!" the nurse said, depositing Leigh at her bedside. "You can stay a minute or two, no more. She needs her rest."

Bess made a visible effort to seem cheerful, but was clearly mortified with her patient status. Dependency was not in her program. "I'm sorry to drag you down here, kiddo," she said regretfully. "I wish they hadn't called you, but when I first got in I thought I'd need a ride home, and then—" Her face reddened as she broke into a spasm of heavy coughing.

The nurse returned instantly. "You're trying to talk too much," she admonished, fiddling with the oxygen machine. "You're going to have to write things down for a while." She produced a pad and pencil from a nearby cabinet and handed them to the patient, leaving only when Bess was breathing normally again.

"Take it easy, please," Leigh begged, sitting down on what little space she could find on the edge of the bed. A trail of her aunt's unnaturally auburn hair had escaped over her forehead, and Leigh pushed it gently back into place. "And stop apologizing. Of course you need someone here with you. Anyone would. What happened? And for heaven's sake, write—don't talk."

As Bess began scribbling, Leigh found herself thinking up more questions than Bess could possibly answer. Not the least of which was why she had called Leigh—rather than Leigh's mother or one of the other Morton siblings. Not that she didn't feel honored—she and Bess had always been good buddies. But it was odd, no doubt about it. And what was the deal with the pastor?

Bess turned the pad toward Leigh. *Ankle broken—needs surgery. Rest is smoke inhalation.* Leigh looked at her aunt in alarm. "Smoke! You had a house fire?"

Bess shook her head emphatically and began writing again. Leigh was relieved. Her aunt's house catching fire would be a terrible disaster, given its numerous furry occupants.

Fire in parsonage, Bess scribbled.

Leigh's eyes widened in understanding. So that was why the pastor was here, and why he had seemed so bedraggled. He had been in the fire too. She waited for more explanation, but Bess dropped her hand to her side and gave Leigh a loaded look instead.

"Okay," Leigh said speculatively, trying to pick up the gist. "So you were at the parsonage. With the pastor. At night. Check." It made sense—superficially at least. But then . . . when she'd seen the two of them together, Bess had hardly seemed enamored of the man. And when she'd seen that he was talking to Leigh, she'd almost looked panicked. What the heck was going on?

"Aunt Bess—" Leigh began, but the other woman shook her head and started scribbling again. She turned the pad around toward Leigh and gave her another emphatic look along with the message.

Our secret.

The words were underlined twice. Leigh sat back and let out a breath. This was weird and getting weirder by the minute. It wasn't Bess's reputation that was the issue—the fact that Bess lived life to its fullest had not been missed by her conservative family at any point in the last forty years, so it certainly didn't matter now. Perhaps the pastor was married? She had always steered clear of that sort of thing, at least.

Bess started scribbling again, and Leigh leaned over to read the pad. *Fell down* my *stairs. Cough—a bug. OK?*

Leigh sighed softly. She hated lying to people. Just because she was the only one in her family capable of keeping a secret didn't mean she was advertising for material.

"I want to help you, Aunt Bess," she said sincerely. "But you have to tell me what's going on. Lying to my mother has certain unpleasant consequences, and I can only be so witty at bending the truth. So you've got a new boyfriend, so what? Mom will get over it. She always does. And you know Lydie doesn't care. He seems like a nice enough man."

Bess shook her head fiercely, her eyes recapturing the same anxiety Leigh had seen before the pastor left. The words on the pad were written heavily. NOT MY BOYFRIEND!

"Time's up, I'm afraid," the nurse interrupted. Her body language brooked no dissent, and Leigh rose reluctantly. She had a feeling this mess couldn't be explained in broken phrases. Bess scribbled frantically, then held up the pad.

Bring clothes tomorrow—for release. Take others away—OK?

Leigh looked around, and Bess pointed at the small cabinet by her bedside. "Her things are all in a bag there," the nurse instructed after reading the pad herself. "You can take them if you want. But she'll need street clothes for discharge."

"When can I take her home?" Leigh asked, opening the cabinet.

"Not until after the doctor sees her tomorrow morning," the nurse answered shortly. "Call first."

Leigh pulled a very large, clear plastic bag out of the cabinet, and her eyebrows arched. Her aunt had a wider range of taste in clothing than most women in their sixties, but "biker chick" was definitely new to the menu. Black leather boots, black leggings, a black turtleneck shirt, and a huge black leather jacket were tumbled in together. No purse, no keys. She looked up at her aunt with several questions in her eyes, but Bess just smiled stiffly and wrote one more note.

You promised.

Chapter 2

Getting Bess out of Leigh's Cavalier proved even more difficult than getting her into it. The broken ankle was twice its normal size, and the bulky splint seemed only to increase Bess's odds of banging into something. Leigh tried to help by supporting her arm, but she grimaced as Leigh touched her.

"I'm sorry. You're bruised all over, I'm sure," Leigh said anxiously.

Her aunt waved off the concern with a weak smile. "I've felt worse." Between Leigh pulling on one arm and her anchoring the other against the roof of the car, she finally managed a stand. A one-footed stand, however.

"Here are your crutches," Leigh said, handing them over. "You've only got a few more feet now, then you can rest all day if you want." She had pulled the car right up to the front walk of Bess's old but nicely preserved farmhouse. It was a country charmer that had once actually been in the country, but now sat nestled in the midst of Franklin Park, one of Pittsburgh's more prestigious northern suburbs. And though developers had been drooling over her rolling ten acres of woods for years, Bess refused to sell. She had a thing about mature trees, and she refused to sacrifice any of hers for the sake of yet more new, unnecessarily opulent houses squeezed together on small, barren lots.

"You've fed everyone already?" Bess asked, making a gallant effort to hoist her unwieldy frame forward.

Leigh cringed but tried not to intercede. At least the walk wasn't icy. In Pittsburgh in January that was hardly a given. "Of course," she answered lightly. "Chester was a gentleman, as always, but the cats were frantic. I didn't think I could finish filling the bowls without needing a transfusion."

Bess chuckled. "What about Punkster? Did he behave?"

Leigh rolled her eyes at the reference to her aunt's most psychotic feline. Punkster's habit of attacking passersby made her own Mao Tse look sociable. "We have an understanding," she said soberly. "I don't come within four feet of him, and he doesn't try to kill me."

They reached the front door, and Leigh held it open. But instead of coming through, Bess paused a moment with her shoulder to the frame, breathing heavily. "Take your time," Leigh said quickly, letting the door close. "You don't want to start coughing again."

She watched as her aunt caught her breath. There had been nothing but small talk in the car, and Leigh hadn't wanted to push. But sooner or later she was darn well going to hear the story behind all this. She had arrived at the house earlier that morning to find nothing much amiss, but just enough to pique her curiosity. Like the fact that the television had been left on, along with several lights. And the fact that her aunt's blue plastic recyclables bin had been sitting on her front porch instead of by the detached garage with the other trash cans. Bess's car was in the garage, her purse and keys were on the hall table where she always kept them, and the front door was unlocked. So why had she been at a burning parsonage in the middle of the night, decked out for a spin on a Harley?

Bess pulled herself upright again, and Leigh opened

the door. Chester, Bess's primarily Pekinese, made an enthusiastic run for his master, but Leigh scooped him up handily. "Take it easy, pal. Let her sit down first, OK?"

The dog appeared offended but licked Leigh's hand anyway. Bess shuffled a few more feet to her couch, then dropped the crutches and plopped down with a sigh. "This may be harder than I thought," she admitted ruefully. "My armpits are killing me."

Leigh lowered Chester to the floor, and when his legs—which had been paddling from three feet down and counting—made contact, he was off like a shot.

"Hello, Chester, love." Bess smiled, pulling the dog into her lap. "Did you keep an eye on the family for me?"

The cats began to spiral en masse, several inching over to examine the swollen foot. Punkster, Leigh noted, was lounging on top of the television. Bess scratched all the cats she could reach. "I can't tell you how much I appreciate what you've done for me, kiddo," she said, turning to Leigh again. "Especially bringing these clothes for me. Er, by the way, where did you put the other ones?"

Leigh's eyebrows rose. "I hung the jacket up in the coat closet. The rest are in a laundry basket by the washer."

"In the hospital bag?" Bess asked quickly, her eyes anxious again.

"No, I threw that away," Leigh assured, just a little proud of her deviousness. "Now, perhaps you can tell me why—"

Her question was interrupted by the doorbell, and Bess jumped. "Oh, Lord. That isn't your mother, is it?"

Leigh walked over to peer through one of the narrow stained-glass windows that flanked the front door. The arrival of Frances Koslow had struck fear in her own heart many times, but Bess seemed unusually edgy. "No," she said, studying the figure as well as she could through a smooth blue pane. "It's a man."

Bess exhaled loudly, apparently in relief. "Good. Let him in, will you?"

Leigh opened the door. A slightly heavy, freckle-faced man in a modest suit and wool overcoat smiled pleasantly at her. "Hello, Ma'am. Jack Brugos, County Fire Marshall's Office. I'm here to speak with Ms. Cogley. Is she home?"

Leigh's stomach churned. The man's tone was pleasant enough, but after her experience the previous fall, the sight of any county crime-investigating sort tended to halt her digestion. She stared at him blankly for a moment before recovering. "Of course. I'm sorry. Won't you come in?" She stepped back and admitted the man into the room, where Bess greeted him warmly.

"Hello, Mr. Brugos. I'm sorry you made that trip to the hospital this morning for nothing. Those nasty doctors—they always come by when it's least convenient." She smiled flirtatiously.

"It's no problem, Ms. Cogley," he answered cheerfully, sitting in the recliner to which she had gestured. "I'm glad you're feeling well enough to be released. I know it's tough to take in a chest full of smoke like that."

Leigh's anxiety dwindled a little at the pleasantness of the exchange. It didn't sound like her aunt was in any sort of trouble. But then with Bess, one could never be sure.

"As I mentioned earlier," the man began, "we need to know anything you can tell us about what you saw last night."

"I'll be happy to help," Bess answered. "But can you tell me—I mean, do you know yet how the fire started?"

Brugos smiled patiently. "The final report isn't back yet. What would help us out is if you could walk me through what you remember from last night, step by step. Could you do that?"

Bess nodded, then swallowed. Leigh, who had settled herself next to Bess on the sofa, watched her aunt carefully. She looked perfectly at ease, but the swallow was a giveaway. It was a nervous habit, and Bess didn't get nervous over just anything.

"Let's start with the flickering light you said you saw out your window. Which window was that?"

Bess waved in the direction of her kitchen. "I was on the back porch, letting the cats in for the night."

"And what time was that?"

Bess hesitated but only slightly. "About ten-thirty, I guess. I'd just finished a *Golden Girls* rerun."

"Go on," he urged. "Tell me exactly what happened after you saw the light."

"Well," Bess began, sounding quite comfortable. "This forest separates my house from the backs of the buildings on Nicholson Road, as you can see. I can't see the church at all in the summer—I can't see ten feet past my back door. But last night I could see an orange light flickering through the tree trunks, and I knew it wasn't supposed to be there. To be honest, I didn't really think it was all the way over at the church. I thought maybe some kids had lit up a campfire in the woods. That's happened before, you know."

Brugos nodded politely and urged her on.

"So I threw on a coat and went out to see what was happening."

Leigh's brow furrowed. *A coat, indeed.* The black leather coat Bess had worn that night was clearly an archive from a past husband—hardly the first thing she'd reach for.

"You were still dressed?" he asked offhandedly. "That late?"

Bess chuckled. "I'm a night owl. What can I say?"

He grinned but said nothing. Leigh gritted her teeth.

"I was just going to walk out a little bit—till I could

see for sure what it was. Then I was going to call the police. But the closer I got, the farther away it seemed, and when I realized it was the parsonage I was already halfway through the woods. I just kept on running, and when I got to it I could tell that the fire was in a back room of the house. I ran around to the front door, and that part wasn't burning yet, so I opened the door and yelled inside."

Brugos interrupted her. "Could you stop here and describe the fire for me?" He asked several specific questions about the location of the flames and smoke, but Bess's careful recounting suddenly grew vague; she insisted she hadn't paid much attention. "Was anyone else at the scene when you arrived?" he continued.

"Not that I could tell," she answered. "When I saw Pastor Humphrey's car in the lot, I was afraid he was still inside. So I went in. I didn't see him downstairs, so I took a deep breath and ran upstairs." She paused and looked at the man—who was probably only a few years younger than she was—with feigned sheepishness. "I've been on the trustees committee many times, you see, so I knew where the master bedroom was."

Brugos just smiled.

"Thank God it wasn't in flames yet. I opened the door and found the reverend lying on top of his bed, his street clothes still on, dead to the world. I shook him and he woke right up—well, I was probably screaming at him too. We hustled back out of the house, or at least we tried to. Yours truly thought it would be fun to take the quick way down the stairs— which is a delicate way of saying I tripped over my own feet, tumbled the whole flight, and landed flat on my patoot. If the reverend hadn't helped me, I might never have made it back out."

Bess paused a moment, and so did Brugos. Finally he asked another question. "And how did the reverend burn his hand?"

"When he was helping me out," she answered. "The carpet had started burning along our path to the front door. He took off his jacket and pounded it as we went." She stopped and looked at the man. "Who reported the fire? Was it the Ivey sisters?"

He grinned a little. "No, apparently this all happened a little late for them. Although I understand they're regular little watchdogs for the Franklin Park Police."

Bess chuckled. "They have the number on their speed dial, you know."

"Actually, the fire was reported by a motorist with a cell phone," Brugos stated, folding up his notebook and rising. "You and your friend were very lucky. And I'd say he owes you no small amount of thanks, ma'am."

Bess never blushed, but she tried hard to fake it. "I didn't do anything. I'd still be at the bottom of the stairs if he hadn't helped me out, you know."

Brugos smiled and held out his right hand. Leigh watched her aunt's eyes dart quickly to his other one. A ring check? Bess smiled and returned a firm shake. "If there's anything else I can do, please let me know." Her smile suddenly faded. "But if you don't mind, could you call before you come? I, um, want to make sure I'm decent."

Brugos laughed. "No problem, Ms. Cogley." He and Leigh exchanged pleasantries, and he exited with a wave. When the sound of his car's engine had faded, Bess sighed dramatically. "Married. The cute ones always are, you know."

Leigh didn't comment. She walked over to the recliner he had just vacated and sat down, leaning forward. It was her turn. "Night owl, eh?"

Bess smiled tightly. "I do stay up late occasionally, kiddo. I'm not out to pasture yet."

Leigh looked straight into her aunt's eyes, which

quickly looked the other way. It was a telltale sign—
one of many.

"I don't suppose you could make us some tea, could
you?" Bess asked casually, pulling a nearby cat into
her lap. The cat protested, but she held it closer.

Leigh had no intention of being distracted. "Do you
always wear black leather boots while watching
Golden Girls reruns in your living room, or was last
night a special occasion?"

Bess looked back at her tiredly. "I do a lot of things
you don't know about, kiddo." She released the cat,
which jumped off her lap and onto the couch, only to
change its mind and circle back again.

"Listen, Aunt Bess," Leigh said slowly, trying to
sound patient. "I don't mean to pry into your personal
life or anything, but I do think I know you a little
better than our friend Mr. Brugos—"

"More's the pity," Bess interrupted, grinning evilly.

Leigh tried not to smile. "And I'd bet my last Her-
shey bar that every word you told that man just now
was a fat, stinking lie. And if you think for one minute
that—"

The statement was interrupted by the simultaneous
sounds of a ringing doorbell and opening door. Within
a second, the hurricane that was Frances Koslow had
swept into the room. "Well, Bess, you weren't kidding,
were you?" she exclaimed, her eyes zoning in on her
sister's foot. "Though how you could break an ankle
just puttering around your own house, I have no
idea."

Leigh and Bess looked at each other and shared a
sigh. Leigh's of frustration, Bess's of going from the
frying pan to the fire. "I told you on the phone already, Francie," Bess answered reluctantly. "I fell
down the stairs. It hurts like the devil, by the way."

"Well, of course it does!" Frances affirmed, remov-
ing her coat and gloves. "Did you think it wouldn't?"

Leigh couldn't help but grin. Her mother and Bess

were really quite fond of one another, but the constant trading of barbs was a long-standing sisterly ritual. Frances hung up her coat and walked in front of the television set, which was a mistake.

As Punkster flew from his perch with paws outstretched and mouth open, Leigh and Bess both shouted a warning. But it didn't prove necessary. Frances hardly flinched as she intercepted the cat at hip level and caught it neatly by the scruff. "I don't know why you keep this creature," she said with disdain, depositing him on the back porch.

"And you!" she said, turning on her daughter without missing a beat, "should be at work. I told Bess I would pick her up at the hospital, but she said you were on the way already. It was nice of you to come, Leigh, but I'll handle things from here. The last thing you need is to lose another j—"

"No problem, Mom. I'm gone!" Leigh said, rising quickly. She had had enough surprises for one morning—Bess could have at least clued her in on the changing of the guard. She had planned on skipping work to help her aunt get adjusted, but three was a crowd, and her mother was better at that sort of thing anyway.

"I'll be working out the care schedule soon," Frances continued, brushing cat hair off the coffee table as she talked. "Leigh, we may need you to stay over Saturday night. Lydie has a class, and your father and I are going to a benefit."

Leigh stole a glance at Bess, whose eyes were filled with an uncomfortable mixture of resolve and regret. She would have trouble getting around for a while, there was no doubt about it. The crutches would take some getting used to—and she was still sore all over from the fall. Being a patient to Leigh's overzealous mother would be brutal, but Frances was the only Morton woman who wasn't gainfully employed. "Sure,

Mom," Leigh said quickly, bestowing a sympathetic glance on her aunt as she left. "I'd love to."

Leigh was exhausted, as usual, when she finally knocked off work at Hook, Inc., the fledgling ad agency she had helped to conceive after her last unfounded layoff. But this Friday there was a spring in her step. Business had been great the last few months—more than they could have hoped for. Still, the twelve-hour workdays that came with it had been wearing on them all, and after they had finished a particularly huge project on Wednesday, she'd made the decision to take her week's vacation ASAP. She had wanted to wait until spring, when she theoretically might have enough money to go somewhere, but as the weeks wore on, that fantasy seemed less and less likely, while the idea of vegetating for a week now seemed more and more appealing. At least it was cheaper. Today she had managed to tie up the last of the annoying loose ends on her plate, which meant her long-awaited week of R and R had finally begun.

Her first project, she resolved as she drove toward her apartment building, would be getting her act together where Warren was concerned. She hadn't been able to get him off her mind for months, and yet she'd hardly seen him. Somehow there was always one more job to be done at Hook—and besides, there was *that thing*. Her feelings about him were all over the board, and if she wasn't careful, he'd pick up on them prematurely. Then what would she do? The car of her attractive ex-lawyer, Katharine Bower, had been a regular visitor in the parking lot for a while now. She had to find out exactly where things stood—or she'd be setting herself up for a major fall.

Her second project, which had been driving her bonkers all day, was to find out what had possessed her normally law-abiding aunt to falsify a statement to the fire investigator. That project, however, would have to wait until Sergeant Frances was no longer hovering around.

First things first.

She knocked on Warren's door with just a touch of anxiety. Not that she hadn't knocked on his door for no particular reason countless times before. They'd had a carefree, comfortable, completely platonic thing going ever since college—twelve years total. It was only after she had moved into his apartment building last summer that things had started getting confusing. Having someone around on a twenty-four-hour basis to share donuts, Chinese food, and Simpsons reruns had been more of a bonus than she'd expected. In fact, it had screwed up her thinking entirely. That— and the way he'd been looking at Katharine Bower.

Was Katharine there now? Several seconds passed with no response to her knocking. Leigh was just about to give up and walk away when she heard footsteps.

The door opened to reveal the surprised face of Warren J. Harmon III, whose political ambitions had earned him the college nickname of "future president of the United States." He was now the Allegheny County register of wills, which wasn't too shabby for a self-made man of thirty. "Excuse me," he said formally, a smile playing on his lips. "Do I know you?"

Leigh grinned and pushed her way around him and inside. "Yeah, all right, I know. I've been a lousy friend. I owe you about six dinners and fifteen Simpsons episodes. I'm sorry, but you know how insane things have been at Hook. There's finally a light at the end of the tunnel, though. . . . I'm taking next week off."

"Excellent." He smiled, pulling a can of Diet Coke from his neatly organized refrigerator. "Let's celebrate. So what are you going to do with yourself? Start that novel again?"

Leigh took the Coke gratefully, then scoffed. "Are you kidding?" she asked, collapsing onto his couch. "For the next nine days I don't even want to *see* a keyboard. I'm going to do nothing. Absolutely nothing."

She wondered for a moment whether that was a lie. She was going to do several things, one of which was to quit living in limbo where he was concerned.

"Nothing sounds good," Warren agreed, dropping down beside her with a Dr Pepper in hand. "Wish I could join you. Unfortunately, I'm buried at the moment with groundwork for my county council campaign. Plus, I've got a family wedding next week."

The sigh accompanying his last statement was slight, but Leigh caught it. "Say no more," she said sympathetically. She knew how good weddings were at bringing out a family's dark side. Her cousin Cara's had nearly killed them all. "Who's getting married?"

"Joy," he answered, his voice turning affectionate.

Leigh smiled. She'd never met Joy, but she knew that Warren thought of her more as a little sister than as a cousin. Her mother had died when she was a child, and Warren's mother had assumed the role as best she could. Joy had even lived with the Harmons for a while, presumably because her father had some emotional problems.

"I like the guy she's marrying," he continued. "Nice fellow, Tim. Smart, treats her right."

Leigh sensed a "but," and said so.

"But Joy's father is a nutcase," he said with concern. "He's got a good heart, but he gets too wound up about things, and he doesn't do well with ceremonious occasions. My mother has pretty much taken over the wedding plans herself."

He paused, and Leigh prompted again. "But—"

"But the wedding's Tuesday night, and my parents are still in Florida. They were supposed to fly back this weekend, but my father has the flu. If he doesn't rebound in a day or two, they'll miss the wedding, which would be a sad turn of events on two counts.

First, because my mother loves Joy like a daughter and really wants to be there. And second, because other than her, the only one in the family who has a chance at keeping my uncle from going off the deep end is me."

From the look on Warren's face, it was hardly a challenge he looked forward to. "I was on the phone with my mother just now when you knocked," he said tiredly. "Everyone's in a tizzy because the church parsonage burned down last night."

Leigh sat up, instantly alert. "The parsonage burned? What church?"

Warren's eyebrows rose at her sudden show of interest. "Little independent outfit—out on Nicholson Road. 'First Church of the New Millennium.'" He chuckled. "If you can believe a name like that."

Leigh sat stiffly, thinking. "What exactly did you hear about the fire?"

Warren studied her face, which meant he was trying to read her mind. He was disturbingly good at it, and today was no exception. He knew, for example, that he wasn't going to get any explanation for her interest until she had heard what she wanted to hear.

"The pastor was at home, but he wasn't hurt badly. A neighbor helped get him out. The house is gone, but it wasn't much of a loss, from what I understand. The real issue for my irrational uncle is whether the fire will make the church off-limits for the wedding next week, and it appears not. The parsonage was fifty yards or so from the main building."

"Do they know how the fire started?" Leigh asked, choosing her words carefully.

"I haven't heard. Why?"

She ground her teeth, as she always did when thinking hard. What had really happened at that parsonage last night? And why was her aunt trying to cover it up? One thing was evident—at least Bess and the pastor had been telling the same story.

"I repeat," Warren interrupted, "why do you want to know?"

Leigh looked up at him—and suddenly forgot what she'd been thinking about. This was the kind of thing that had been plaguing her. He was the same Warren she'd met in freshman volleyball at the University of Pittsburgh—but then again, he wasn't. That Warren had been tall, gawky, uncoordinated, and in need of Clearasil. And though she had enjoyed his company immensely, she'd never been attracted to him. This Warren was tall, sophisticated, successful, and all of a sudden—seriously tempting.

Get a grip, woman.

She averted her eyes and tried to remember what they were talking about. Mercifully, it came back to her. "I can't explain, not just yet," she said quickly. "I promised somebody I'd keep my mouth shut. Suffice to say that your crazy family and my crazy family may already know each other."

His eyebrows rose. "Now, that's a scary thought."

She laughed. "Tell me about it."

Chapter 3

When Leigh approached the front door of her aunt's farmhouse late Saturday afternoon, she was not in a particularly good mood. Partly because she'd spent half the day scrubbing her shower with Tilex and the other half wiping up kitchen grime. But mostly because she'd hoped to spend the day with Warren, and he'd had other obligations.

Other obligations. And he wouldn't even tell her what—a very bad sign.

She sighed to herself and stretched out an arm to open Bess's door, but the door came out to meet her instead, followed closely by an agitated-looking Frances Koslow.

"You can go in in a minute," Frances said shortly, grabbing her daughter's arm and propelling her back onto the front walk. "First, we need to talk."

Leigh resigned herself to the inevitable. "About what?" she asked innocently.

Frances let out a frustrated breath. "About your aunt, of course. She's not telling me the whole truth about this accident. Yesterday she insisted she fell down her own stairs, then it's all over the TV news and the papers that she's a hero for dragging a man out of a fire. We both know perfectly well that Bess isn't capable of modesty. There's something fishy going on with her, and I intend to find out what it is. What did she tell you?"

Leigh bit her lip. What her mother said was true. If

Bess had actually saved someone from a fire, she'd probably be calling the local news stations herself, offering interviews and distributing autographed pics. "She didn't say much," Leigh answered honestly. "We haven't really had a chance to talk about it."

Frances humphed. "Well, I've had plenty of time with her, and it hasn't accomplished a thing. That woman is as stubborn as a mule." Frances's voice trailed off as her eyes lit up with inspiration. Wanting no part in whatever scheme her mother was concocting, Leigh moved slowly toward the house. It was a fruitless effort—she'd only gone a few inches before her mother's hand had clamped back down on her arm.

"*You* can get her talking," Frances ordered. "She's always been loose-lipped with you. Find out what's she's hiding. And do it soon, or God only knows what will happen."

"I'll take good care of her," Leigh answered, forcing a smile.

Frances frowned. It was the look she always got when she suspected her daughter was duping her, but couldn't prove it. She released Leigh's arm, straightened her coat, and hiked her purse up higher on her shoulder. "Lydie will come relieve you as soon as church is over tomorrow. Don't let Bess go up the stairs on any pretense or she'll kill herself. And don't go driving all over town with her either—her lungs can't take it."

"Got it, Mom," Leigh said, inching away again.

"And, Leigh," Frances said sternly, her eyes fixing on her daughter like cruise missiles ready for launch. "We'll talk more tomorrow."

At the sound of Frances's Taurus revving up for departure, Leigh and her aunt shared another sigh. Bess wasn't looking so good this morning. In fact, she looked awful. "Bad night?" Leigh asked, concerned.

Bess rolled her eyes in an exaggerated motion—one of several honed to perfection during her years in community theater. "Your mother is an angel—and Satan incarnate."

Leigh suppressed a smile as she looked around the living room. Since Frances's arrival yesterday morning, a transformation had occurred. The house was now spotlessly clean, without so much as a cat hair in sight, much less a cat. Bess's entourage of potted plants, animal figurines, and food and water dishes were missing from the floor, and the furniture had been rearranged with wide aisles connecting the living room, kitchen, and bathroom. The carefully stacked pillows and blankets on the coffee table gave evidence that Bess had been sleeping on the sofabed, and the air—which normally carried the faint mingled scents of antique wood and cat litter—reeked of Pine Sol.

"You must admit," Leigh said playfully. "It is practical."

Bess glared. "Francie's been waiting for years to get her paws on my dust. Now I haven't a clue where anything is, and the pets are all out freezing to death on the porch. Let them in, would you?"

Hoping that Frances would not be returning unannounced, Leigh did as she was bid. The "porch" was actually a bright, semi-heated sun room with large, louvered-glass and screened windows, and only a few of the cats (Punkster thankfully not among them) wanted in. Chester, on the other hand, could not return to Bess's lap fast enough.

A teakettle began whistling as Leigh made her way back through the kitchen, and she smiled. Frances had set out two cups with tea bags—St. James, no less. Leigh poured the water with a grin. Her mother did have her moments. Tea was just the ticket for a relaxing—and enlightening—conversation.

When the tea had cooled enough to be drinkable, Leigh settled herself next to Bess on the couch and

started the interrogation as innocently as possible.
"You remember my friend Warren, don't you?"

Bess smiled. "Warren Harmon III, future president
of the United States? Of course, dear. I voted for him
for register of wills. I'll vote for him for president too,
if I ever get a chance. What about him?"

The last question was delivered with an insinuating
tone that Leigh didn't miss, but chose to ignore. "He
told me that his cousin is getting married next week.
Oddly enough, she's being married in the First Church
of the New Millennium, where your pastor friend is
from. Small world, eh?"

Bess paled slightly. "I never said he was my friend."

"He did. The night I met him at the hospital."

"What else did he say?" Bess's eyes had widened,
and Leigh started to feel guilty again. Bess was a
pretty together lady, but this person, whoever he was,
really had her rattled.

"Nothing really," she answered soothingly. "He just
introduced himself, and said he had to run because he
needed to find another place to stay. In retrospect, I
understand why."

Bess ground her teeth on one side. "Frances found
out about the fire. I should have known she would—
I just didn't think about it. I thought I could keep
everything quiet, but that was pointless. I just can't
have her nebby little nose mixed up in all this!"

Leigh set down her tea and leaned forward. She was
getting more and more worried. Bess was not above
getting into a tizzy over life's little annoyances, but
she wasn't the fearful type. This whole thing was really
eating at her. "Aunt Bess," she asked gently, "what
is it you're afraid of?"

The older woman stared down at her hands and
continued grinding her teeth.

"Just tell me," Leigh urged. "Maybe I can help."

After a long moment, Bess exhaled loudly. "All
right. But you have to swear to me that you won't

go blabbing all this to Frances, or Lydie, or anyone, understand? It could ruin everything."

"I'll do my best," Leigh promised.

"Just tell your mother that I said whatever happened is my life and it's nobody else's business? OK? It'll even be true. 'It's my life and nobody else's business!' "

Leigh grinned. "Check."

Bess took a long swig of tea and began. "I've been going to the First Church of the New Millennium for a while now, but I haven't told anyone in the family about it because I didn't want to hear your mother lecture me about what wackos they are."

Leigh's brow furrowed. Bess had always been, if not an exemplary Presbyterian, a very discerning person. She wasn't the type to shell out for an overpriced warrantee or buy into the health claims of the latest dietary supplement. She knew when she was being sold, and she rarely got taken. All in all, she seemed an unlikely candidate for a charismatic religious movement. Perhaps the First Church of the New Millennium was more legitimate than it sounded?

"Why would anyone think they were wackos?" Leigh asked carefully, taking a sip.

Bess humphed. "Because they're outside the box. Because they don't cling to any of your standard boilerplate Protestant theologies. Ergo, they must be nuts, right?"

Leigh took another sip of tea in lieu of answering. Her aunt's brand of sarcasm was hard to decipher sometimes, and she didn't want to make a translation error. "But you went to the church because . . ."

"Because of the Presby people, of course. And because of Reginald Humphrey. If that's even his name—which I doubt."

Leigh was getting more confused, not less. Bess went on.

"You know what happened to my old church,

Franklin Presbyterian—I'd been a member there almost as long as you've been alive. We had three duds
in a row for pastors, all our young people defected,
and at the end we were left with forty or so old fogies
who didn't want to support the church on their own.
We met and discussed and met and discussed, and
finally decided to disband and throw our support elsewhere. The church buildings went up for sale, and
this brand-new group—the First Church of the New
Millennium—bought them for a song, thanks to *his*
powers of persuasion."

Bess paused and took another swig of tea. Leigh
wanted to urge her on but refrained. Bess's stories
were always high drama—if you tried to skip the the-
atrics, the curtain came down.

"He visited each and every former member of Presby, even brought flowers and candy to the widow
women. He went on and on about how bad he felt
about Presby losing its young people, and how his
congregation had the opposite problem—they were a
group of young, enthusiastic Christians who needed
the wisdom of an older generation to guide them."

Leigh's eyebrows rose. "That's a heck of a pitch,"
she admitted.

Bess sighed. "Yes, it was. As I said, he was quite
persuasive. So, a few at a time, people started coming
back to the building. After all, many of them still felt
like it was *their* church. Only now it was alive again.

"The 'First Churchers' seemed like nice enough
people, and they welcomed the Presby folks with open
arms. But from the first time I met Reginald Humphrey, I couldn't shake the feeling . . ." She paused
again. "Well, let's just say a little warning buzzer went
off in the back of my head. Only at the time I wasn't
sure why. His theology wasn't too far out of the mainstream, even if it was hopelessly vague. And he oozed
so much charm no one seemed to care. The people
were all so energetic, so excited to have a real church

building. Apparently they'd started out in Cranberry by meeting in people's homes, then they rented space. Now they've got almost two hundred members, and they're still growing strong."

Bess's eyes turned wistful. "There's something terribly appealing about being needed, you know. And they certainly knew how to make the old Presby crowd feel needed. The others kept asking me what I thought—I'm the ringleader of that crowd, you know—and I told them I couldn't see anything wrong with the church's mission, which I couldn't. So we all kept going back, and by the time I realized what the little alarm bell had been clanging about, it was too late."

"Too late?" Leigh asked. "Did something happen?"

"Not yet," Bess replied uncertainly. "But something will. Right now Humphrey *is* the First Church of the New Millennium. That's why I couldn't let it go."

Leigh was lost again. "Let what go?"

"Him, of course!" Bess's voice rose. "That man wants something from them—money, power, their firstborns . . . I'm still not sure exactly what. But the Reverend Reginald Humphrey is a class-one, grade-A con artist. I'd stake my life on it."

She drew in a quick breath, then dropped her voice to a whisper. "And unfortunately, I think I might have."

Leigh sat for a moment, blinking at her aunt stupidly. The last line sounded ominous, but since all the women in her family were consummate exaggerators, she didn't take it too seriously. Bess's feelings about the church and the pastor were getting clearer, but unless she had missed something, there was still a big black question mark hanging over the parsonage fire. Not to mention the biker outfit.

Before she could formulate more questions, Bess started to struggle up. "Don't!" Leigh protested. "Whatever you need, I'll get it."

But Bess waved her concern away and carefully positioned her crutches. "I'm not an invalid, although I would be if I had to spend another day with your mother." She hoisted herself forward and began making progress toward an antique rolltop desk. Stopping in front of it, she opened a drawer, pulled out a yellowed envelope, and laboriously turned herself around. Leigh resisted the urge to help her. If she herself were on crutches, she doubted she'd want help either.

Bess made it back to the sofa and dropped down with a grunt. "Here," she said, extending the envelope to Leigh. "Open that, and you'll see."

Leigh finished her tea and set down the cup, then took the envelope and flipped it over. It was postmarked Fort Jackson, South Carolina, and dated April 13, 1952. She looked at her aunt questioningly. It was a sad story in the Morton family—Bess had married for the first time at eighteen, and had been widowed the same year. The letter must have been written from her young husband's basic training camp—perhaps one of the last he wrote before heading off to a tragically short stint in Korea.

"Open it," Bess encouraged. "It's all right."

Leigh extracted the folded yellow paper carefully. A black-and-white photograph was nestled inside.

"I have better shots of Dan," Bess said fondly. "I don't like to remember him as a soldier, so I've never had this one framed. But I've spent countless hours staring at it. Look at it carefully. Go ahead."

Leigh peered at a moment in time a half century before, when six teenage boys in army duds had huddled together to mug for a picture. They must have been only weeks away from an uncertain future in a foreign war, but there was no trace of anxiety on their faces at this moment. They were all laughing heartily, and Leigh couldn't help but wonder what the joke had been.

"Can you pick out Dan?" Bess asked, her voice optimistic.

Leigh pointed at the heaviest of the four, a boy with a stubby nose and toothy smile whose face had decorated her aunt's piano for decades.

"That's right," Bess said with a smile. "Now, who else do you recognize?"

Leigh studied the other faces, but none seemed particularly familiar. It was only on the second pass that she stopped over the image of a short boy with a freckled nose and wicked grin. It was the same engaging smile that had greeted her Thursday night in the intermediate-care ward. "Oh, my God," she whispered. "It couldn't be. Could it?"

Bess's eyes twinkled. "And why not? He's the right age. There's more—look on the back."

Leigh flipped over the picture and tried to decipher the smudged ink. Dan had labeled his buddies by their nicknames, with a little comment about each. Her eyes skimmed over "Jelly Roll," "DoDo," and "Tooter" and went quickly to the words describing the short boy. *"Money"—who'll swindle the Reds down to their skivvies.*

Bess let the implication sink in for a minute. "Now do you see why I'm convinced Reverend Humphrey is a fake? There's more about 'Money' in another letter. Dan says he was quite an accomplished con, and was always in trouble with their sergeant. He hadn't cheated any of the boys in their unit, though—apparently he wasn't that stupid."

Leigh considered a moment, then folded the picture back into the letter and replaced it in the envelope. "It could be him, Aunt Bess," she admitted. "But even if it is, it was an awfully long time ago. He could have changed."

Bess looked at her niece with disappointment. "Oh, please. You mean maybe he 'found religion?' Hogwash. Once a con, always a con. These people's brains are wired wrong or something."

The theological backing for such a statement was questionable, but Leigh knew better than to take her aunt to task over it. "All right. So you're convinced Reginald Humphrey is a con artist. Why haven't you tried to expose him?"

Bess narrowed her eyes. "I *have*, of course! I've been working on it for weeks. But it's not as easy as just calling the police. I have no proof. And what's worse, the congregation really believes in him. There's no doubt the young folks would take his side over mine, if it came to that. Even the Presby folks who were hesitant at first have swallowed up his spiel hook, line, and sinker. I have to have irrefutable evidence that he's cheating them in some way. And in order to get it, I have to keep playing along. The trouble is, every day I can't get evidence is another day the whole situation is getting worse. And frankly, I've gotten a little desperate."

Leigh looked at her aunt thoughtfully. Bess was a woman of passion—a woman who thrived not only on joining crusades but on staying with them to the end. This was a woman who still had hopes for the ERA amendment. No way was she giving up on the salvation of the First Church of the New Millennium.

The contents of the hospital garment bag flashed again across Leigh's mind. The serviceable black boots, the leggings, the turtleneck. All items Bess might normally wear—just not together. The leather jacket, Leigh realized, hadn't completed the ensemble because it cut the wind on the open road. It fit because it was black.

Her aunt hadn't meant to be a biker chick after all. She had meant to be a burglar.

Chapter 4

"Aunt Bess," Leigh asked slowly, afraid of the answer. "Please tell me you didn't break into the parsonage Thursday night."

Bess just looked at her.

Leigh sighed. "Of course you did. You were looking for evidence. Evidence that Humphrey was a con."

Bess touched a finger to her nose and grinned. "You *have* got a devious mind, kiddo. I like that in a niece."

Leigh sighed louder. "But, Aunt Bess! Breaking and entering is a felony—at least I think it is."

"It wasn't *really* breaking and entering," Bess wheedled. "As it so happens, I had a key, and the parsonage is the property of the congregation, not the pastor. Still, you're right—if Humphrey kicked up a fuss, I could be in some trouble."

Leigh shook her head. "Some trouble" was a place she had visited before, and she had no desire to return. "Well, as long as he doesn't find out what you were really doing there, I guess there's no harm done." The words weren't even out of her mouth before she remembered the fire. "Oh, my God. The fire. You didn't—I mean—was it an—"

Bess drew her back up straight. "I'm going to assume you're asking me if I started the fire by accident. Well, naturally not. I have no idea what started the fire. I couldn't see a blasted thing from that accursed attic."

Leigh was beginning to think that getting through

this conversation would require a lot more tea. Perhaps something stronger. But somehow she couldn't seem to move. Instead, she sputtered out the obvious question. "The attic?"

Bess nodded grimly. "It's not like I planned it that way. Humphrey was supposed to be at the men's Bible study. They meet every Thursday night in members' homes, and they usually stay till around ten. I was going to sneak in the parsonage around nine—I figured the Iveys would be going to bed around then."

"The who?" Leigh asked.

"Betty and Louise Ivey," Bess answered with a sigh. "The definition of busybodies. They're both in their early eighties—nice women at heart, but experts at making trouble. They live across the road from the church, and their living room looks right out on the parking lot and the parsonage. For years they've loved nothing better than to spy on the pastor and whoever's coming and going. They even installed a big picture window about ten years ago." Her eyes narrowed. "It was their meddling that made Pastor Morley leave back in the late eighties. She was young and single, and they suspected she was fooling around at the parsonage, which was none of their business even if she was. But the church never recovered."

Leigh tried to drag Bess back to the present day. "So you went to the parsonage late, so the Ivey sisters wouldn't see you?"

Bess nodded. "I don't think they did, either. I used a dim flashlight just in case." She smiled to herself. "I even left the TV and lights on over here, so anyone who drove by would assume I was home. But I guess you already know that, don't you?"

Leigh nodded. That explained one odd thing she'd noticed this morning, at least. "So why did you put your recyclables bin right next to the front door?" she asked, remembering the other. "I put it back by the garage, by the way."

Bess's eyebrows arched. "I didn't put it anywhere—maybe the trash men moved it." She took a swig of tea and continued with her story. "I'm not sure exactly what I was looking for at the parsonage, to be honest. Maybe some identification. I didn't find much of anything. The parsonage is full of old, donated furniture, and there was a desk, but it didn't look like Humphrey used it. The one in his church office is much better." Her eyes drifted off as her thoughts wandered. "That's where I really need to look . . ."

"Aunt Bess!" Leigh chided. "Don't even think about it. Now, how did you end up in the attic?"

"I'm getting to that," the older woman answered, lowering her chin. "Be patient. I looked around the living room and kitchen, and couldn't find anything interesting. Not many personal items, just some framed pictures of him and his wife."

"He's married?" Leigh asked, surprised. "Where was his wife during the fire?"

Bess scoffed. "Where is she, period? Zaire, Zimbabwe . . . some Z place. He says his wife is a foreign missionary, and that as much as it pains them, their calling is to live apart. No one at the church has ever met her."

Leigh's eyebrows rose. "Sounds a little fishy to me."

"I don't think she exists," Bess announced. "I think she's a scam too, to protect him from the attentions of his parishioners. And to make him look like a family man. At least there are no fake children in the package. Could you make more tea?"

Leigh started at the quick change of topic, then complied. She gathered their cups and went back to the kitchen to heat more water. She kept waiting for Bess to go on, but her aunt seemed intent on delaying the good part of the story. After the stove was turned on, Leigh returned to her chair. "So you went to the attic to see if he had personal items stored up there?"

Bess sighed. "Not exactly. I was searching the upstairs—and still finding nothing—when I heard a car door slam. I shut off my flashlight and went to the window in the master bedroom, and sure enough, it was him. Home way early. He was already opening the front door, so I couldn't go back down the stairs. I started to panic, and then I remembered that the door to the attic was in the master bedroom closet. He came straight up the stairs to the bedroom—I barely had time to get through the panel and reset it before he opened the closet door. I guess he was changing clothes. I sat there squatting on the steps for a long time, and then I thought I heard him leave. My legs were killing me, so I climbed the rest of the way up and sat down in the attic. It was freezing up there, and filthy. I felt like a complete dolt."

Leigh wisely decided not to comment, and Bess continued.

"I kept listening for him to come back to the bedroom. My only chance to get out without him catching me was just to wait until he fell asleep. I didn't hear much, a door opening and shutting now and then, but I was pretty sure he wasn't in bed yet. It seemed like ages passed. I was cold and stiff and getting annoyed. I was about to bag the whole thing and confess when I heard the glass shatter.

"Glass?" Leigh asked. The teakettle whistled, and she rose to pour the water. As soon as the cups were full she hightailed it back to her chair. "What glass?"

Bess shook her head in disgust. "Darned if I know. But glass broke, and then another door slammed. A few seconds later I smelled smoke, and that was that. I was getting the heck out of there." She paused again. "Is the tea ready?"

"No," Leigh answered as quickly as possible. "How did you get out?"

Bess threw a look toward the kitchen as if doubting her niece's word, but kept talking anyway. "I climbed down the ladder, moved the panel, and hightailed it for the stairs. When I got to them, I could see that the downstairs was on fire—there were no flames at the foot of the stairs, but I could see light flickering on the walls, and I could feel the heat. I'm not proud of it, mind you, but I panicked. That's all there was to it. I started down those stairs like a bat out of hell and wound up at the bottom like Humpty Dumpty."

Bess gestured toward the kitchen, and Leigh jumped up. She grabbed Bess's cup and carried it as quickly as she could without burning herself. Then she carried it a little quicker.

"Ouch!" she cursed under her breath, dropping the cup onto Bess's saucer and dabbing the burning liquid from her wrist.

Bess was neither sympathetic nor critical. "I'm glad I'm not the only clumsy one in the family," she said with a smile.

"Not hardly," Leigh agreed ruefully. "You were saying?"

"What was I saying?" Bess mused playfully. Leigh glared.

"Oh, yes," Bess began again. "My daring escape. I was lying there at the foot of the stairs, in some sort of shock, I assume. I couldn't move for the life of me. And then I could see him standing there, and all I could see behind him was the flames. He didn't say anything, just started to help me up. It seems like I fought him at first, but then my mind started to clear. He got me up, and I leaned on him and hopped with one foot toward the door. The carpet was on fire, like I told the investigator, but we made it out OK. Then we just sat in the parking lot and waited."

"Waited for . . ." Leigh prompted.

"For the fire trucks. We could hear sirens already."

"And what did he say to you?"

"Nothing, at first." Bess frowned, blew on her hot tea, and frowned again. "Right before the firemen got there, he said not to say anything to anybody until after he had had a chance to think. Of course, I was coughing so hard I couldn't say much anyway."

Leigh looked at her incredulously. "He didn't try to get you to explain what you were doing there?"

Bess shook her head. "Not only did he not ask right away, he didn't ask at all. He still hasn't asked."

Leigh pondered that odd fact, then remembered the anxious exchange she had witnessed in the intermediate-care ward. "Right before I saw you in the hospital, you two were talking."

Bess nodded. She tested her tea gingerly, then took a sip. "That was my debriefing, kiddo. He told me the story he had just told the authorities—about what a great hero I was."

Leigh was finally beginning to understand the alarm she'd seen on her aunt's face that night. "He was covering for you, even when he must have known you were snooping in his house? Why would he do that?"

Bess took a deep breath and shrugged. "I suppose if I weren't the suspicious type, I'd say he was just being a good Christian. But since I am the suspicious type, I think he's doing me a favor because he wants something."

"Like what?"

"I don't know yet," Bess answered, her eyes losing the amusement they'd held earlier. "That's what worries me."

The sanctuary of the First Church of the New Millennium was a little cramped for the crowd that gathered the next Sunday morning. The pews, and some folding chairs behind them, were packed with an odd assortment of casually dressed young and formally dressed older parishioners. Leigh felt slightly out of place in her dress and hose—she was probably the only woman under forty who wasn't wearing slacks.

Bess had managed, with only a little help from Leigh, to squeeze into an appropriately doctored pair of thigh-highs and a bizarre Middle Eastern–looking wrap dress. Leigh couldn't help but admire her aunt's chutzpah. Though the rest of the Morton women were decidedly pear-shaped, Bess was bountiful at both ends. Far from worrying about her weight, however, she had always considered herself sexy, and that view seemed to be contagious, at least to the opposite sex. The modified beehive took some getting used to, but those who knew Bess came to understand it for what it was—a harmless badge of nonconformity.

Leigh squirmed a little in her seat. There was space on the end of the pew still, and she knew that if people kept coming, the ushers were going to squeeze someone in beside her. She didn't relish the idea of sitting shoulder to shoulder with someone she didn't know, particularly after her aunt had complained about how long the Sunday service normally lasted. "His sermons are powerful, but when he gets wound up he just won't quit," Bess had griped. "I can't sit that long today with my ankle throbbing. If he preaches past noon, there'll be hell to pay." Leigh was more than a little daunted by the prospect of a marathon service, but her curiosity about the Reverend Reginald Humphrey won out. She simply had to see him in action.

An instant before the processional began, a tall man in a dark suit slipped onto the pew beside Leigh. She stiffened up, then realized who it was.

"Fancy seeing you here," Warren whispered.

Leigh smiled. Her friend's punctuality was legendary, but she'd had no idea he was coming. "I brought my aunt Bess," she whispered back. "This is her church."

"So I gathered. My mother told me last night that a woman named Bess Cogley had saved the pastor's life." Warren leaned around Leigh to greet Bess, the famous Harmon charm in full swing. Bess cooed and

twittered like a schoolgirl, then sat back and elbowed
Leigh meaningfully in the ribs.

Leigh ignored her. The service began, and the crowd
grew silent. She wasn't sure what she expected, but
Reginald Humphrey did not disappoint. The service
was fabulous—warm and friendly, with upbeat music
that made her toes tap and a classic hymn or two
thrown in for good measure. The crowd was obviously
enjoying just being there—one would never have
guessed that a tragedy such as the loss of a parsonage
had so recently taken place. After forty-five minutes
of good cheer, the sermon was up next. Leigh got the
distinct feeling that it was greatly anticipated, though
she suspected that had a lot to do with the parsonage
fire. It was the first time Humphrey had preached
since it had happened. What was he going to say?

Reginald Humphrey clicked on his lavaliere microphone and moved the podium to the side of the altar.
"My friends," he said loudly, beginning to walk among
the crowd. "We are here today to rejoice. To rejoice
about the good things that God has given us this
week."

Being in a charismatic church, Leigh expected to
hear an "amen" from the pews, but none came. Perhaps that was a Southern thing.

"First off," he continued, illustrating his speech with
gestures, "I want those of you who don't already know
to realize that the parsonage building was fully in-
sured, so the church should not suffer any financial
hardship."

Someone coughed, but otherwise the church was silent. "Secondly, and more importantly, we have lost
nothing that should be of value to us. I have lost pictures of my wife—but my beloved Noel is still alive
and well. I have lost my clothing—but as Alida de
Vries will tell you, that's probably a good thing for
the fashion world." He approached an older woman

behind Leigh and smiled at her warmly, laying his hand on her shoulder as she blushed.

"These material losses are of no consequence. Our joy should be in the fact that we are all safe. I was the only one in the building when the fire started, and thanks to the courage of Ms. Bess Cogley—who risked her own life to save mine—I am here today as healthy as a horse." He had come to the edge of the pew next to Warren, and was extending a hand to Bess. "I owe this lady my life, my friends, and I thank her from the very bottom of my heart."

He bestowed a look on Bess that was akin to worship—a look so bold and piercing that Leigh, knowing what she knew, couldn't bear to witness it. She was sure her aunt would like to crawl under the pew as well, but Bess held her cool, even as the entire congregation turned to stare at her.

"Don't be ridiculous," she chastised, speaking toward the mike. "I didn't do anything more than anyone else would have done. And if you hadn't helped *me* out, I'd still be stuck at the bottom of the stairs."

Humphrey stepped back but continued to hail her presence with an outstretched arm. "Just listen, friends, to the modesty of a good Christian servant. What a wonderful role model we have in Ms. Cogley. Please, let's give her heroism and selflessness a big round of applause."

The crowded sanctuary nearly shook with the noise, and Leigh felt sick to her stomach. Bess must have too, because her face was a tad green. Warren watched them curiously. The applause seemed to go on forever, and it might have if Humphrey hadn't stepped back up to the altar and motioned for silence. Then his tone turned serious.

"My friends, we have much to be thankful for. But we must also be wise. We cannot ignore those forces in the world that would seek to stop our mission."

The room grew deathly quiet again. Humphrey

paused a moment, letting the silence fester. Just when
it seemed unbearable, he spoke again, barely above a
whisper. "I have news, my friends. Frightening news.
The chairman of our trustees committee was notified
just this morning as to the official cause of the fire."

There was more silence. Then the fateful word, spoken very, very softly. "Arson."

Some members of the congregation started in their
seats, others looked fearfully at each other, and those
with less than perfect hearing began looking around
asking, "What? What did he say?"

Reverend Humphrey answered them. Loudly.
"*Arson*, my friends!!" he railed, this time causing almost everyone to jump off their seats. "Your building
was burned to the ground not because of faulty wiring,
not because of an untended stove, but because some
misguided soul threw a Molotov cocktail straight
through the kitchen window!"

Bess turned to look at Leigh, and Leigh looked
back. Neither could think of anything to say. Apparently, no one else in the congregation could either.

"I know what you're thinking," Humphrey continued in a calmer voice. "You're thinking that we must
be the random target of a hate crime. There was that
string of church fires in Pittsburgh a while back, and
maybe this is a copycat crime. But I would caution you
about those thoughts. Because it wasn't our beautiful
sanctuary that this soul chose to burn—and praise
God for that—it was only the house beside it. Just
a small, old, ordinary house. Nothing fancy. Nothing
valuable. Just right for a servant like me. And I ask
you, should we believe that the individual who threw
that fire bomb intended only to harm God's people at
large? To harm them with an relatively innocuous act
of property vandalism?"

He answered his own question quietly. "No. It
might be easier to think that, but we can't. Because
as I said, there is evil out there, waiting for a chance

to spread its dark wings and fly. And I must tell you, though it pains me to do so—"

He broke off, his dazzling green eyes brimming with tears. "I believe with all my heart that this fire was no random prank. I believe—" He broke off again and steadied himself by leaning on a pew. "I believe someone is trying to kill me."

Chapter 5

When the sermon ended at twelve fifteen, Leigh and Bess sat motionless in their seats. "A Molotov cocktail," Bess repeated. "I can't believe it."

"It explains the glass breaking," Leigh said distantly. "I wonder why Humphrey didn't tell you this before. He must have seen what happened."

Bess shook her head. She looked around them to make sure no one close by was paying attention, then spoke softly into Leigh's ear. "According to our story, he was passed out on the bed, doped up with antihistamines and painkillers. He really did leave the Bible study early with a sinus headache, you know. But he can't very well admit to having heard glass breaking when I claimed I woke him up afterward."

Their conversation was soon interrupted by a long stream of people offering sympathy and appreciation to Bess. Feeling only slightly guilty for abandoning her aunt, Leigh slipped out and took refuge on a folding chair in the corner, gesturing for Warren to join her.

"So what brought you here today?" she asked as he sat down beside her. "Casing out the joint before the wedding?"

He smiled ruefully. "You got it. My mother's worried, seeing as how my uncle doesn't have the best judgment about such things. She suggested I come and make sure they weren't all snake handlers."

Leigh grinned. "And your assessment?"

He shook his head. "Jury's still out."

"My aunt thinks—" Leigh cut herself off, then felt her face flush. Had she really been about to blurt out everything Bess had told her in strictest confidence? Was she nuts? She looked into Warren's soft brown eyes and decided it was his own fault—he was so damn easy to talk to. "My aunt thinks these are very nice people," she corrected. "A lot of the members are from her old Presbyterian church."

Warren cocked his head to one side and looked at her closely. "Your aunt didn't really save Humphrey from the fire, did she?"

Leigh's face flushed redder and hotter. Then she got mad. "Dammit, Warren! I hate it when you do that!"

"Do what?" he asked innocently.

"You know what!" she ranted. "Read my mind! Now cut it out!"

Warren dissolved into laughter. "Calm down, Leigh. I'm not psychic. It was obvious to anyone with half a brain that you were both miserable in that spotlight. I don't know your aunt very well, but I'd think that if she were a hero, you would at least look proud of her. You looked like you wanted to crawl under the pew."

Leigh just glared. She had no intention of confirming his accuracy. "Aunt Bess doesn't like the spotlight," she lied without thinking. "I was just worried about her, that's all."

Warren lifted his hands and tried to stop smiling. "Fine. Let's change the subject. How about if I take you and your aunt out to lunch? It will give me an excuse to dodge my uncle."

Leigh's anger started to melt. Warren's mind-reading abilities could work in her favor sometimes—he knew, for example, that food was a sure means of pacifying her. Besides, she was starving. "That sounds great," she answered, looking to see how many more well-wishers remained in Bess's line. There were quite a few—almost as many as were in the pastor's. A thought struck her, and she turned back to Warren. "You heard the sermon. Do you believe someone could be trying to kill him?"

Warren shrugged. "All I know is what's been passed on from my uncle, and he's hardly a reliable source. A Molotov cocktail is a little rough for petty vandalism, but I can't buy the bit about the dark side trying to thwart the up-and-coming Jedi either."

Leigh narrowed her eyes at him. He was talking that gibberish again. "In English, please?"

He translated. "If someone's out to get him, it's not because he's started up a successful church. He must be involved in something else."

Leigh felt a sudden twinge of panic. A mobster? Her aunt had gotten herself indebted to a mobster?

"Warren! How're you doing, my boy? Good to see you!"

Her thoughts were interrupted by a large, loud individual she assumed was Warren's uncle. He clapped his nephew on the back with one long arm and wrapped the other around the tiny woman beside him. "Shannon and I are so glad you could come. You're still planning on being a groomsman, I hope!"

"Of course, I wouldn't miss Joy's wedding for anything." Warren answered politely, standing up. "And how have you two been?"

The man shook his head and wiped a hand across his damp brow. Leigh was a bit warm herself. The tiny, crowded church had gotten progressively stuffier, even though it was freezing outside. "Things have been sticky lately," the man said heavily. "I guess your momma told you about the parsonage."

Warren nodded.

"Now Humphrey thinks someone's out to kill him." The man shook his head as if he didn't believe it, but said nothing more.

Warren seized the lull in the conversation to introduce Leigh. "Uncle Ted, this is a good friend of mine,

Leigh Koslow. She's Bess Cogley's niece. Leigh, this is my uncle, Ted Hugh, and his wife, Shannon.''

Leigh rose, and the three shook hands. Ted Hugh was a strong-looking man, at least physically. He was tall and broad-shouldered, and his shining head—bald except for a thin line of black hair arching from ear to ear—made him look even more imposing. His mannerisms were equally unsettling—he fidgeted almost constantly as he stood, and his dark eyes darted back and forth as he talked. "Bess's niece, eh? My little girl's counting on your aunt to coordinate one heck of a wedding. It had better be perfect too!"

His tone was jovial, but it seemed to hold a serious undercurrent as well. Before Leigh had a chance to be offended, however, the slight, easily overlooked woman who clung to his arm broke in gently. "It's so nice to meet you, Leigh. We think the world of your aunt, of course. Everyone in the church does."

Shannon was almost striking in her plainness, with short, straight ash blond hair devoid of any styling. A neat, prim-looking pantsuit hung on her thin frame, and large, thick glasses hid what were probably a pretty set of pale blue eyes. "Bess is such a wonderful volunteer," she continued. "We couldn't possibly have afforded to pay a professional wedding coordinator, but she just jumped right in."

Leigh smiled and nodded. Bess did have a habit of doing that.

"We were just on our way out to lunch," Shannon continued sweetly. "Won't you join us?"

"Yeah!" Ted chimed in loudly. "How about it?"

Warren hesitated only a millisecond, but Shannon's soft voice broke in swiftly. "Please, Warren. We'd enjoy your company. It's been such a long time since we've seen you, and I'd love to hear how your campaign is going."

"Of course, Shannon," Warren said graciously.

"We'd love to come. Will it be all right if Bess joins us?"

"I sure as the devil hope so!" a boisterous voice insisted. "Because otherwise I'm going to start eating the carpeting." Bess hobbled up on her crutches and clapped Ted soundly on the back. "So you're Warren Harmon's uncle! Small world. Where're we going?"

Ted didn't answer but turned to confer with his wife, and Bess's cheerful expression vanished instantly. She clutched Leigh's shoulder and whispered intently in her ear. "Please tell me Warren Harmon is *not* this man's blood nephew!"

Leigh shook her head, trying hard not to grin.

Bess relaxed visibly. "Okay, then. You're allowed to have his children."

Leigh glared fiercely, but before she could think of a suitable retort, Ted Hugh's unnecessarily loud voice scrambled her brain waves.

"To Kings, then!" he boomed, heading out the door. *"My treat!"* It was a generous offer, but delivered in Ted's offbeat tone, it sounded suspiciously like an imposition.

Warren looked at Leigh and Bess apologetically, but Leigh just grinned and started walking. She had too many nutcases in her own family tree to be disconcerted by anyone else's. Either way, it took more than one loony uncle to make her lose her appetite.

Leigh walked through the doors of her apartment building late that afternoon with a heavy feeling that went beyond the fried clams she'd had for lunch. Two days of vacation down, and she felt more drained than ever. She was supposed to be either indulging herself or relaxing—preferably both. Yet all she seemed to be able to do was worry about her aunt's predicament—and stew about Warren.

She never did get a chance to be alone with him. After lunch he had made some vague excuses and departed, and judging by the absence of his neon-blue Beetle in the apartment parking lot, he hadn't come home. So where was he?

Leigh entered her apartment and swept up the black Persian that tottered out to meet her with a lilting whine. "I know, Mao Tse—I've been neglecting you. That nasty Warren has been feeding you on schedule, hasn't he?"

She surveyed Mao's food and water dishes, and found both well filled. He was reliable, she'd give him that. She'd asked him if he could drop in Saturday night—and he'd evidently made a morning visit as well. That certainly made up for his refusal to touch the litter box.

She collapsed horizontally on the couch, and Mao Tse quickly curled up on her chest, purring loudly.

It's your own fault, you know. Her conscience chided her as she reviewed what a quandary she'd gotten herself into with Warren. She'd never even considered the possibility of his being more than a friend until this fall, when he had started getting serious about another woman. Then it had hit her. How much she would miss him. He would marry someone else, and she would be relegated to an entry on his Christmas card list. The more she had thought about it, the more unbearable the idea became. But naturally, she hadn't done anything about it. She hadn't had time.

Oh, come off it. She'd just been too damned chicken.

A knock interrupted her thoughts. She put an arm around Mao Tse and carried her to the door. A glance through the peephole made her heartbeat quicken, and she opened the door. Warren must have gotten home right behind her.

"Are you busy?" he asked, walking in as he spoke. "I want to talk to you about something."

Leigh shook her head and settled back down on the couch with Mao, gesturing for him to join them.

He did. "Sorry about running off so soon after lunch—"

"That's OK," Leigh jumped in. Her voice sounded nervous, which annoyed her. Why should she be nervous? She was only going to hassle Warren about his social life. She'd been doing that for years. "I assume you were with Ms. Bower?"

Warren looked surprised. "Not just now, no. I was talking to my mother again."

Leigh felt stupid. "Oh." She buried her face in her cat, hoping he would ignore the question and move on.

Of course he didn't. "What made you think I was with Katharine?"

She peered at him over a horizon of black fur. He looked amused. *Dammit.* "Because you've been joined at the hip lately, that's why." She put Mao Tse back down in her lap and decided to go for broke. "So, has she popped the question yet?" Once the words left her mouth all she could do was wait—and listen to the sound of her own heart racing.

But Warren just looked at her. After a few years, he cracked a smile. "If you're hoping my marrying Katharine will get you a retroactive legal discount, you're out of luck. I already got you her rock-bottom criminal-defense rate."

Leigh digested this little bit of non-information and decided it didn't mean anything. But he was definitely dodging the question, and that wasn't a good sign either. She dove in for another cuddle with Mao Tse and tried not to hate Katharine Bower. After everything the woman had done for her last fall she owed her a lot, not the least of which was money.

"A girl can dream, can't she?" she said flippantly, emerging again from cover of cat. "I keep hoping one day she'll show up at my doorstep, tear up her bill, and say, 'Never mind, friend copywriter. You need this money more than I.' "

Warren smirked. "Keep dreaming."

Leigh was wondering if she had any choice. "Seriously," she said, getting brazen again, "are you and Katharine getting serious, or what?"

Warren looked at her even longer this time. Unfortunately, the traitorous Mao Tse had jumped down from her lap as she spoke, and now she had to look back at him. She tried hard to look like his answer didn't matter, but she doubted any Oscars were heading her way.

He leaned a little closer to her. "Why do you want to know?" he asked softly.

Leigh's heartbeat leapt skyward again, and she was certain her face had turned into a tomato. Why was this happening to her? She was a thirty-year-old woman shooting the breeze with a man she'd known almost half her life, yet she felt like a sixth grader at a school dance.

Why did she want to know? Really? Because she couldn't stand the thought of him being with anyone else, that's why. Because for some inexplicable reason she wanted him all to herself, in every way, for the rest of their lives. And if he didn't want that too—

"Leigh," he said in a low voice, with just a hint of a smile. "I asked you a question. Why you do care what's going on with Katharine and me?"

She stared back into his eyes, wondering if she already knew. Surely he must. He knew everything else about her. But if he already knew how she felt and he felt the same way, he wouldn't be dating Katharine. Would he?

She jumped up from the couch in one motion. "No reason," she chirped. "You want a Coke?"

It took him a moment to answer. "Sure."

Leigh drained half of hers before delivering his to the couch. She had to get a hold of herself—supreme humiliation was only one step away. "So," she began more soberly, "what's the word on your dad? Are they going to make the wedding?"

He shook his head sadly. "I don't think so. It sounds like my father has pneumonia. It's killing my mother to miss Joy's big day, but she won't leave him. I offered to fly down and stay with him so she could come up, but she wouldn't hear of it."

"She stands by her man," Leigh said with an attempt at cheerfulness. She had always liked Warren's mother, who was just about the sweetest woman alive. His father was nice too. The uncle was another matter. "I'm sure everything with the wedding will go fine," she said supportively. "Shannon seemed nice."

"Shannon's a saint," Warren said sincerely. "She's been wonderful for him; I don't know what would have happened if she hadn't come along when she did. She's been wonderful for Joy too, but more as a sister than as a stepmother. My mother always kept that role." His expression suddenly turned somber. "You know, my mother got me worried about all this mess with the church; and now I'm more worried than she is."

Leigh's brow furrowed. "What do you mean?"

He sat up, exhaling sharply. "That's what I came here to talk to you about. You'd never met my uncle before today. Based on his behavior at lunch, how would you guess he feels about the Reverend Humphrey?"

Leigh paused a moment. She preferred not to remember much about lunch, except perhaps the monster salad with blue cheese dressing she'd enjoyed before stuffing herself silly on the clams. She certainly didn't care to recall Ted's frequent insinuations regarding the parentage and general deportment of Reginald Humphrey—nor how uncomfortable his comments had seemed to make Shannon. "He doesn't like him," she answered simply.

"It would appear not," Warren agreed. "Would you

be surprised to learn that for the last six months my uncle has sung the praises of the fabulous reverend virtually nonstop?"

She nodded. "Uh-huh."

"Well, join the crowd. I found it very odd, so I asked my mother if she had noticed the change—and she had, though just recently. Before, he couldn't say enough good things about Humphrey or the church, and he boasted about how proud he was to be appointed to the executive board. In fact, when Joy and Tim got engaged, he insisted they have the wedding at the First Church of the New Millennium, even though she wanted to be married in a private ceremony on a cruise ship. Being so newly formed, the congregation hadn't had a wedding yet, and he thought it would be fabulous if his daughter was the first."

"And Joy agreed," Leigh assumed with pity.

"They compromised," he answered. "She insisted on setting the date for her mother's birthday—a Tuesday—with her and Tim leaving on a cruise the next morning."

Leigh grinned. She loved rebel brides. "A weeknight wedding. Didn't everybody hassle her about the inconvenience?"

Warren threw her a heavy look. "Please, don't remind me. You have no idea what kind of crisis *that* was."

Leigh grinned more. She did too know. He should have seen the carnage in her family when her cousin Cara had announced she was getting married in a red dress. "Good for Joy. I don't blame her for wanting to flee the country afterward."

An image of her own fantasy honeymoon floated awkwardly in front of her eyes. The sky was blue, the ocean was blue, the sand was warm, and Warren was—. She blinked back the images forcefully. "So anyway," she said, a little too loudly, "you're worried about what's behind your uncle's change of heart?"

He nodded and took a swig of Coke. Luckily, he hadn't been watching her during her last brain drift. "His reaction to the fire seemed odd to me at the time. Now I can't help wondering if he knows something else about this supposed attempt on Humphrey's life."

He finished the Coke and let out a deep breath. "Or maybe he's just flipping out because he wants the wedding to be perfect, and he's blaming Humphrey for attracting trouble. I don't know." He looked at Leigh. "I wanted to ask you, since your aunt is obviously a part of the inner circle over there, do you have any idea what might be going on?"

Leigh paused. She couldn't betray Bess's confidence, but she might be able to sidestep it—just a little. "Bess doesn't know for certain that anything fishy is happening," she said carefully. "She has her suspicions, but she's trying not to show them to anybody—so please, don't pass that along."

Warren studied her for a moment. "All right. I won't ask what your aunt was really doing over at the parsonage the night of the fire. But if you find out anything that could affect Joy's wedding, would you let me know, please?"

Leigh nodded, but then a worry struck her. What if Reginald Humphrey wasn't even a licensed minister?

He caught her distress immediately. "You know something already, don't you? What is it?"

Leigh wavered. Surely her aunt wouldn't care if Warren knew part of the story? After all, his being suspicious shouldn't affect Bess's ability to gather evidence. "My aunt is concerned that Humphrey isn't all he claims to be. Are you sure—I mean, is all the legal paperwork in order?"

His brow wrinkled. "Bess thinks Humphrey's a fraud, eh? I suppose it's possible. But thankfully, it won't matter to this ceremony. They're officially being married by Tim's best friend—a Methodist minister imported from Erie. Humphrey's just assisting."

Leigh breathed a sigh of relief. Her aunt undoubtedly already knew that.

Warren glanced at his watch, then threw his Coke can into Leigh's recyclable bag and headed for the door. "I've got to run," he announced. "Dinner plans. But thanks for the information." He put his hand on the doorknob and waved good-bye. "If we can hold the First Church of the New Millennium together for another forty-eight hours—Joy and Tim just might make it on that cruise ship as man and wife."

Those pesky sun and sand images started floating around Leigh's head again. "Hey, Warren?" she asked as he started out the door.

"Yes?"

"New *Simpsons* at eight. How late is your dinner going?"

He smiled. "You got microwave popcorn?"

"Low-fat butter flavor."

"I'll do my best."

Chapter 6

Leigh was fairly certain that if her mother didn't take off soon, Bess was going to send Frances flying through the front door with a well-placed kick from her formidable new splint. The surgery had gone well, but both Frances and Leigh's Aunt Lydie had baby-sat Bess at the hospital all morning and at the farm-house all afternoon, and their smothering attentions had apparently not worn well on their fiercely self-reliant big sister. By the time Leigh arrived to begin her scheduled overnight shift, Bess was edgy as a razor.

Lydie had already left, but Frances pulled on her coat with excruciating slowness, barking orders as she dawdled. "And I want you to make absolutely certain she doesn't go *anywhere* or try to do *anything,* you understand?"

"I'm right here, Francie," Bess snapped with exasperation. "You don't have to talk like I'm not in the room."

Frances ignored the outburst and continued instructing her daughter. "She's a little testy from the anesthesia. Don't let her bully you. Understand?"

Leigh nodded cooperatively, trying not to laugh at the murderous gestures Bess was making behind her mother's back. "She'll be fine, Mom. I have medical training, remember?"

Frances tilted her chin down and glared at her daughter. "Making a stubborn woman take care of

herself and helping your father put an IV in a dachs-
hund are two different things." The coat was finally
in place. "Call me if you have any trouble."

"Well, don't call here!" Bess insisted. "I'm going to
bed early tonight."

Frances looked at her sister skeptically and waggled
a finger at her as she headed for the door. "Just *don't
overdo*. The only one you'll be hurting is yourself."

Bess returned an exaggerated salute, and Frances
left, pulling the door shut behind her. Bess muttered
something under her breath, and Leigh's eyes widened. "Um, what was that, Aunt Bess?"

Bess looked the other way. "Nothing, kiddo. Just
saying what a pleasure it is to be around your mother
for prolonged periods of time. Incidentally, how the
Sam Hill did you grow up normal?"

Leigh grinned. She didn't get called normal too
often. "Because you took pity on me and let me hide
out here once in a while, that's how."

Bess smiled back. "I did, didn't I? Right. So now
you owe me. Grab my coat and hand me those
crutches. I've got a wedding rehearsal to coordinate—
and I'm late already."

Leigh sank down in a pew midway through the sanctuary, her shins propped irreverently on the back of
the pew in front of her. She was easy, there was no
doubt about it. But Bess had managed getting in and
out of the car surprisingly well, and she had sworn
she wouldn't move all night from the comfortable
chair Leigh had parked her in. There wouldn't be any
harm done. Unless, of course, Frances found out.

She shuddered at the thought, then returned her
attention to the rehearsal, which was proving quite
dramatic indeed. Bess had been late in arriving, but
not quite as late as the Reverend Humphrey. And
though the pastor had sauntered into the sanctuary
with a ready smile and a pleasant apology, Ted Hugh's

answering glare had quickly enveloped the whole room with tension.

Within half an hour Ted was sweating like a horse and bellowing like a mule. The slightest little problem seemed to set him off, and his wife was working overtime to pacify him, her face pinched tight with concern. The bride and groom were doing their best to ignore him, but Bess was clearly ready to duct-tape his face to the baptismal font when Warren intervened. He put his arm around his uncle's shoulders and they exited towards the parlor, while the rest of the wedding party decided to take a short break.

Leigh watched them curiously. Shannon went straight to Joy, presumably to apologize on Ted's behalf. But it didn't look as though the bride was going to let her father's bizarre behavior get to her—she and the groom still beamed at each other as if they were alone. The imported minister made a joke Leigh didn't catch, and everyone at the front of the church shared a laugh. It was a nervous laugh, however, and the sound rang hollow over the wooden pews.

Leigh was wondering if Ted's outbursts were the only problems with this wedding when a warm hand squeezed her shoulder. "Miss Koslow? We meet again. I'm delighted."

Reginald Humphrey extended a hand that was still lightly bandaged. "It's all right," he said with a smile. "This hand got a good workout on Sunday and I'm no worse for the wear." His green eyes twinkled at her, and she took the opportunity to look into them closely. He certainly seemed sincere to her. But then again, she'd been wrong about people before.

She extended her hand and shook his gently. "I'm glad you're recovering so well. My aunt Bess is doing wonderfully too."

He smiled. An honest, open smile with absolutely no guile. Leigh found herself smiling back. Damn, he was good.

"Your aunt is one of my favorite parishioners—but if you quote me on that, I'll deny it," he said, continuing to grin. "I thank God for women like her in the church. We'd all crumple up and blow away without them. Do you have a church home, Ms. Koslow?"

And he's a smooth recruiter too, she thought wryly. "Call me Leigh. And yes, I've belonged to Greenstone Methodist all my life."

"Ah," he said, scratching a chin whose weathered skin was shaved smooth. She studied his face, her mind flashing back to Bess's army picture. The older man had gained no small amount of wrinkles, which seemed to lessen the shine on his cheeks and obscure some of his freckles. But otherwise, the image was dead on. This was the boy nicknamed Money. She was almost sure of it.

"Greenstone," he continued. "That's in Avalon, right?"

She nodded.

"Excellent church, I'm sure. But don't get so attached to it you never come visit us again, you hear?"

Leigh offered a smile, but the wheels in her head were turning deviously. She had to know whether the man beside her was a saint or a scumbag. But how could she find out for sure without tipping Bess's hand? "Have you ever been a Methodist?" she asked pleasantly, hoping for a brainstorm.

"Oh, yes," he answered proudly. "And a Presbyterian, and a Disciple of Christ, and a Congregationalist. All good churches, but there's room for other ways of thinking. Ways with a little less baggage."

Leigh thought hard. She knew where she wanted the conversation to go, but she wasn't sure how to get it there. "My mother has always been a Methodist," she began, as inspiration came. "But my father used to be an atheist." She tried not to dwell on the fact that she was lying through her teeth. Perhaps fibbing to a con artist was a lesser sin?

Humphrey took the bait. "Used to be?"

Leigh nodded. "It was the war that changed him. Korea. He almost died."

The pastor nodded soberly. "I understand completely. Nothing like mortal combat—staring into the face of death—to make you think about what's really important in life. I've been meditating on that myself lately."

He was clearly thinking about the Molotov cocktail, but now that things were rolling, she had no intention of letting him change the subject. "Were you in combat, too?"

He smiled a small half smile. "Not really. I was drafted during the Korean War as well, but Fort Jackson was as far as I ever got. I never saw a battlefield."

Bingo. "Fort Jackson, South Carolina?" she asked innocently. "My father went through basic training there!"

"Indeed?" he said, eyes widening.

She smiled at her own slyness, and watched his face carefully for the coming reaction. "I still remember the funny nicknames my father's old army buddies had. There was Jelly Roll, and DoDo, and Tooter. Any of those sound familiar?"

Humphrey's eyes gazed off into the distance for a moment, and she looked anxiously for the lightbulbs she knew would pop up in them. But there weren't any. "I'm sorry," he said, looking at her sympathetically. "But the names don't ring a bell. A lot of boys went through Fort Jackson, you know. It was an awfully long time ago, and not a very good time for me. But I'm happy that the experience brought your father to God."

Deflated, Leigh sat for a moment trying to remember what he was talking about. *Oh, right. The atheist thing.* Her shoulders sank a little. Unlike her, compe-

tent liars probably managed to keep their stories
straight for more than five seconds. She was struggling
to come up with some intelligent response when Bess
spared her by calling the party back to action. Humphrey rose and applied another fatherly squeeze to
her shoulder.

"It was nice visiting with you, Leigh. If you ever
need someone to talk to, just drop in. No strings
attached. OK?"

She nodded, and he gave her a friendly wink.

Magnetic, Leigh thought, watching him rejoin the
group. There was no other word to describe him. She
rose from the pew and went to check on Bess, who
sat with her ankle propped up on a soft ottoman imported from the parlor.

"Do you need anything?" Leigh asked.

Bess shook her head. "I was going to ask for my
shotgun, but I see your friend Warren has gotten Ted
under control again. Let's hope it lasts."

She glanced at Ted, who did appear much calmer.
He sat on the bride's side and smiled at his daughter
as she practiced her vows. Shannon, who was serving
as matron of honor, watched him nervously out of the
corner of her eye.

As the rehearsal dragged on less eventfully, Leigh's
mind wandered. The wedding party was strictly a family affair, with the groom's father serving as best man
and the groom's sister and bride's cousin (a.k.a. Warren) completing the ranks. But despite the small cast,
the church at large was buzzing with activity. A group
of middle-aged women roamed about decorating the
sanctuary with flowers and ribbon, and occasional
bursts of raucous laughter drifted up from the youth
meeting down in Fellowship Hall. Leigh was tempted
to leave her post and go exploring, but after a last
blocking run-through, Bess declared everything flaw-
less. The bride and groom practiced their kiss again,

and Warren beat a hasty retreat from his perch on the altar steps. Leigh grinned at him as he walked over.

"Having fun?" she asked.

He narrowed his eyes. "Let's just say I'm glad Joy's happy and leave it at that." He glanced at his uncle, who was smiling pleasantly as he talked with Tim's father.

"Was it Valium or threats of violence?" Leigh joked, following his eyes. "What exactly did you do to him?"

"We just had a little talk, that's all," Warren insisted. "He wants everything to be perfect for Joy—he just doesn't know how to go about it. I gave him some pointers." He smiled a little. "Will I see you at the wedding tomorrow?"

She nodded. "It looks like I'll be hanging out with Bess most of the week—at least until she can handle the stairs without killing herself. It's not exactly the vacation I had in mind, but that's all right. She keeps begging me to keep my mom away from her—and I do have a heart. Are you sure you don't mind checking on Mao at night? I'll pop in during the day."

"Pizza and donuts!" a voice rang out pleasantly. "The youth ordered plenty to go around, so if you guys have any room left, just come on down to Fellowship Hall!" The invitation was delivered by a jovial young man Leigh assumed to be the youth director, and though the food combination was questionable, either component was sufficiently tantalizing. She, after all, had not had the luxury of a nice rehearsal dinner.

But tonight neither entrée was in the cards. Bess looked exhausted, and the Frances in Leigh knew enough was enough. "I'll take care of her imperial majesty," Warren replied, referring to Mao Tse. "But don't stay away too much longer, or she may start to like me."

Leigh grinned. Mao Tse didn't like anybody but her

master, which of course was part of the cat's charm. Still, anything was possible. Mao was a cat after her own heart.

The shrill ringing of an old-fashioned rotary phone vibrated inside Leigh's foggy head, and it took a few seconds for her to remember that she was in her aunt's spare room. She rolled off the comfortable four-poster twin bed and started to reach for the telephone, but when no ring followed the first, she sat back down. Bess must have gotten it. Her eyes focused lazily on the unoccupied bed beside her, and she smiled. She and her cousin had spent many a happy night in this room when they were growing up. Bess had insisted they sleep over once in a while to keep her company, then had spoiled them with popcorn and late-night games of Clue and Rummy.

A shuffling sound drew Leigh's attention to the doorway. Bess stood poised on her crutches, still dressed in a nightgown. "Good, you're awake. I hate to ask you this, but I need a ride to the shelter. The manager just called—there's been a break-in."

Leigh blinked twice and rose. "The homeless shelter?" Her aunt's list of nonprofit board memberships had always been too long to keep up with.

"No," she answered. "The animal shelter. The one by the church, of course."

Leigh nodded, feeling stupid. Though the shelter hadn't existed during her formative days working at her father's veterinary clinic, she'd certainly heard a lot about it since. Bess had founded it herself a few years before, on a patch of land purchased from her old Presbyterian church. The shrinking church had sold off the narrow end lot partly because of financial trouble, and partly because Bess had sweet-talked the session into it. What she had had to do to gain the approval of the zoning board, however, Leigh and the rest of the family preferred not to know.

Leigh dressed hastily and went to see if Bess needed any help. She was amazed to find her aunt already dressed and ready to go—modified beehive in place. She seemed rather stiff, however, and they took the trip down the stairs and out to the car slowly.

The ride itself was almost instantaneous, as the nondescript concrete-block building sat right around the corner on Nicholson Road, with only a thin patch of woods separating it from what was now the First Church of the New Millennium. Like the church building, it would have been within easy walking distance of the farmhouse had Bess been able to walk.

With the shelter itself in sight, Bess's mission seemed to become more urgent, and Leigh was hard-pressed to keep her aunt from slipping perilously on the frosty concrete walk. The manager, an efficient-looking woman about Leigh's age, opened the door and ushered them inside. "I called the police—they said they're on their way," she announced with distress, running a hand through her hair. "I don't understand what happened. I'm telling you, nothing's missing, nothing's even out of place, besides the door."

Bess hobbled across the bright linoleum in the reception area, moving behind the main desk and inspecting it carefully. Once satisfied, she moved over to a heavy metal door marked DOGS and promptly heaved it open, releasing a deafening chorus of barks. She started to step into the run, but the recently mopped concrete floor was still slick, and her good foot immediately started to slide. Leigh sprang into action, barely preventing another disaster. "If you break a hip too," she whispered harshly, "you really will be an invalid." Bess responded with a flippant glare, and Leigh proceeded with her trump card. "*And* you'll have my mother living with you twenty-four hours a day, because once she finds out I let you get hurt, I'll be deader than a doornail."

Bess scowled and let the door swing shut.

"All the dogs are present and accounted for," the shelter manager assured, bringing over a chair. "The cats too. Please don't hurt yourself. There's nothing to see except in the basement, and there's no way you can get down there safely."

Bess allowed her niece to lower her to the chair, where she sat miserably. "I'll have a look around for you, okay?" Leigh cajoled. "You know I have a way with crime scenes."

Given Leigh's history, it was a bad joke, but it did bring the ghost of a grin to Bess's pouting lips. "Fine," she said. "But I'll expect a full report."

Leigh gave her aunt a dutiful salute, then followed the manager through the door marked DOGS and around the corner through another one labeled STAFF ONLY. They filed into a multipurpose room with an exam table in the middle and a kitchen counter and cabinets along the walls. "Everything was fine in the dog run—and in the cat room too," the manager explained. "I didn't notice anything was wrong until the puppy food bin ran low and I went down to the basement for another bag." She tilted her head toward a narrow staircase leading down, and was in the process of leading Leigh to it when they heard Bess's voice ring out.

"Police are here!"

The manager turned back toward the front. "Well," she said, "you can see for yourself, I guess."

Sensing that her time to roam would be limited, Leigh nodded and walked quickly down the staircase. She wasn't sure what she expected, but what she found was a basement that looked much like the one at the Koslow Animal Clinic, complete with stacks of dry food bags, a deep freeze, isolation cages, and a washer and dryer. Everything was clean and tidy; there were no muddy tracks on the floor and no open cabinets. She remembered that the manager had mentioned something about a door, and cautiously approached the back exit.

Light filtered in around the basement door, which was lodged an inch or so out of whack, its displaced screws hanging limply from sagging hinges. The key lock appeared to have been wrenched out of position, and in Leigh's admittedly uneducated opinion, she was not looking at the work of a locksmith as much as the result of a few powerful, well-placed kicks. Or maybe a battering ram.

Heavy footsteps squeaked on the wooden staircase behind her. "Excuse me," a familiar voice said formally, "but I'm afraid you'll have to wait upstairs with the others."

Leigh considered making a run for it, but decided that would be pointless. She straightened her back and turned around.

The newly promoted county detective who stood at the bottom of the steps ordinarily stood about six foot two inches, but at the sight of Leigh, her body sagged down into the five-foot range.

"Tell me I'm hallucinating," she said dryly.

"Sorry, Mo," Leigh said sheepishly. "It's really me. But don't worry—it just so happens that this time I have nothing whatsoever to do with anything."

Maura Polanski looked at her ex-college roommate with a skeptical glare. "That's what they all say."

"Really!" Leigh protested. "I've just been helping my aunt Bess get around since she broke her ankle. She dragged me down here with her when the manager called."

"Well, she can drag you right back out," Maura said firmly, grabbing Leigh's arm and pulling her away from the broken door. "Call me crazy, but every once in a while I like to write a report that doesn't have your name in it. Good-bye."

"Come on, Maura," Leigh cajoled. "I was just looking around; I didn't touch anything. And congratulations again on the promotion. The city's loss is the county's gain."

One corner of Maura's mouth lifted, but only slightly. She had spent eight years on the Pittsburgh city police force, and had been only a stone's throw from making detective when her father's death and mother's Alzheimer's disease had forced her to take a job closer to home in the borough of Avalon. But after her mother was happily relocated to an assisted-living complex, she had started working for Allegheny County—and had earned a particularly speedy promotion. It wasn't the city job she'd always wanted, but she was a detective, and Leigh was proud of her.

"So you investigate break-ins, eh?" Leigh asked, sitting down on the steps. An idea came to her. "What about arson? Are you working on the parsonage fire?"

Maura frowned. "Arson's a separate division. General Investigations handles burglary, robbery, and fraud. Now get out. Do I look like I'm joking?"

Leigh got up again and began her ascent. After four years as college roommates and several more years as grown-up friends, she knew Maura like she knew the back of her hand. And the detective definitely wasn't joking.

Chapter 7

Leigh hoped that Joy and Tim would enjoy their wedding day, because it certainly wasn't shaping up nicely for anyone else. Bess had been greatly distressed by the break-in at the animal shelter, even though she did eventually prove to herself that nothing had been disturbed, much less taken. Maura had declined to offer her opinion of the incident to Leigh, but eavesdropping had produced a few theories, including that someone might just have wanted a warm place to sleep. It seemed an innocuous enough crime, but coming so close on the heels of the Molotov cocktail, it had Bess more than a little rattled.

Which explained why the seasoned wedding coordinator wasn't taking the Tuesday evening pre-wedding chaos with her usual good humor. She had worked her way from distressed to perturbed, and was getting more perturbed by the minute. Her cast was misbehaving. Ted was completely manic, racing about the church and alternately dialing and slamming phones. Shannon dogged his every step, distraught. Even the bride and groom looked a little unsettled as a long-haired photographer ordered them and the groom's parents about, staging awkward prenuptial shots. The church members who were helping out fluttered back and forth between the Fellowship Hall and the sanctuary, wringing their hands and talking in hushed voices.

The inciting factor for most of the distress was clear.

The wedding was scheduled to begin in ten minutes, and Reginald Humphrey was nowhere to be found.

"No one seems to know where he moved to," Bess told Leigh with disgust. She had settled herself in a back pew near the bride's entrance, and was less than pleased with her lack of mobility. "Barbara thought he told Shannon, Shannon thought he told Cindy, and Cindy thought he told Barbara. The upshot is, nobody knows where he is."

"Isn't he staying with someone in the congregation?" Leigh asked.

"He was," Bess said tightly. "But after the parsonage fire was ruled arson, he gave the board this song and dance about not wanting to endanger anyone. So he's on a living allowance, at least until the apartment Joe Antram volunteered becomes available. Humphrey told Shannon he'd found a temporary place, but he didn't give anyone the address. Just a phone number."

Leigh figured that explained the endless phone calls Ted was making. Wherever Humphrey was staying, he obviously wasn't there.

"Long time, no see," a voice called cheerfully from over Leigh's shoulder. "But in my profession, that's usually good news. How have you been? Busy at your new agency, I hear."

She turned to see a smiling, petite redhead decked out in an extremely flattering bright green dress. "Hello, Katharine," she said, trying not to sound as stiff as she felt. She didn't need to ask who had passed along her work habits. "We've been swamped, all right. But I'm taking a week off. How about you? Doing well enough without my business, I hope."

Katharine Bower, attorney at law, smiled good-naturedly. "Oh, there are still plenty of people out there who need defending. Even an occasional innocent one. They can't all be as gratifying as your case, though."

Leigh wondered whether Katharine was referring to the case itself, or the fact that it had given the single, fortyish lawyer a chance to get her hooks into Warren Harmon III. She decided she didn't want to know. "Katharine, this is my aunt Bess, who's coordinating the wedding. Aunt Bess, this is Katharine Bower, my ex-attorney."

"And a fine attorney at that, I hear," Bess said, shaking Katharine's hand firmly. "Are you here for the bride or the groom?"

"I don't know either, actually," Katharine answered. "I'm here with—this handsome devil."

Leigh almost didn't recognize Warren as he strolled up and wrapped an arm around Katharine's pencil-thin waist. He was wearing a black tuxedo, and he looked divine.

"Everything's going to be fine, Bess," he said, his words more confident than his voice sounded. Being fundamentally honest, Warren was an even worse liar than Leigh, a handicap that made his success as a politician nothing short of amazing.

"Humphrey's here?" Bess said fiercely, sitting up as if to confront the man.

"No," Warren answered, gesturing for her to relax. "We still don't know where he is. But the wedding can go on without him. The other minister doesn't have a problem with picking up the homily and prayers, and he was going to do the actual ceremony anyway." He ran a hand through his hair and exhaled. "It may be for the best. Once we made the decision to go on without Humphrey, my uncle calmed right down. If I didn't know better, I'd think he never did want Humphrey involved."

When Katharine and Warren had excused themselves to find their places, Leigh sank down beside Bess. "Why would Humphrey miss a wedding?" she whispered as the music started. "He certainly seems to love the spotlight."

"He also loves to grandstand," Bess muttered. "I bet you a dime he's hiding out down the street, waiting to make an entrance at the last minute." Her voice was angry, but her eyes flickered with dread. "At least," she said heavily, "he'd better be."

Leigh stuffed another cheese cube into her mouth and tried not to stare at Warren and Katharine, who were laughing playfully by the piano on the other side of Fellowship Hall. Despite all odds, the wedding had gone off without a hitch. And without Reginald Humphrey.

She tried not to dwell on the fact that Warren had hardly spoken to her all evening. She also tried not to dwell on the fact that Ms. Katharine Bower had had the nerve to catch the bouquet. Instead, she volunteered to help clean up the food, a task that brought with it the moral responsibility of not letting anything go to waste—a duty she took very seriously indeed.

She disposed of a few more cheese cubes and rounded up the crackers. The guests were dwindling, some no doubt disturbed at being offered stand-up hors d'oeuvres in a church basement instead of a sit-down dinner at a posh reception hall. But the bride and groom had been determined to take off early in preparation for their cruise tomorrow, and since Warren's uncle Ted had grown up in the South, he hadn't considered kielbasa and the hokeypokey to be obligatory wedding traditions.

Leigh set aside the empty tray and began on the next one, picking up a yellow sliver of pepper and coating it with dip. She really should be trying to make Bess leave, but that was proving difficult. Bess was relaxing on a couch nearby, basking in the glory of having directed the First Church of the New Millennium's first wedding perfectly. Interestingly enough, she seemed to be keeping an eye on the couple at the piano as well. Katharine, bouquet still in hand, ap-

peared to be telling some sort of story, and Warren
was laughing heartily.

Leigh grabbed up both trays and turned away
toward the kitchen. "Hasn't anybody heard from him
yet?" she heard a woman ask as she swung the trays
onto the counter.

"Not that I've heard," another woman answered.
The two were standing by the sink, drying a stack of
serving spoons and platters. "And I just don't believe
he could have forgotten. I'm really getting worried
about him, and I think everyone else should be too."

Leigh lingered, making a pretense of rearranging
the remaining pepper slices.

"Oh, Barbara," the first woman said skeptically,
"you don't really think someone is out to get him, do
you? Who on earth would want to hurt a man like
Reginald Humphrey? I know he thinks that there are
people in the world who resent new churches, but—
well, that's a little far-fetched."

"You never know," the second woman said heavily.
"What about all those church fires we had a few
years back?"

The first woman shook her head. "He could have
had car trouble. Or a fender bender."

"I called the police earlier, and they said there
hadn't been any serious traffic accidents. But it could
be something to do with his wife. She's in constant
peril down in Zaire, you know."

Leigh could have lingered longer, partly because she
wanted to hear more about Humphrey's absentee
wife, and partly because the artichoke dip sitting on
the counter was awesome on the Triscuits. But a
movement in the doorway outside the kitchen caught
her eye, and when she realized her aunt was gesturing
to her, she quickly hustled over.

"Are you okay?" she asked, wishing Bess would
quit getting up when no one was around to catch her.
"Are you ready to leave yet?" She hoped fervently

that her aunt's answer was yes. It had been a stressful day, and artichoke dip or no artichoke dip, she wasn't sure how much longer she could watch Katharine and Warren bonding in formal wear.

Bess put a finger to her lips and shook her head. "Not quite. There's one more little job I have to do. This way." She pivoted quickly on her crutches, swung a little off balance, and righted herself just as Leigh swooped in with a hand.

"I've got it," Bess said firmly. She hobbled down the hallway to the base of the back staircase and took a deep breath. "Now I see why old lady Hodowanec never went down to Fellowship Hall," she said ruefully. "She had to get back up."

Leigh sighed. She had tried to talk Bess out of coming downstairs in the first place, but reminding her aunt of that would serve no purpose now. "Why don't we take the main staircase?" she suggested. "I don't think those steps are as steep, and they're carpeted."

Bess shook her head determinedly and began her slow and careful ascent. "I don't want anyone to see us."

Leigh got a sinking feeling in her stomach. It was a familiar sensation—the one that always popped up when someone was about to convince her to do something stupid, and she was about to agree to it. She sighed. "Where exactly are we going, Aunt Bess?"

"To find some answers," Bess said gravely. She didn't say any more until she had worked her way laboriously up the rest of the stairs and then stopped to rest a moment. "I don't know what Humphrey's trying to pull," she said finally, having caught her breath at last, "but I'm not going to let him get away with it." She set off again down the upstairs hall, and Leigh trailed her anxiously.

When they reached the door to the main church office, Bess glanced through its glass window, then turned to her niece with a whisper. "Good, it's clear.

Follow me." She moved silently past the office and swung open the next door down.

Leigh followed her aunt inside and instinctively shut the door behind them. Whatever her aunt planned on doing, it was undoubtedly better if she didn't get caught. "So," Leigh asked, studying the dark, musty-smelling room she assumed was Pastor Humphrey's office, "what exactly are we looking for?"

"I'm not sure," Bess answered. "But I'll know when I see it." She sat down in the swivel chair behind the desk and leaned her crutches against the wall.

Leigh looked around critically at Humphrey's modest, uninspired workspace. The walls were pale yellow, a tired-looking brown shag carpet covered the floor, and one burnt-orange curtain was stretched over the single window. An ancient mahogany desk sat in the center of the room, flanked only by a file cabinet and a dorm-sized refrigerator.

Hardly the lap of luxury, she thought to herself, wondering why any non-legitimate pastor would put up with such a hole. She was about to pose that question to Bess when a large picture on the wall caught her eye. It was a black-and-white portrait of a much younger Humphrey, his arm around a tiny woman with long, dark hair. It had all the earmarks of a wedding photo, including a bouquet, though the couple wore modest dress clothes instead of a tux and gown. The man looked happy as a clam, smiling gleefully, his freckled skin still smooth and glowing with youth. Just like the boy in the army picture.

"You can really see it there, can't you?" Bess said proudly. "Take off the wrinkles and the age spots, and there's no doubt about it. Reginald is Dan's 'Money,' sure as I'm alive."

Leigh didn't comment. "And this is the missionary?" she asked, referring to the bride. "I thought you didn't think he was really married."

Bess waved a hand toward the picture dismissively.

"Who knows? Maybe he was married once. Whoever that woman is, he didn't dump her immediately. There were more recent pictures of her hanging in the parsonage."

Leigh took another look at the picture, trying to determine if Humphrey looked like a man in love. "He seems happy enough," she mused out loud. "But his eyes aren't really twinkling. I wonder if a photograph can capture that."

"I need a screwdriver," Bess lamented, interrupting her thoughts. "Humphrey never locks his office, but he always locks the desk drawer when he leaves. The scoundrel."

Leigh watched as her aunt pulled on the handle of the thin center drawer—and slid it out easily onto her lap. "Well, I'll be darned!" Bess said with surprise, digging quickly into the contents. "It wasn't locked after all." She picked up a small key and studied it carefully, then dropped it unceremoniously into a breast pocket.

"Aunt Bess!" Leigh protested. "He could come back anytime, you know."

Bess ignored the comment. She rifled through the remainder of the drawer's contents, then fixed her eyes on the refrigerator. "Open that for me, would you, kiddo?"

Leigh stepped over to the mini-fridge and popped open the door, clueless as to why Bess would care. "There's nothing but some pop and some mustard," she said with frustration. "Can we go now?"

Bess sat back in the chair and propped up her chin with her hands. She looked at the window, and her brow furrowed. "What did he do that for?"

Leigh assumed she was referring to the less than stylish window dressing. "Do what for?"

"Stretch the curtain like that. There used to be two. What could he have done with the other one?"

Leigh couldn't see how Humphrey's taste in interior

decorating mattered to anything. "Aren't you going to look at the file cabinets?" she asked, eager to get the operation over with. "You've seen everything else."

Bess shook her head, her eyes still staring at the curtain. "He never locks the file cabinets—ergo, there's nothing incriminating in them."

Leigh sighed. She had always thought her aunt Bess was sharp, but her behavior in this case was a little over the top. Humphrey might be a con artist working an elaborate scam—then again, he might not. Granted, he looked an awful lot like the boy in the army picture, particularly when he was younger. But she could swear that the silly boot-camp nicknames meant nothing to him, and it was hard to believe he could have forgotten his old army buddies completely. Besides, other than the picture, Bess had no evidence at all that the reverend wasn't a reverend. What's more, he had saved her from both a fire and the embarrassment of being exposed as a burglar—no questions asked. So, what was his crime?

"It's time we leave, Aunt Bess," Leigh said firmly, retrieving the crutches. As she did, her eyes were drawn to a metal wastebasket on the floor beside the desk. It was filled with crumpled-up paper—and hypodermic syringes. Her eyes widened. She tapped Bess's arm and pointed.

Bess glanced briefly into the wastebasket, then took the crutches and struggled up. "Good eye, but that's nothing," she said with disappointment. "Humphrey's a diabetic." She led the way out of the office, and her niece closed the door behind them.

"Can we *please* go home now?" Leigh begged. "I'll bring the car around to the door by the office."

Bess nodded. She put a hand over her jacket pocket and smiled. "You'll be around tomorrow, won't you?"

Leigh had a strong instinct that the best answer for all concerned would be no, but that wasn't what she said. "Sure. Why?"

Bess grinned. "I need a ride to the S.P.E. Mini-Storage in Wexford. It seems I have a date with a padlock."

Leigh had slept fitfully, and she felt it. She was tired all over the next morning, and her stomach was still complaining about last night's lengthy hors d'oeuvres spree. When Bess announced she was ready to leave, Leigh gave up on breakfast and helped her aunt into the Cavalier. "You don't look so good this morning," Bess noted cheerfully once the car was moving. "Is the bed OK?"

"The bed's fine," Leigh answered glumly.

Bess let silence hang in the air for a moment, then cleared her throat. "She certainly was attractive, wasn't she?"

An image of Katharine Bower in her form-fitting green dress popped immediately into Leigh's mind. She squelched it. "Who? You mean Joy? Yes, she was gorgeous."

"No, silly," Bess said with a grin. "I mean your competition. The lawyer."

Leigh hit the brakes hard to catch a stop sign she'd almost missed. "I don't know what you're talking about. I'm not competing with anybody."

Bess scoffed. "Spare me. You were so green last night I thought you'd sprout roots. And you always insisted Mr. Harmon was just a friend."

"He is just a friend," Leigh said stiffly.

"Things change. Stop pussyfooting and tell him how you feel."

Leigh sighed inwardly. Either everyone around her was amazingly perceptive, or she was the most transparent person on earth. Either way, it was irritating. "It's complicated," she said noncommittally.

"Oh, bosh," her aunt said sternly. "Heaven knows what sort of rubbish your mother has been feeding you about men all these years, but as a woman who's

been married three times and only divorced once—let
me tell you this. Men don't like mind games. Play
it straight."

Leigh said nothing. She was normally averse to taking advice on her love life, particularly from family.
But her aunt did have some prowess in the area. Besides, she'd been ignoring advice her entire life, and
it hadn't gotten her squat.

"There it is!" Bess shouted as the mini-storage
came into view. She pulled the key out of her purse
and checked the number that was handwritten on the
back of the plastic S.P.E. key chain. "Number forty-
seven. Pull over there."

Leigh swung in front of the appropriate metal door
and parked. She tried not to dwell on the fact that
this marked the third time in less than a week that
her aunt had trespassed in, on, or through Reginald
Humphrey's private property. She also tried not to
dwell on the fact that for two of those crimes she had
been an accessory.

She helped Bess out of the car and onto her
crutches. "You realize, of course, that it's broad day-
light and there are any number of people around here
who might remember seeing us."

Bess's arms were occupied, but she waved the concern away with a flick of her wrist. "It doesn't matter.
I'll just say I was concerned about him and thought
there might be a clue to his whereabouts inside."

Leigh's eyebrows rose skeptically.

"Then I'll think of something else later," Bess said
impatiently. "Can you get the door up?"

Leigh took the key from her aunt's hand and turned
it in the well-oiled padlock. She slid the open lock out
of position and pulled up on the handle below. The
door opened easily.

Bess was in no position to limbo under the rising
door, but in her haste she came as close to it as a
woman on crutches possibly could. She swung inside,

pivoted in place, and smiled with glee. "See there! I could have told you."

Leigh surveyed the piles of boxes without enthusiasm. "Told me what?"

It took a moment for Bess to answer, as she began hobbling around, lifting box lids and grinning at the contents. "Don't you see? Furniture and a motorcycle I could understand. But this is all just little stuff. *Personal* stuff. Here's a CD player, and an electric screwdriver. This one's full of clothes."

When Leigh didn't respond, Bess sighed a little and went on. "He's been living in the parsonage for months now. Why wasn't all this stuff there with him? Why is he storing it at his own expense?"

Leigh shrugged. "Maybe this is like a retreat for him. Maybe he comes and communes with his stuff on his day off. Who knows?"

Bess shook her head. "If he planned on staying with the First Church of the New Millennium indefinitely, he'd have no reason to maintain a storage unit. There's plenty of room in the parsonage for all these boxes. I expected to find boxes in the attic when I went up there. You know what I found? Nothing. Not so much as an old pair of bowling shoes."

Leigh considered. It was on the strange side. The unit was a small one; everything in it could probably by packed into one van. Why *not* keep it at the parsonage?

"I'll bet my bottom dollar that at least some of this stuff *was* at the parsonage," Bess said pointedly. "People helped him move in—there'd be witnesses to know just how much stuff he had. But then he moved it here. Little by little, I'm guessing."

Leigh started to get a sick feeling as she realized where her aunt's theory was headed.

"Which can only mean," Bess said, her voice dropping to a theatrical whisper, "that he knew the parsonage was going to burn."

Chapter 8

"It would have been less suspicious if we'd just stayed," Bess chastised. "Running out like that only made us look guilty of something."

"We *are* guilty of something!" Leigh retorted. She didn't care if the patrol car *had* just been passing through. One look at it was more than enough to make her bundle Bess into the Cavalier and skedaddle.

"We'll just have to go back later, then," Bess proclaimed. "We didn't get a chance to open the boxes that were sealed—and you know they had the good stuff."

Leigh had no intention of taking her aunt anywhere near the mini-storage again, but she knew better than to debate the issue now. "So let me get this straight," she said as they drove toward the First Church of the New Millennium. "You think that Humphrey isn't a real minister at all, that he's nothing but a con artist. The whole church is just some power trip for him, and he threw a Molotov cocktail through his own window because he wanted more privacy?"

"Not *his* window," Bess corrected. "The church's window. He lost nothing—seeing as how he'd already moved out everything he cared about." She paused, and sighed a little. "Many a happy Presbyterian pastor has lived in that house over the years, but let's face it. The place was a bit of a dump when it burned. It hadn't been kept up for years, and it was always cramped and drafty in the winter. Not to mention the fact that it was under constant surveillance by the Ivey sisters. With the parsonage gone, Humphrey would be free to live in a nicer place, without being watched."

Leigh chewed on the theory as she pulled into the church parking lot. "But wouldn't arson be risky? I mean, if he was suspected, the police would check out his background. And if he's a veteran con, he'd surely have a rap sheet."

"He covered his tracks," Bess insisted. "Since he didn't own the house, he had no financial incentive that could raise suspicion. Plus, I think he planned on burning himself—a little. He could say he was too drugged up to notice the place was burning until it was pretty far gone." She let Leigh help her out of the Cavalier and onto her crutches. "I bet he never even had a headache."

"But if all he wanted was to move out, why the high drama?" Leigh continued, playing devil's advocate. A part of her still wanted to believe that Reginald Humphrey was legitimate—if only because she hadn't seen through him immediately herself. "Why would he tell everyone at church that he thought somebody was out to get him? Why would he use something as violent as a Molotov cocktail instead of rags in the garage or a broken toaster?"

Bess's mouth twisted in frustration. "Do I know everything? Give me some time, kiddo. I'll figure it out."

Despite her aunt's bravado, Leigh could sense the nervousness that still brewed underneath. She also knew what was causing it. The fact remained that Humphrey had gone out of his way to cover up Bess's burglary attempt. And he probably had a less than pure reason for doing so.

An unpleasant possibility struck her. "Aunt Bess," she said heavily, stopping before they reached the church door. "Humphrey didn't know you were hiding in his attic. All he knew was that you were upstairs. What if he thought you had *seen* him set the fire? Maybe he was trying to buy your silence!"

Bess stopped too, and considered. "That's possible," she said thoughtfully. "But if the whole truth did come out, he'd have a lot more to lose than I would. Who would care about my harmless snooping once they knew he was an arsonist?"

"The whole hero thing," Leigh thought out loud. "Maybe he was just upping the ante—giving you further to fall if you did tell."

Bess considered a moment more, then shook her head. "He'd need more than that to keep me from exposing him. Unless—" She swallowed, her pupils widening. "Unless he planned to hedge his bets by pinning the arson on *me*."

An image of a flaming bottle flashed across Leigh's mind, and with it another image she'd almost forgotten. Her blood ran cold. "The morning after the fire," she said weakly. "Your recyclables bin was up on the front porch, right next to the door. It had glass bottles in it. Those expensive flavored-water things. Kind of a weird shape."

"I don't drink anything like that," Bess said with surprise. "And I told you I didn't put the bin there."

"But it was out front and center first thing Friday morning," Leigh continued. "If I hadn't moved it, it still would have been sitting there when the fire investigator showed up."

Bess's voice turned icy. "And ten-to-one odds say the Molotov cocktail was the same kind of bottle." She looked up at her niece, her eyes flashing with fire. "That S.O.B. was setting me up."

Their conversation was interrupted by a short, stout woman about Bess's age. Her gray hair was cut short like a boy's, and she wore a western-style shirt decorated with embroidered vegetables. Leigh recognized her as one of the women she'd overheard talking in the kitchen last night—the one that had been so sure something terrible had happened to Humphrey.

"Come on in! Don't stand in the cold!" she called, holding open the door for Bess.

"Of course not. Thank you," Bess said, recovering quickly. She hobbled through the door. "Leigh," she said when they were all inside, "this is Barbara Jodon. She's one of our church secretaries."

Leigh and the woman exchanged greetings, and the threesome walked down the hall to the church office. The First Church of the New Millennium had two other secretaries—Ted's wife, Shannon, and a chubby bleach blonde whom Bess introduced as Cindy. Barbara's husband, Ed, a frail-looking man at least a decade older than his wife, sat at a desk stuffing envelopes. Shannon and Cindy stood in the center of the cluttered room, looking nervous.

"What is it?" Bess asked, worried. "Has he still not shown up?"

Shannon and Cindy shook their heads. Barbara began to pace. "No one's heard a word," she answered. "It doesn't look good. Shannon called the police earlier; they're going to trace the number."

Shannon nodded. Her eyes were wide with alarm, but she kept her voice calm. "They were really very helpful about it. I explained how unusual it was for him to be out of touch, not to mention missing a wedding."

"I made her remind them about the fire too," Cindy piped in, her voice a frightened whine. "He was sure someone was out to get him. It looks like he was right!"

"Please don't say that," Shannon pleaded. "It could just be his diabetes."

"Hello, ladies. Mind if I come in?" The booming male voice came from the doorway behind them, and Leigh turned to see a Franklin Park policeman stride into the office. "Ms. Hugh?" he asked, scanning the room. Shannon caught his eye, and he proceeded. "I thought I'd give you the news in person. The number you gave me matched up with a private boarding house in Ohio township. Little place—just four units. The manager said he had rented a unit to Humphrey over the weekend, but hadn't seen him since. He let me in the place, and I had a look around, but there's not much to tell. Suitcase full of clothes, half unpacked. Toiletry items. No signs of foul play."

There was another moment of silence as the news sank in, then Cindy whispered breathlessly, "He wasn't there?"

"No, ma'am."

Another moment of silence. "What about his car?" Bess asked.

"No green Buick Skyhawk on the property," the policeman answered, "but we'll start looking for it. I'll need some additional information."

None of the three women staffers seemed capable of movement. Barbara stood dumbly with her mouth open, Shannon had gone pale as a ghost, and Cindy was sweating profusely. "I'll do what I can," Bess offered, propelling herself toward the officer. "I'm a board member here. What information do you need?"

Leigh walked over to Shannon, who of the three church employees looked most likely to pass out imminently. "Are you OK?" she asked softly.

Shannon nodded and pushed her thick glasses higher up her thin nose. "I'll be all right," she said, struggling unsuccessfully to keep a tremor from her voice. "I just don't know what could have happened to him. We should have started looking for him sooner."

Despite Shannon's efforts to sound brave, she was obviously close to tears, and Leigh couldn't help wondering what was it about this man that made people care about him so much. If he was a con, he was a damn good one.

"Ladies?" Bess called from her position by the policeman. "Have any of you ever seen Reginald Humphrey go anywhere without his insulin kit?"

The three women exchanged glances, then shook their heads.

"A diabetic can't go without one for long," Bess explained. "Yet Officer Ward here"—she paused a second, bestowing a fawning look—"says there was nothing fitting that description at the boarding house. Ergo, Humphrey took it with him. Ergo—he meant to leave!"

The women all stared at Bess. Even Barbara's husband, Ed, who had continued to lick envelopes throughout most of the previous conversation, stopped suddenly and looked up.

"It's a good sign, of course," Bess clarified, not without a touch of exasperation. "If Humphrey had met with foul play at his apartment, his insulin kit would have been there."

"You're right!" said Cindy, her face brightening. "It is a good sign."

What Leigh's peripheral vision caught at that moment, however, was not. She'd had that "hand in the cookie jar" feeling all morning, and it appeared her come-uppance was now due. She walked toward the figure in the office doorway with foreboding. "Hi, Mom," she said with as much false enthusiasm as possible. "What are you doing here?"

Frances Koslow performed one of her favorite maneuvers—the dreaded chin-down, eyes-up, knitted-brow glare. "You're asking me? Your aunt had major orthopedic surgery less than forty-eight hours ago, and yet the two of you have been out cavorting for hours. I know, because I've been calling for hours. She should be at home with her feet up—"

"Oh, lay off, Francie!" Bess said quickly, hobbling up. She grabbed her sister's arm and rotated her back toward the door and away from the general conversation. "Leigh's been doing a wonderful job of keeping me company, and we were just on our way out to lunch. If you promise to behave yourself, I'll even let you join us."

Leigh steered her Cavalier out of the church parking lot and onto Nicholson Road with trepidation. Driving her mother anywhere was hard on the digestion, but having both Bess and Frances as passengers was a copayment waiting to happen.

Bess had clearly been eager to keep her little sister out of the church's problems, but since Frances's trouble sensors were second to none, Leigh feared the attempt was ill-fated. To make matters worse, in this isolated instance she *almost* agreed with her mother. Bess had been up and around entirely too much since the surgery, and that couldn't be good for her ankle. Leigh was pretty sure that Bess had been ready to go home for a while before Frances appeared, but now she would probably hobble till she dropped.

"How about Chinese?" Bess suggested cheerfully. "Or we could have fish sandwiches at the Fox Trot."

"I think we'd all be better off with something light," Frances announced. "A good salad bar, perhaps."

Bess scoffed. "You want to pretend you're a rabbit, fine. I want some real food. Hey, Leigh, how about the Franklin Inn? Francie can scrape the lettuce off my tacos."

Leigh wondered if it was possible to laugh and churn out stomach acid at the same time.

"Pothole, dear!" Frances informed from her position in the back seat. "Bear left. I'm sure I can find something healthy to eat at the Franklin Inn, but you'll have to turn around, you know. You're going the wrong way."

Leigh clenched her teeth. She hadn't been going the wrong way for Chinese, but two women bickering in the car was enough. The Franklin Inn it would be.

Without warning, Bess lurched across the front seat and nearly into Leigh's lap. "Turn around!" she ordered, sitting up and looking back over her shoulder. "I think I saw something!"

Leigh pulled into the next driveway and back out again, like she'd been planning on doing anyway. "Saw what? You mean at the park?"

"Yes!" Bess said excitedly, "pull in there!"

Leigh steered the Cavalier into the entrance of Winterhaven Park. "Now, what are you talking about?"

"Down there!" Bess said excitedly. "I saw it down by the ball courts!"

Leigh drove down the hill to where a green Buick rested in an odd position off the road, half in, half out of a clump of shrubs. "You think that's Humphrey's car?" she asked, parking.

"I know it is," Bess said smugly. "How many green '85 Skyhawks do you think there are around here?"

The car had hardly stopped moving before Bess opened the door and tried to get out by herself. Leigh cursed under her breath and ran around to the passenger side just as her aunt collapsed in a heap on the grass.

"You can't possibly walk over there," chastised Frances, who had emerged quickly from the backseat and was reaching down to pull her sister up. "The ground's uneven and there's frost on the grass."

Bess struggled back to her feet, shaking off Frances's steadying hand. "I'm all right," she insisted, her voice taut with pain. "Just give me the crutches."

"You're staying right here," Frances commanded, tossing the fallen crutches onto the Cavalier's backseat. "What on earth is so important about that car?"

Bess sighed. "Leigh, you go check it out, would you? I'll fill your mother in."

Wondering what version of the truth Bess was planning to tell, Leigh headed toward the rusted Buick.

Her insides churned as she looked for the outline of a head above the driver's seat. Of course he wouldn't be in it, she told herself. The car was in plain view from the ball courts; surely *someone* had been here in the last two days.

She moved closer, her guts still anxious. One foot slipped in a hole and her ankle twisted slightly. She looked up self-consciously, but Bess and Frances were deep in conversation.

Leigh looked back at the space above the driver seat. It looked empty. That was good. She kept moving forward until she was close enough to look in the back window. She wanted to look there first. She wouldn't admit why.

The Buick's backseat looked much like her own backseat, except with male-type junk. A necktie, leather gloves, boots, a paper sack from Wendy's, empty pop cans, and an ice scraper. She took a deep breath and stepped farther forward, looking into the front seat.

A winter coat on the passenger side. Nothing more.

She let out the breath and leaned against the car for a moment.

"What is it?" Bess yelled.

She shook her head. "Nothing," she called. "It's empty. Just a coat and some snow gear."

Bess was quiet for a second, then yelled again. "What about the insulin kit? It's a black plastic case."

Leigh turned around and examined the inside of the car more closely. There didn't appear to be any black case, but then, she couldn't see under the coat. Her hand reached for the door handle, and she pulled it skeptically. She was surprised when the door popped open without protest.

"It's not locked?" Bess said loudly, sounding equally surprised.

Assuming the question was rhetorical, Leigh leaned down and lifted the coat. There was no black plastic case underneath it. Nor, she decided after a quick but thorough check of the rest of the interior, was there a black case anywhere else in the car.

She closed the door and stood up.

"No kit?" Bess yelled.

She shook her head.

"Check the trunk!"

Leigh looked at the green metal trunk apprehensively. It wasn't a big trunk, but it was big enough. She walked over and put her hand on the latch, then paused. She should be curious. And she was curious. Just not *that* curious. Not with her knack at discovering things she didn't want to find. And at this particular moment and under these particular circumstances, she did *not* want to find Reginald Humphrey. She let her hand rest on the latch a moment. "It isn't opening," she announced.

"Try it again!" Bess yelled.

"It must be locked," she reiterated. It wasn't a bald-faced lie, she reasoned, walking back toward the Cavalier. After all, she didn't know that it *wasn't* locked.

"If the case is gone too, that's good," Bess said approvingly as her niece came within speaking-voice range. "It confirms my theory." Bess lowered herself carefully back into the car, and Leigh and Frances returned to their own seats. "Leaving the coat inside was a nice touch. Makes it look more like foul play. But he should have known that someone would look for the insulin kit."

"You don't seriously think he staged his own disappearance?" Frances asked skeptically. "What good would that do him?"

"It could do him a lot of good," Bess proclaimed smugly. "I'll bet you a nickel that the First Church of the New Millennium is about to receive a hefty ransom request."

"Oh, please," Frances scoffed. "No two-bit con

could succeed in pulling that off. He'd do much better
to keep embezzling, *if* that's what he was doing."

Leigh's head spun as she drove out of the park, her
eyes searching earnestly for a pay phone. It was bad
enough when her aunt played detective, but if her
mother started in as well—. She shivered. The possi-
bilities were too horrible to contemplate. How much
had Bess told Frances about Humphrey, anyway? And
why did Frances have to care? Didn't the Koslows'
oven need cleaning or something?

"He can't embezzle forever," Bess debated. "Particularly if he's onto me being onto him. Which, of
course, I am." She smiled proudly. "Like ugly on a
frog."

"And what if you're wrong?" Frances countered.
"What if he really was abducted? Or what if he went
for a walk around the park, took his insulin, then went
into hypoglycemic shock somewhere?"

Bess faltered only for a second. "Nonsense. If he
was going for a walk he'd have taken his coat. I'm
telling you, he planned this whole vanishing act from
day one. Reginald Humphrey is alive and well—and
busy planning his next scam."

Which had better not be setting you up for arson,
Leigh thought grimly. There was no phone in sight,
so she continued driving until they were back at the
church. She parked the car near the office door and
jumped out, leaving the engine—and the women's
mouths—running. Let them debate all they wanted to.
As far as she was concerned, this was a matter for the
police. They needed to know that Reginald Humphrey's car had been found, and they needed to check
that trunk. Whether it was empty or not, she didn't
know. But she did know one thing Bess and Frances
didn't. If the reverend had gone off intentionally, his
coat wasn't the only thing he had neglected to take
with him. His car keys were still in the ignition.

Chapter 9

How Bess could plow happily through three beef tacos and a margarita, Leigh couldn't imagine. Not with the possibility of her being framed for the Molotov cocktail just hanging there. Sure, putting a batch of similar bottles on her porch had been a long shot. Bess might have seen them herself, or the fire investigator might have missed them. But maybe it didn't have to be a sure thing. Maybe it was just a warning.

Leigh picked at her plate, wondering exactly how much Bess had told Frances about the situation. Clearly, she had not divulged everything. Frances seemed to know about the old photograph and to understand why her sister had gone to the parsonage. But she couldn't possibly know about Leigh's role in the "visit" to the mini-storage or she would be hyperventilating, to say the least. There was certainly no way Bess had mentioned the recyclables bin.

Yet Frances did pick up on one thing. She knew that no matter what her sister said, the quest to debunk the reverend was still very much in progress. Between carefully chewed bites of salad, Frances enumerated a long list of horrible things that could and would go wrong if Bess didn't keep her nose out of it. Bess responded by batting her eyes at the men at the bar, and Leigh kept her eyes on her plate, wishing fervently that her mother were at home doing mother things—like cooking pot roast and dusting off refrigerator tops.

"Lydie will be over at dinnertime," Frances announced as they returned to the church parking lot, where her Taurus was parked. "She's bringing a casserole, so don't cook anything." The comment was directed at Leigh, but both women knew that Leigh cooking was a non-issue. "Lydie has a class in the morning, though, and I have music club. Can you be at Bess's by seven-thirty?"

Leigh yawned mentally. "Sure."

"I really don't think this will be necessary much longer," Bess insisted, annoyed as always at the fuss. "I can almost handle the stairs by myself now, and there are plenty of people I can impose on as chauffeurs." Bess leaned toward Leigh. "But I may need your help with some other things," she whispered.

Leigh smiled hesitantly. Frances revved up her car and departed, and Leigh and Bess headed out behind her in the Cavalier. When Frances was out of sight, Bess pointed across the street. "We're not going home just yet, kiddo. Head right over there. You're about to meet the notorious Ivey sisters."

Not having the energy to argue, Leigh steered the Cavalier across the road and parked in the driveway of a small brick ranch with a giant picture window across the front. Before Bess was even up on her crutches, the house's front door opened. "Bess, dear," chortled the elderly woman who opened it. "We were hoping you'd come by. You're recovering beautifully. Come in and sit down—we'll set up a place for you to prop up that foot."

"Thank you, Betty," Bess cooed sweetly, then delivered a wink to Leigh. They followed the concrete walkway up to the door and were shown inside.

For a spinster who'd spent her entire life living with her sister, Betty Ivey was surprisingly attractive. She had high cheekbones and a profile like a china doll, with dark brown eyes and black hair that showed only a few strands of gray as it disappeared into a tightly

coiled French braid. She shut the door behind her
guests and ushered them into the living room. Leigh
noticed she walked with a limp.

"Here's tea!" rang a merry voice from the other
side of the room. "Specialty of the house. Almond
raisin herbal." Carrying a tray laden with four un-
matched china cups, Louise Ivey shuffled in. She
looked very similar to her sister, though the crop of
snow white hair on her head was obviously a wig. Her
limp was even more pronounced, but she had no trouble keeping the tray level. From the look of their
shoes, Leigh suspected both sisters were clubfooted—
a sad reason for their spinsterhood if true.

"My goodness, tea already! And you didn't even
know we were coming," Bess praised, after the obligatory round of introductions. She pulled her splinted
foot up onto the stool provided and centered it on the
cross-stitched cushion.

"Of course," said Betty with a smile. "You know
we always keep a little extra brewing for company."
The guests had been given places of honor on the
sectional couch that formed a semicircle around the
treasured picture window, while the Ivey sisters sat in
stiff, Victorian-looking furniture nearby.

Leigh took in the view uncomfortably, feeling like
she was doing something she shouldn't. The view was
panoramic—offering a sweeping spread of the whole
north and east corners of the church, the entirety of
the parking lot, and what used to be the front of the
parsonage. The window stretched from the floor to the
ceiling, with mint green curtains pulled back tightly to
either side.

"Do you know if the police have checked out the
reverend's car yet?" Louise asked innocently.

Leigh sputtered some tea over her hand, then wiped
it delicately on her jeans. She could only hope none
had landed on the cream-colored couch.

"The car?" Bess asked, sounding equally innocent.

"Of course, dear," Betty answered. "We saw the police car at the church this morning, so naturally we called over to find out what was going on. Then when you left and came back so quickly, we just had to call again. Barbara said that Reverend Humphrey must have left his car at the park."

"Apparently," Bess answered.

"I can't imagine what could have happened to him," Betty said worriedly, twisting her hands. "We haven't been able to watch over him like we used to—before the fire. That was such an awful tragedy."

Louise nodded soberly, but her eyes gleamed with excitement at the memory. "We were up all night. Sirens, fire trucks. It was terrible."

"After that we've been very careful to keep an eye on the church," Betty said seriously. "People count on us, you know. Ordinarily we're in bed by nine, but lately we've been trying to spell each other. We get nervous, just two old ladies out here all alone, with all this funny business going on!"

Leigh got the distinct impression that what the Ivey sisters said and how they felt were two different things.

"When was the last time you saw Reverend Humphrey?" Bess asked, moving things along.

"Monday night," the sisters answered together. They looked at each other, and Betty continued alone. "He was at the wedding rehearsal, of course. There were a lot of cars coming and going earlier, what with the youth meeting, but the reverend was there late, as usual. Louise went on to bed, but I stayed up. I wanted to make sure he took off safe, you know."

Leigh took another swallow of the bizarre-tasting tea and hoped she didn't look as skeptical of her hostesses' motives as she felt.

"Did anyone else stay late with him?" Bess asked.

"People trickled off," Louise broke in. "The wed-

ding party was the last to go. Shannon and Joy walked
out to their cars together about nine-thirty, I'd say."

"Nine thirty-eight," Betty corrected. "You went to
bed at nine forty-five."

"Did I?" said Louise, sounding miffed. "I know that
Ted Hugh's car and the reverend's car were still
there."

"Right," Betty responded smugly. "Then the reverend left."

Bess sat up. "Ted Hugh stayed late with Humphrey? Just the two of them?"

Betty nodded. "I think I had just drifted off when
the reverend's headlights woke me up." She gestured
toward the couch. "It's really comfortable to snooze
on, you know. Anyway, I checked the clock when I
saw him. It was 10:42. He took off in that awful old
green car and headed north."

"And hasn't been seen since," Louise declared dramatically. "The poor, poor man."

"I can't imagine what Ted Hugh was doing there
so late," Betty continued, ignoring her sister's interruption. "He didn't leave till after eleven."

"Eleven-oh-three, I think," said Louise.

"You weren't even awake," Betty snipped.

"I know when you came to bed," Louise protested.
"You came in and said that Ted had finally gotten off,
and I looked at my clock and it was 11:05."

Leigh started to feel a little queasy, and wondered
whether it was the bitter tea or the sour-cream and
green-onion enchiladas she'd just eaten. Perhaps it was
a combination effect.

"It is odd that Ted stayed at the church so long,"
Bess mused out loud. "Especially after Humphrey
left."

Betty and Louise Ivey exchanged a look that Leigh
couldn't interpret, and she wondered if the sisters
were really as precise with times as they seemed, or
if they just got a kick out of pretending.

"Would you ladies like some cake?" Louise asked suddenly. "The bridge club bought me such a huge one for my birthday; I doubt we'll ever finish it."

"We really must be going," Bess insisted, much to Leigh's dismay. A little cake was probably just what her stomach needed. "But happy birthday, Louise. Which one is this now, fifty-seven?"

Louise laughed heartily. "I'm eighty-one, you know. But I'm still the baby of the family. Betty's almost eighty-three."

"I'm eighty-two and a half," her sister replied without humor. "And never felt better." She turned to Bess. "Do you think the police will want to talk to us? We'd be happy to help, you know."

Louise nodded her head vigorously. "We can write down everything we remember. From the fire on. Should we call them, do you think? They haven't seemed so interested in our reports in the past," she added ruefully.

Bess smiled. "I'll think they'll appreciate this one. Just tell them about the last time you saw Humphrey's car."

The sisters stared at each other in delight, and their guests rose to leave. The almond-raisin tea lay heavily in Leigh's stomach as she departed, though she was beginning to think her gastric distress had more to do with the conversation than the menu. She had been trying to put a mental finger on what was bothering her, and she was getting closer. It had something to do with Warren's uncle Ted being the last person to see Humphrey before he disappeared.

The inconsistency didn't hit her until later that evening, as she was finishing up a generous helping of her aunt Lydie's sausage-rice casserole. But it bothered her enough that she left before dessert.

Please, be home.

Leigh knocked on Warren's door with apprehen-

sion. He had no obligation to be home at seven
o'clock on a Wednesday night, or to be alone if he
was. She could only hope.

The door opened, and he smiled tiredly. "Hey,
Leigh. What's up?"

He wasn't opening the door as wide as usual, but
he wasn't exactly blocking her way either. She scooted
inside quickly.

"You look beat," she said honestly. "Am I interrupting something?"

"Yes," he answered with equal honesty, motioning
her to the only chair in his living room that was not
covered with papers. "But I can use a short break.
You want a drink?"

Leigh smiled. There was nothing like being offered
refreshments by a handsome man in well-fitting jeans.
"A Diet Coke would be nice," she said. "Remind me
to replenish the kitty sometime."

Warren waved away the concern and brought her a
cola. For someone who was an expert in finance, he
was always generous.

"The wedding came off really nicely, I thought,"
she began, somewhat nervously. "I trust you gave your
mother a good report?"

He nodded. "She was quite pleased, but a little distracted." His voice turned serious. "My father was admitted to the hospital last night."

Leigh's eyes widened in alarm. "I'm so sorry. Is he
going to be all right?"

"He'll be fine," Warren answered optimistically.
"But it's definitely pneumonia. He'll be there a few
days."

Leigh felt terrible. Warren obviously had enough
worries without her coming to inform him of more.
She decided to delay the dirty work for a moment by
telling him about the time Bess had had her gall blad-
der out and had been chastised by the nurses for flirt-
ing with the orderlies. When she finished, he was

smiling again, and she couldn't help remembering how good he'd looked in that tux—smiling and laughing with someone else.

"Katharine looked nice," she said incongruously.

Warren looked at her curiously, then the ghost of a grin appeared on his face.

"What?" Leigh said, suddenly annoyed. "She did look nice! Can't I say that?"

He laughed out loud. "You can say whatever you want. She looked fabulous."

Leigh knew her cheeks were turning red, and it infuriated her. She buried her face in her Diet Coke and tried to think of another, less dangerous line of small talk.

Warren spared her the effort. "So, enough about my social life. What's been going on with you? Slipped any dates into that hectic work schedule of yours?"

Leigh swallowed. The answer was no, of course. In fact, being on a date was about the only thing that could ruin her joy in obtaining a free meal. "No dates," she confessed. "All the good ones are taken." She hadn't meant to include the last line, but it popped out anyway.

"Define 'taken,'" Warren said quickly.

Leigh raised her eyebrows. It was an odd question, but it played right into her hands. "Taken means married, engaged, or living together. Don't you think?"

"What about dating exclusively but not living together?"

Her heart rate increased. Was he talking about himself and Katharine? If so, what was he getting at?

"No," she said without thinking. "If they're not engaged or living together, they're fair game."

"I see," he said, his smile fading somewhat. An awkward silence followed, compelling Leigh to dive on into her real agenda.

"Have you heard about Reginald Humphrey's disappearance?" she asked.

His eyebrows arched. "You mean he's still AWOL? Since last night?"

Leigh nodded. "Since Monday night, actually. The women in the church office got worried when he didn't show up this morning, so they called the police. There's going to be an investigation." She went on to describe the discovery of the car, being careful to leave her aunt's hypotheses out of the picture, at least for now.

"The keys were in the ignition?" Warren asked incredulously. "That doesn't sound good. Maybe his sermon on Sunday wasn't just paranoia after all."

Leigh took a deep breath and forged ahead with the sticky part. She'd had enough unfortunate brushes with the law to know what made trouble, and Warren's uncle was brewing a batch of it.

"Do you remember before the wedding, when your uncle was ranting and raving about where Humphrey could be?"

"You think I could forget?" he asked, sounding tired again.

"Well, it seems like I remember him saying, 'He was fine when I left last night.' Do you remember that?"

Warren considered. "I can't swear he said that verbatim, but I do remember him talking about how he had a meeting with Humphrey after the rehearsal. He implied that they had gotten some things straightened out, which made everyone doubly surprised that Humphrey hadn't showed for the wedding."

Leigh sighed. Was she remembering things right? "Maybe it's nothing, then," she said hopefully. "But I could swear he said those exact words, 'He was fine *when I left.*'"

She took a moment to explain about the Ivey sisters and their picture window, then repeated their version of events for the night of the wedding rehearsal. "According to Betty and Louise, your uncle stayed at the church a good half hour after Humphrey left. Now, why would he do that?"

Warren's brow creased. "I can't imagine."

"Whatever he was doing," Leigh said hesitantly, "I'm wondering if he didn't want anyone to know about it. If he intentionally turned things around a little to cover it up. It might not have mattered, but if something really did happen to Humphrey, he's likely to be questioned, and I'm sure the Ivey sisters have already given their statement. I was just worried that—well, do you think he might—"

"Lie to the police?" Warren finished, following her train of thought easily. He leaned over and picked up the phone. "Hell, yes, he would."

Chapter 10

Warren returned the phone to its cradle without dialing. "No," he said thoughtfully, "this demands a personal visit. Shannon's always telling me I should drop by more often." He turned to Leigh. "Do you want to come along?"

She nodded quickly. Hanging with Ted Hugh was not exactly her idea of fun, but if it meant more quality time with Warren, she could manage. She had gotten the distinct impression that he and Katharine had reached some critical juncture, and that he was close to telling her about it. If the mood struck, she wasn't going to miss it.

A half hour later, she and Warren were settled comfortably on a billowy brown couch in Ted and Shannon Hugh's dark family room. She had expected Warren to bring up the subject at hand immediately, but instead he opened with family chitchat. He was probably trying to get his uncle warmed up, but Leigh had no patience for that. She wanted to know what the Franklin Park police had reported about Humphrey's car. Particularly about that trunk.

"So, Shannon," she said quietly, as soon as she could get the other woman's attention away from her husband, "what did the police say about the car?"

Shannon paled a little, and Leigh's stomach flip-flopped. She knew in the back of her mind that if a less than breathing Reginald Humphrey had been discovered in the trunk, she would have heard something hours ago. But the possibility still made her nervous.

"They just confirmed what you said you saw," Shannon answered.

Leigh let out the breath she'd been holding. She could chalk up another failure for her instincts, but in this case that was a good thing.

"They did say," Shannon added in a somewhat shaky voice, "that the key to his new apartment was on the chain with his car keys."

As Leigh digested this information, she noticed that Warren and Ted had at some point started listening to the conversation.

"It doesn't look good for Humphrey," Ted announced, his voice once again a little louder than appropriate. "Guess he had some real enemies after all."

His tone held a distinct lack of empathy, and Leigh threw a sideways glance at Warren to see if he had noticed.

It appeared that he had. "So I hear you were the last one to see him before he disappeared," he asked his uncle smoothly. "Did the police ask you anything about how he seemed when you left him?"

Ted's eyes flickered over to his wife, who studied her shoes. He answered with a calmer voice. "They came and talked to me at work this afternoon, actually. Shannon had told them I had a meeting with Humphrey after the rehearsal."

"I was so embarrassed that they bothered Ted at his office," Shannon broke in, distressed. "But after the car was found, the police seemed to get a lot more serious about the whole thing. I really think they suspect foul play now." She stumbled over the last words, her chin quivering.

"It's all right, honey," Ted said tenderly. Leigh looked at him in surprise. She would have classified him as a lout across the board, but judging from the expression in his eyes, his concern for his wife was genuine.

"They wanted to know just when Shannon and Joy left, and just when I left," he continued. "I didn't pay much attention, but Shannon says I got home at quarter after eleven, so I figure I must have left the church around eleven." He sighed and shook his head. "And nobody's seen him since."

There was a brief silence before Leigh jumped in to ask the fated question. "He was still at the church when you left?"

Ted didn't bat an eye. "Oh, yeah. He's a night owl—stayed late a lot, working on the computer. He didn't have an office in the parsonage, and—well, I guess he didn't have one at that boarding house either."

A silence hung thickly over the cozy family room as Leigh shot a glance at Warren. He looked stricken, an appearance she no doubt wore herself on the many occasions when her own relatives self-destructed. She looked to see if Shannon and Ted had noticed, but they seemed comfortably oblivious to the problem.

Leigh started to speak, but Warren stopped her with a hand on her knee. "I have to tell, you, Ted," he said seriously. "You may have some trouble with the Ivey sisters."

At the name of the First Church of the New Millennium's celebrated "caretakers," both Ted and Shannon sat up. "They were still awake?" Ted asked with surprise. "I thought they went to bed at nine!"

"They told Bess and me that they'd been taking turns staying up late ever since the parsonage fire," Leigh explained, noting that the sisters' bedtime seemed to be common congregational knowledge. "I think they felt guilty about not being more help."

Ted did not appear interested in the Ivey sisters' guilty consciences. "What did they say they saw?" he asked, growing agitated. "Did they tell the police?"

He had risen from his chair and was advancing on Leigh when Warren stood up in between them.

"We don't know that they've told the police anything," Warren said calmly. "But they told Bess and Leigh that Humphrey left the church a half hour before you did."

Ted's face registered an odd jumble of emotions. At first he seemed frightened. Then relieved. Then confused. "They said . . ." He faltered. "OK. I guess, I mean . . ." He paused a moment and swallowed, then spoke in a steadier tone. "They don't know what they saw."

Warren looked at his uncle worriedly, and Leigh didn't blame him. He motioned for Ted to sit down again, which the man did—heavily enough to make his recliner walk a step backward. Shannon's face had gone stark white, with beads of sweat forming on the bridge of her nose as she sat motionless in her rocker.

"It will be all right, Ted," Warren said firmly, slipping into politician mode. "But I do think you should consult a lawyer. It never hurts to have a professional's opinion about how to protect yourself. You must realize, there could be a criminal investigation coming out of this. You don't want a minor misunderstanding about your comings and goings to muddy the waters."

"Of course not," Ted said quickly. "That's all it is. A misunderstanding. He was fine when I left him. Just fine."

Leigh stewed in silence for a few minutes as Warren drove them home, then decided she couldn't take it anymore. "He was lying through his teeth, you know," she said with frustration. "Why didn't you just ask him what really happened?"

"You'd have to know my uncle," Warren answered patiently. "He doesn't deal well with accusations, and getting him angry wouldn't help anything. What he needs to do is talk to Katharine. She can get the real story, and she'll know how to coach him." He sighed. "I'm not sure I even *want* to know the real story."

Leigh did. "And did you see how upset Shannon got? I think she's afraid that there's a lot more going on than just a misunderstanding."

"Shannon," Warren responded, "lives in daily fear of what incredibly stupid thing her husband is likely to do next. I don't know how she stands it." He looked over at Leigh and chuckled. "Or maybe I do."

She looked back at him, puzzled. Was he talking about her or Katharine? The lawyer certainly wasn't in the habit of doing stupid things. Whereas she— *Well, anyway.*

Leigh knocked on Bess's door the next morning at 7:42. It was the best she could do, since she'd gotten next to no sleep the night before. She had failed once again in her attempts to make Warren spill his guts about Katharine—in fact, he had retreated to his apartment immediately after their return, to call *her,* of course. She had then tossed and turned all night with a wide assortment of bad dreams—ranging from red-haired, green-eyed pastors packing semi-automatic weapons to Katharine Bower in a wedding dress. She still wasn't sure which one was worse.

"Good morning, honey," Leigh's aunt Lydie said pleasantly, opening the door and stepping outside. "I wish I could stay and chat with you a while, but I've got a class, you know."

That sort of statement was as close to a reproach as Lydie ever got—one of the more obvious contrasts between her and Leigh's mother, her identical twin. "Just two things you should know. One, I talked to Cara last night, and she told me to ask you if you'd— and I quote—'made your move' yet."

Leigh rolled her eyes. Even in the middle of a two-week family vacation to Sanibel Island, her cousin found time to hassle her. "Tell her the timing's still not right," she answered. "And to give baby Matt a kiss for me. Next?"

"Number two," Lydie continued, "I put in a new shower head with a hose sprayer and a tub bench. Bess can handle it all by herself. She just needs to conquer those stairs, and then she can get rid of us all." She waved good-bye with a wink and headed out to her car, whistling.

Leigh smiled. Her father was handy too, but family appliance emergencies had always been Lydie's domain. Leigh watched her aunt saunter off student style—in jeans and a long denim coat, with a backpack dangling over one shoulder. Lydie had not had an easy life—her husband had deserted her when she was pregnant with Cara—and she had had to work at least two jobs for years to make sure that her daughter got through college. Now Cara was returning the favor, and Lydie was on cloud nine.

"A sitting-down shower!" Leigh remarked to Bess as she walked inside. "You think Lydie'd make me one too?"

But Bess couldn't respond, as she was in the middle of a phone call. "Calm down, Mary Rose," she said soothingly. "I'll come down and we'll pick it up, all right? Dr. Koslow will take care of it. You just sit tight till we get there, okay?"

Leigh didn't bother to take off her coat, but went to fetch her aunt's instead. Bess hung up the phone and reached for it gratefully. "Thanks, kiddo. We've got to make a quick run to your father's place—there's a groundhog at the shelter that was hit by a car. Somebody left it in the drop-off run last night, and the kennel girl says it's cold as ice and barely breathing. I'm not sure what your dad can do, but we can't let the poor thing suffer."

Bess waited in the car while Leigh ran into the shelter, but it was clear when she arrived at the treatment room that a trip to the Koslow Animal Clinic wouldn't be necessary.

"It's dead, isn't it?" asked the nearly hysterical teenager who appeared to be manning the shelter by herself. "I hated to bother your aunt, but the other kennel guy called in sick, and I couldn't get the manager on the phone—"

"It's okay," Leigh said calmly. "I'm sort of a vet tech. I'll take care of it." She took off her coat and looked at the deceased creature with curiosity, having not seen a wild groundhog up close and personal before. To the shelter worker's credit, she had done a good job of rescuing it from the drop-off pen, bundling it in a large blanket and getting it inside without further injury to it or—as the case might have been if the animal were feeling better—to herself. "Why don't you go and break the news to my aunt?" Leigh suggested. "Tell her I'll be out in just a minute."

The girl smiled gratefully and made a quick exit, obviously glad to be spared the rest of the process. Leigh placed the groundhog's body carefully into a doubled plastic bag and tied it up tight. Looking around the treatment room, she wondered briefly if the break-in earlier in the week might have been drug-related. Her father did come out to the shelter to do treatments and the occasional euthanasia, but she knew he would never keep controlled drugs on site. Those he kept locked up at the clinic, which had a suitably elaborate security system. Still, not every ketamine-seeking junkie would know that.

She opened the door to the basement and went back for the bundle, which was heavier than she'd thought. Like the giant deer who were more numerous than squirrels in the well-groomed Pittsburgh suburbs, the local groundhogs lived well. And this one, she surmised, had also lived long, which made her feel at least a little better about the task at hand.

She descended the stairs into the basement, where

she noted that the broken door had been replaced by a considerably more hardy metal one. Complete with lock, dead bolt, and chain.

Using a spare elbow to pop open the chest-style deep freeze, she lifted up the awkward bundle and leaned over to lay it inside. Something wrapped in a ragged orange blanket took up most of the available floor space, but she managed to find an unoccupied corner just as the bag began to slip from her grasp. She was in the process of straightening up when her eyes rested on a round edge of black poking out from under the orange wrap. She'd seen big paw pads before, but this one had to come from a wolfhound.

Curious, she lifted back the blanket, and her blood went cold. The black object wasn't a paw pad. It was the heel of a man's dress shoe. And judging from the wrinkled black sock and hairy, snow white flesh above it, the shoe was connected to a man.

Chapter 11

Leigh stood a few feet back from the freezer, staring at the open lid. It would be better if what she had just seen—and recoiled from so hastily—had been only her imagination. But she'd never had that kind of luck.

She stood another moment, knees knocking, then took a deep breath and stepped up to the freezer again. Forcing herself to look down, she surveyed the shape under the orange blanket, then let her eyes rest on the part she'd uncovered.

Damn.

She closed the freezer lid quickly, having seen all she needed—and certainly all she wanted—to see. Rubbery legs carried her quickly up the stairs, through the treatment room the oblivious teenager was cleaning, and safely into the lobby. She sank into the chair behind the reception desk, picked up the phone, and dialed 911. Somebody explained the situation to the dispatcher—she supposed it was her. Then she hung up the phone and moved mechanically out the door and over to the Cavalier, where her aunt sat waiting with the engine running.

"What's wrong?" Bess said anxiously, rolling down the car window. "Why are you standing there without your coat?"

Leigh looked down at the thin turtleneck she was wearing, and it occurred to her that she was freezing. Trembling all over, she moved quickly around the car and slipped in the driver's side. As she rubbed her hands in front of the heating vent, she thought about saying something. But nothing happened.

"You're scaring me, kiddo," Bess said seriously. "What's up?"

Leigh sat for another second before answering. "I put the groundhog in the freezer."

"Thank you," Bess said impatiently. "I'll tell your dad we need another crematory run. Now, what the devil's wrong with you?"

Leigh exhaled and shook her head, trying to clear the fogginess. She then turned reluctantly to face her aunt. "The freezer wasn't empty," she said with a struggle. "There was a person in it."

Bess's pale blue eyes bore into hers, the pupils widening. "A dead person?" Leigh nodded, and they both sat dumbly for a moment.

"Was it—" Bess broke off her statement, then swallowed. "Was it *him*?"

Leigh hesitated, then shrugged. She hadn't seen past the man's calf, and she didn't want to presume, no matter what her gut was telling her.

But Bess studied her niece's face, and an exchange of words wasn't necessary. They both knew what the other was thinking. Reginald Humphrey was no longer missing.

He was dead.

It seemed like a lifetime later when Detective Maura Polanski weaved her way through the crowded reception area of the animal shelter and plopped down on the plastic chair next to Leigh.

Leigh braced herself.

"Are you OK?" Maura asked with a sigh.

Leigh looked up at her friend and smiled. The words were sincerely spoken, albeit a bit strained. "I'm all right," she answered sheepishly. "Thanks for asking."

Maura said nothing more for a while, and neither

did Leigh. Her sixth sense was well aware that although Maura was trying her best to be supportive, a part of her wished she had never heard the name Leigh Koslow. And no wonder. There seemed to be no jurisdiction where the policewoman was safe from Leigh's particularly onerous brand of bad luck.

"Are you working on this one?" Leigh asked finally, unable to stand the silence. "The homicide detectives have already questioned everybody. I thought you just did burglaries and stuff."

Maura glanced at her uncomfortably. "This started out as a burglary, remember?" she said grimly.

Leigh nodded. It didn't take a brain surgeon to make the connection, though it was considerably more obvious in retrospect. Reginald Humphrey's body had probably lain in that freezer for three days—since sometime after the wedding rehearsal Monday night. She shivered. It must have been there the whole time she had been down in the basement the next morning, messing with the broken door. And the whole time Maura was investigating . . .

Ouch. Was that a problem? Surely not. The shelter staff had all insisted that nothing had been stolen. They'd never even thought to look in the freezer— and why should they? There was nothing in it to steal, after all.

Leigh searched her friend's face for signs of guilt. Guilt was an emotion she knew well. She was a master at it, in fact. She just didn't know how to get rid of it.

"You had no reason to look in the freezer," she stated, fishing.

Maura started a little, then looked miserable.

Guilt confirmed. "You didn't!" Leigh insisted. "None of these other bozos would have checked it either, that's for sure." She had no independent knowledge of the prowess of the county detectives, but the ones she had met in the city hadn't impressed her. Maura, on the other hand, was one in a million.

"Don't," Maura said sternly, shaking her head. "No excuses. I just want to get busy and close out my part of this ASAP." She cleared her throat. "So tell me, off the record, why were you and your aunt snooping around after Reginald Humphrey?"

Leigh bristled a little. She never "snooped." That was Bess's area. "I was just helping my aunt get around," she answered defensively. "She, like everyone else at the church, was interested in knowing what happened to the reverend."

Maura looked at her skeptically. "You reported the car."

Leigh started to say something but stopped. Perhaps she was a little more entwined in the whole mess than she wanted to admit. Bess had lied about her role in the parsonage fire, and she and Bess had broken into Humphrey's mini-storage after he died. Had they left prints? Of course they had. *Fabulous.*

She sighed. The homicide detectives had not yet probed beyond this morning's events, but it was clear she would eventually have to come clean about the whole week's worth of debacles, or things were going to get nasty. And how could she explain her actions without getting Bess into trouble?

"Look," she said tiredly. "It's a long story, and I really don't think you want to hear it now."

The detective's eyes looked pained. She obviously assumed the worst, which made Leigh bristle again. "It's not like I *want* to find bodies," she protested. "I didn't even look in the trunk!"

Maura raised an eyebrow. But as Leigh was debating whether or not to explain, she was interrupted by one of the homicide detectives. The crime-scene unit was done. It was time for her part in the identification process.

She rose, irritated by the fact that her knees had started to knock again. The coroner's van was waiting out front; a covered stretcher was next to it ready for loading. She approached it and took a deep breath. The detective pulled back the sheet, and she nodded once before turning away. She barely knew Reginald Humphrey, and it wasn't as if she took his passing personally. But recognizing his frozen face confirmed the sinking feeling she had been harboring all morning. Finding the good reverend had produced as many questions as answers, and it was bound to produce no small amount of trouble. For her family—and Warren's.

"Let's get on with it," Bess said miserably, shutting the door of the Cavalier. They had finally been given clearance to leave, and despite Leigh's best efforts to convince her aunt to go home, they were on their way to the First Church of the New Millennium instead. It was only a few hundred yards away, but walking even that short distance was out of the question for Bess, who looked far more exhausted than she would admit. When the word spread, she had insisted, people would start to gather at the church, and as a board member she had an obligation to be there.

But Leigh was beginning to see that her aunt's role at the First Church of the New Millennium went beyond board meetings. Bess seemed to have set herself up as an incognito protector of the flock, and it was a crusade she showed no signs of backing down from.

"I'm truly sorry the man is dead," Bess announced soberly, more to herself than to Leigh. "But I still say he was a con. Nothing's changing my mind about that."

Leigh didn't disagree. It made a lot more sense for someone to have murdered Humphrey the con artist than Humphrey the saint.

"But it doesn't matter now *what* he was," Bess continued. "He won't be cheating the congregation anymore, so they may as well have fond memories of him. In fact, it's best now that they never know."

Leigh looked at her aunt with surprise. She had often wondered if Bess's desire to bring down Humphrey wasn't some sort of personal vendetta, but it was clear to her now that Bess's first priority was—and had always been—the church. Unfortunately, her thinking in that vein seemed a little blind.

"But, Aunt Bess," Leigh said carefully, "*somebody* else already knows about Humphrey, because *somebody* had to murder him."

Bess stared at her niece indignantly. "You don't think a church member killed him!"

Leigh squirmed uncomfortably. She didn't want to cast aspersions on Bess's fellow churchgoers—particularly those related to Warren Harmon. But the facts were hard to forget. Not only had Ted Hugh been the last person to see Humphrey alive, he had lied to the police about it.

"That's preposterous," Bess said defensively. "*You* didn't see the evidence they brought out of the basement!"

Having reached a parking spot at the church, Leigh pulled her keys out of the ignition and turned to face her aunt squarely. "What evidence?"

"The bags, of course," Bess answered, somewhat smugly. "I was surprised you weren't outside watching with me. Before they brought the body out on the stretcher, they brought out a few things in plastic bags. One of which was Humphrey's insulin kit."

Leigh blinked. The insulin kit that Humphrey was supposed to have taken with him everywhere. Why on earth would his killer dump it in the freezer with him?

"So, you see," Bess continued, "we don't know that it was murder after all."

Leigh stared at her aunt in amazement. *"We don't?"*

"Weren't you listening to what all those detectives and forensics people were saying?" Bess asked accusingly. "Well, I was—very discreetly, of course. They couldn't find a murder weapon. They couldn't even find a murder wound. No bashed-in head, no cut throat. Just a man all curled up, frozen solid."

Leigh read her aunt's thoughts with incredulousness. "No," she said firmly. "Reginald Humphrey did not *accidentally* lock himself and his insulin kit in an empty freezer. That's insane."

Bess pursed her lips and looked at her niece with disappointment. "I suppose you have a better theory?"

Leigh didn't answer but got out of the car and walked around to help her aunt into the church. She had a theory, all right, and it made a heck of a lot more sense than Bess's. She just hoped it wasn't correct.

Chapter 12

The news of Reginald Humphrey's passing had spread quickly, indeed. Bess had called the church staff from the animal shelter shortly after the body was found, but even if she hadn't, the procession of police cars that streamed down Nicholson Road past the church would have been hard to miss. The phone chain had begun in earnest, and by the time Bess and Leigh entered the parlor of the First Church of the New Millennium, it was already crowded with people and platters.

Leigh settled her aunt in a comfortable armchair and immediately escaped out into the hall. Her aunt might be able to sit around with a somber expression on her face saying wonderful things about a man she thought was a monster, but Leigh didn't feel so obligated. Besides, there was something she needed to see. She made her way quietly down to the door of the pastor's office, then opened it and slipped inside.

The little room still seemed dark, even with the lights on and the cold winter sunlight streaming around the single curtain. She began to walk toward the window, but a familiar voice stopped her.

"Leigh? Are you all right?" Warren caught up with her in a single stride and wrapped one arm comfortingly around her shoulders. It was a brotherly gesture at best, but the wave of warmth it sent through her made her spine tingle.

Chill out, she reminded herself quickly.

"I heard you were the one who found the body," he continued, looking at her with concern. "I'm sorry. That must have brought back bad memories."

The empathy in his soft brown eyes made her stomach twitch, and she looked away. Had he come to the church just to see her? "I'm all right," she said with a smile, trying to sound more cheerful than she felt. "You know me, I just have bad karma."

Warren didn't smile. "Are you really OK?"

She nodded. It was nice of him to worry about her, but his uncle was the one in real trouble. Speaking of which . . .

She turned and walked to the window, then lifted a corner of the ancient curtain and rubbed it between her fingers. "How is your family holding up?" she asked over her shoulder.

"The Florida contingent is doing well," he answered. "My father should be out of the hospital soon. As for Ted and Shannon—"

"Warren?" The interruption came from the office doorway, where Katharine Bower had appeared, laptop case in hand. "Good. You're here. Hello, Leigh," she added with a polite wave.

Leigh's heart sank, but she nodded politely back. So much for Warren having come to see her.

"Your uncle says we can talk in one of the classrooms," Katharine announced, turning back to Warren. "You'd like to be there?"

He nodded and started to follow her out.

"Wait a minute," Leigh said hurriedly, her voice nervous. "I think there's something you two should know."

The Sunday school room was chilly, but Ted Hugh's brow was dotted with sweat. Leigh almost felt sorry for him as he sat holding his wife's hand, looking like a little boy in a principal's office. She felt rather uncomfortable being there herself, but Katharine had

asked her to come and repeat exactly what the Ivey
sisters had said.

She watched Ted Hugh's face as he told his side of
the story, and she watched Warren's face as he
listened.

"Humphrey and I had a fight," Ted proclaimed, a
bit melodramatically. "I wanted to talk to him after
the rehearsal, because I wanted to tell him that if he
did anything to ruin my little girl's wedding, I was
going to kill him."

Shannon's pale face tensed as her husband talked,
and Warren's color didn't look so good either. Katharine sat impassively, her fingers clicking rapidly on
the laptop.

"I didn't mean it, of course," Ted recanted quickly,
with a glance at his wife. "But I was angry. When I
met him that night, I exploded—and I suppose I made
him nervous. He's—I mean, he *was*—such a little guy.
He tried to calm me down, promised nothing would
happen, said that everything would be fine. Then he
said he had to leave, and he skedaddled. End of
story."

Katharine's fingers continued to click on the keyboard for a few seconds, after which she asked the
obvious question. "Why were you worried about him
ruining your daughter's wedding?"

Ted stole another glance at his wife, who nodded at
him encouragingly. Leigh wasn't certain, but it almost
looked as though Shannon was anxious to hear the
answer herself.

"We had another argument a while back," Ted answered tensely. "What it was about isn't important.
But I felt like I'd made an enemy out of him, and I
was afraid he would take it out on Joy."

Leigh felt, rather than saw, Warren take a deep
breath beside her. He started to speak, but Katharine
cut him off with a raised hand. "That's fine," she said
to Ted. "Now, Leigh," she said without turning her

head, "would you please repeat what the Ivey sisters told you they saw the night of the rehearsal?"

Leigh repeated the story succinctly, feeling guilty again for being the bearer of bad tidings. Katharine recorded everything she said, then turned back to Ted. "And this contradicts the statement you gave the Franklin Park police?"

He winced slightly, then gave Katharine a look that bordered on pathetic. "Who do you think they'll believe?"

"The most credible person without a motive to lie," she answered tonelessly. "What exactly did you tell the police?"

Ted repeated what he had told Leigh and Warren before, then tried to explain. "It was just a harmless little lie—I didn't think much of it. But I didn't want anyone to know I was the last person to leave the church that night. There are procedures for closing up everything, you see. I hung around and stewed a while, then I left. I don't think I even locked the door. When the police came to question me, I panicked—I was just trying to cover my tracks. I had no idea Humphrey would get killed there."

His last word struck Leigh with a jolt. Katharine looked up from her laptop, and Warren tensed in his seat. Shannon remained pale and stricken, staring at an empty spot on the table. "You think Humphrey was killed at the church, then?" Katharine asked smoothly.

A few extra sweat beads broke out on Ted's brow. Shannon looked up at him in alarm, then tightened her grip on his hand.

"I don't know," he said defensively. "I guess I just assumed. Since he was found so close and all." His voice trailed off.

The room fell silent for a moment, and Leigh opened her mouth to say something, but she hadn't gotten a word out before Katharine cut her off with a fierce head shake.

"I'm not feeling so well," Ted announced. "Could I grab a drink?"

"I'll get it for you," Shannon said quickly, jumping up.

"If no one minds, I'd like to get it myself," Ted said shakily, rising. "It's stuffy in here."

"That's fine," Katharine said cheerfully. "Can we start back up in five minutes or so?"

Ted nodded and left the room on Shannon's arm. As soon as they were gone, Warren rose and let out a frustrated breath. "I know it looks bad, but I'm telling you, Kath, Ted wouldn't kill anybody. He's obviously lying about something, but he's not a killer."

Katharine had begun to type again and didn't look up when she answered. "It's hard to know sometimes, Warren. I didn't get the idea you two were close."

"We're not," he responded, a bit stiffly. Leigh sat quietly in her chair. She didn't want to seem like a vulture, but it was hard not to notice the absence of the conviviality Warren and Katharine had shared at the wedding. Had they been fighting?

"But I've known Ted all my life," Warren continued. "And I know that he's just a harmless hothead. He blows his top easily and he makes a lot of noise, but that's where it ends. I've never seen his anger get physical, not ever. He's simply not a violent man. He was good to my aunt, he's been good to Shannon, and he's always treated Joy like a princess."

Katharine paused, looked up from her laptop, and took off her glasses. "You don't have to defend him to me, remember?" she said in a whisper, looking at Warren with an ardor that made Leigh's cheeks burn. "Defending him is my job, and I'm going to do it very well."

Warren sat back down. "Of course you are," he said softly. Then he sighed. "I'm sorry, Katharine. As you can obviously tell, I've had my own doubts about the man. How he knew Humphrey was killed here I don't even want to guess."

The lawyer glanced at Leigh. "I'm sorry I cut you off before, but I didn't want Ted to know what you suspect—at least not yet. There'll be plenty of time for that after I get him to tell me what really happened. But in order to do that, I'll need to talk to him alone, because it's clear he's trying to hide something from his wife."

"I'm sure you're right," Warren said admiringly. "We'll go, then." He rose, and Leigh did the same. "Thanks, Kath," he said, giving the lawyer's shoulder a squeeze on the way out. "I'll call you later."

Leigh's insides churned as she watched the affectionate gesture. So much for the fighting theory.

"And, Leigh," Katharine called out as they were about to leave, "it would be in my client's best interests if the information you remembered does not come to the attention of the police any sooner than necessary. I thought you should know that."

Leigh nodded, and left the room.

"Are you staying here for a while?" Warren asked when they were alone in the hall. He didn't seem himself, and Leigh looked at him sympathetically. It was rough having someone in your family in trouble with the police. At least, that's what her family kept telling her.

"I need to be with Bess," she said with a sigh. "Has anyone called Joy about all this?"

Warren shook his head. "I'm hoping we won't have to. She'll be coming home soon enough anyway." He broke off his next statement, but Leigh could read his thoughts. *And her father may very well be in jail.*

"If there's anything I can do—" Leigh began.

But he quickly cut her off, laying a hand on her arm. "No, this isn't your problem. What Katharine said back there—about information that could hurt my uncle's case—forget about it. If the police ask you about the curtain, I want you to tell them the truth. Not that you wouldn't, but . . . I just want to make it clear that you're under no obligation to protect my relatives. Understand?''

Leigh saw the concern in his eyes and agreed with a smile. Warren said good-bye and headed for the exit, and she started back toward the parlor, pausing at Humphrey's office on the way.

How *had* Ted Hugh known that the reverend was killed at the church? Other than the police, she was the only one who had seen the wrapping around the body. And besides Warren and Katharine, she was the only one who knew that that wrapping was actually a curtain—an ugly orange curtain whose abandoned mate still hung right in front of her—over Reginald Humphrey's office window.

The parlor at the First Church of the New Millennium held only the living, but the atmosphere was as oppressive as any wake.

Leigh stood in the doorway and cast her eyes over the glum crowd. Shannon had arrived—evidently she had been dismissed by Katharine too—looking paler than ever and zombified to boot. Bess sat in the same place Leigh had left her, surrounded by a throng of church members talking in awkward, hushed tones.

"Hard to believe, isn't it?" Leigh turned to see Ed, the office envelope licker, at her elbow, leaning on a cane and nibbling on a celery stick. "Hiding in a freezer like a little kid. Don't know what could have possessed him."

Leigh's eyes widened. "Who told you that?"

He looked at her with surprise. "I don't know— that's just what everyone's saying. That it had to be some sort of accident." He studied her confused face. "You know something different? You saw the body too?"

Leigh threw a glance at her aunt, who just happened to be watching her at the same moment. Bess's expression turned sheepish, and she looked away. Leigh sighed. Evidently, the facts at hand had gotten slightly embellished, and there was no doubt by whom.

"It's too early to draw conclusions," she answered. Then, hearing a formal voice in the hall behind her, she turned around.

"Excuse me, Miss Koslow. Are you a member here?" It was one of the county homicide detectives that had interviewed her earlier that morning. No, she thought, glancing over his shoulder, it was two of them.

"I'm not a church member, no," she answered, grateful of the fact. "I'm here with my aunt, Bess Cogley. She's a member."

"I'm on the executive board," Ed said proudly, drawing up to his full height. "We're the ruling body in the absence of a pastor. Can I help you?"

The detectives conferred. "We'd like your permission to have a look around the church. Are any of the other board members here?"

Leigh could swear that Ed's eyes flickered with fear for a moment, but he recovered quickly. "I suppose I could round up a quorum," he said congenially. "In the meantime, help yourselves to some refreshments."

The detectives waited patiently in the hallway while Ed hobbled around the crowded parlor, tapping Bess and several others, who followed him—at various speeds—back to the doorway. Leigh recognized Betty Ivey among them, as well as the youth leader who had offered pizza and donuts to everyone at the wedding rehearsal. She tended not to forget men like that.

"Ted Hugh's around here somewhere too," Ed said, breathing a little more heavily from his effort. "But we've got a majority—not counting Humphrey, of course."

The detectives explained their mission, and the board

members nodded in agreement. Bess's eyes sparked with curiosity, and she didn't waste a moment in pulling Leigh aside once the detectives had departed.

"What do you think they're looking for?" she whispered.

Leigh knew exactly what they were looking for—and she knew it wasn't going to take them more than five minutes to find it. She was just grateful not to be a part of it. She opened her mouth to answer, but her words were interrupted by a light tap on her arm.

"Excuse me," a squeaky woman's voice asked politely. "I'm a little confused. Could you tell me what's going on here?"

Leigh turned around and surveyed the newcomer with wide eyes. For a moment it seemed that Marlo Thomas had gotten caught in a time warp—or perhaps it was Mary Tyler Moore? The woman in front of her was wearing a dark brown minidress, tights, and wedge heels under a short, fur-trimmed coat with matching beret and muffs. She was as petite as an elf, with a face that looked fresh and young—yet at the same time artificially preserved. Her dark eyes looked questioningly at Leigh from behind overlong bangs, while the rest of her odd, brownish-gray hair flipped up at shoulder level.

"I'm sorry," Leigh said, distracted. "What did you say?"

The dark eyes seemed perturbed, but the woman's voice was smooth. "I was hoping you could tell me what all these people are doing here. Is this some sort of reception?"

The noise level in the room gradually diminished as more and more people turned to stare at the woman in the doorway. Leigh looked out over the crowd, surprised by their reaction. Granted, Marlo/Mary didn't blend in perfectly, but she wasn't nude on a horse either.

"Please come in," Leigh answered, feeling a little

sorry for her. "This isn't a funeral, but it is an informal visitation of sorts. You haven't heard the news?"

"What news?" the woman said, stepping fully through the doorway. Leigh heard a gasp from behind her as her aunt got her first good look at the visitor.

"Oh, my God," Bess said softly.

"The news about Reginald Humphrey," Leigh answered, wondering what her aunt's problem was. "He was the pastor here."

The woman's dark eyes turned up to Leigh and widened. "*Was*? You mean he's gone?"

Bess tugged furiously on Leigh's sleeve, but the words were already out of her mouth. "He's passed away, I'm afraid. Did you know him?"

The woman didn't answer, but walked a few steps past Leigh and out into the room. "Catch her!" shrieked Barbara, the office secretary, who had been watching the exchange from a few yards away. Leigh stood still, wondering why on earth Barbara thought the woman was trying to escape. It was only after the miniskirted figure had crumpled to the floor that she got the drift.

A circle formed immediately around the prone figure, with Bess shoving her way to the front on hands and knees. "Give her some air!" she commanded, taking the woman's hand and gently patting it.

"Gosh damn!" Ed remarked, his cane shaking beneath him. "Is it really her?"

"Really who?" Leigh asked frantically, guilt at her obvious faux pas coming on strong. "Who is she?"

At first no one seemed willing to answer her. Then Bess spoke up with a sigh. "This," she announced, patting the woman's cheeks, "is Reginald Humphrey's widow."

Chapter 13

"If that woman is a missionary," Leigh said emphatically, "I'm the Ayatollah."

It was late afternoon, and she had finally managed, after no small amount of coercion, to get her aunt home. "I don't believe it. Do you?"

Bess sat on the couch, her bum foot propped up on the coffee table and surrounded by cats, several of which seemed to like the taste of plaster. The primarily Pekinese Chester lay upside down in her lap, enjoying a belly rub. "Of course not," she answered smugly. "I never did. I don't even believe she's really his wife."

"But what about the picture in his office?" Leigh asked, smarting a little. She was annoyed at having been one of the few people in the church parlor not to recognize Noel Humphrey, but she was at a fair disadvantage. Though no one at the church had ever met Noel, most had seen more recent pictures of her hanging in the parsonage. All Leigh had had to go on was a black-and-white photo from the sixties.

Bess shrugged. "I'm not saying they weren't ever married. What I am saying is that she's anything but the loving, devoted wife he always portrayed her as. The bit about being called to live on separate continents indefinitely is a crock—as anyone with half a libido should know. I always thought she was just a prop."

"Well, if that's true," Leigh reasoned, "why would

she show up in person now?" She poured herself a glass of Lemon Blennd and returned to the living room, giving a wide berth to the television set on which Punkster was crouching, ready to spring again.

"I'll bet she was part of the plan," Bess said confidently. "I still think Humphrey was trying to pull some grand vanishing act. Only something went terribly wrong." She paused, as if thinking something she didn't want to say out loud. "Or perhaps she was just passing through and wanted to say hello," she finished dismissively. "In any event, I agree with you. No way was that woman ever a missionary."

Leigh shook her head thoughtfully, replaying Noel's actions after she had come to. They hadn't made any sense at the time, and they still didn't. The woman had immediately started crying buckets, explaining how she had come back from Africa with plans to surprise her husband. How a person was supposed to react to news of a spouse's sudden death, Leigh wasn't sure, but she suspected most would ask questions. Noel hadn't asked anything. She had just gushed on melodramatically about how much she loved her husband, and how she didn't know what she would do without him. Then she had suddenly bolted outside to her "borrowed" Monte Carlo, claiming she needed to be alone for a while. For all anyone knew, she might never come back.

The Lemon Blennd was lukewarm, but Leigh drank it anyway. Given the day's long chain of disturbing events, she would have preferred something stronger, but she still had to drive home tonight. *Home.* It had a nice ring to it. She glanced at her watch; Frances was supposed to be staying with Bess tonight. Ordinarily she didn't look forward to seeing her mother, but—where the heck was she? Given the inevitable publicity surrounding Humphrey's death, she should have arrived in a panic hours ago.

Leigh got up and looked out her aunt's front window. "I've been wondering about Francie myself," Bess said, mind-reading. "I can't believe she knows yet. She's going to have one serious conniption when she finds out you trampled onto another body. And me—I'll catch hell about the parsonage fire all over again. If there's an investigation into Humphrey's death—"

"If?" Leigh asked incredulously. "What do you mean, 'if'? You can't really believe Humphrey locked himself in a freezer!"

Bess tilted up her chin stubbornly.

Leigh sighed. She hadn't told Bess about the curtain yet, but there was no point in trying to keep it a secret. Shortly after Noel's departure, the detectives had asked everyone to leave, explaining that the church would be sealed off temporarily. They had clearly discovered the curtain's mate, and were probably looking for more evidence to prove that Humphrey had been killed at the church. If they found it, Warren's uncle would be suspect number one.

She had managed to work it all out in her mind, and she knew the detectives wouldn't be far behind her. Someone had taken the curtain down from Humphrey's office window, wrapped up the body—and the insulin kit—inside it, and carried the bundle through the woods to the animal shelter. The Ivey sisters couldn't see anything on that side of the church, and there weren't any other houses close by with a good line of vision, so barring a passing car, getting there unnoticed wouldn't have been too difficult. Getting rid of the insulin kit made sense if the person had not wanted Humphrey's absence to be noticed right away—and putting the body in the freezer made more sense than dumping it in the leafless forest, where the bright orange curtain would stick out like a sore thumb.

Even the Ivey sisters' timeline made sense, if you considered that they were really identifying cars—not people. They saw Humphrey's car leaving first, but it would have been too dark to identify the driver. The killer could have driven Humphrey's car to the park to get it out of sight, so that, at least temporarily, everyone would think Humphrey was alive and well someplace else. Then the killer could have walked back to the church and driven his own car home.

Leigh didn't want to say what she was thinking out loud—it might be a jinx. Things looked bad for Ted Hugh, but things had looked bad for her once too, and she had been innocent. More important, Warren was convinced that his uncle wasn't a killer, and Warren was an excellent judge of character. She had to give Ted the benefit of the doubt.

"I realized something back at the church, Aunt Bess," she began. Her aunt didn't need to know her suspicions about Ted, but she did need to know that what had happened to Reginald Humphrey was no accident. "The body wasn't wrapped up in a blanket, like I said at first. When I thought about it, I realized it was a coarser piece of fabric. A curtain."

It took only a moment for Bess to understand. When she did, her face fell. "The missing curtain in Humphrey's office," she said dully. "So. You think he was moved from there."

Leigh nodded. They were both quiet for a moment before Bess spoke. "Well, I guess that explains why his desk drawer wasn't locked, doesn't it?" She laughed humorlessly, then her voice turned sad. "I wanted to believe it was all Humphrey's fault, you know," she admitted. "That it was all a stupid accident he brought on himself."

"I know," Leigh said sympathetically.

"But if someone really did kill him, and it happened at the church . . ."

Bess's voice trailed off, and Leigh didn't ask her to complete the sentence. She knew what Bess was thinking. If Reginald Humphrey had been murdered, there was corruption within the First Church of the New Millennium that went beyond simple fraud. And there was another criminal still out there, someone more dangerous than Humphrey had ever been.

"Why do I get the idea you didn't ask me out here just for my company?" Maura asked skeptically, scooping up a large slice of the pepperoni and black olive pizza Leigh had ordered.

"You're paranoid by nature?" Leigh suggested.

"Only where you're concerned," Maura quipped.

Leigh feigned offense. "My rep is largely undeserved, you know." She pulled two slices of pizza onto her plate and dug into them hungrily.

"I forgot to ask," Maura said between bites, "how'd your mom take the news?"

Leigh grinned. "I wouldn't know. She was in Grove City all day shopping the outlet malls—she still hadn't heard when she showed up at Bess's."

Maura raised her eyebrows. "And you took off in a flash?"

"Wouldn't you?"

"No comment."

They both ate quietly for a while, and Leigh rehearsed what she was going to say. Her role in this whole mess was so confusing she could hardly keep it straight, and Maura's being involved in the investigation only made things worse. She couldn't let on that Bess had broken into the parsonage—or the ministorage—yet the fact that Humphrey was very likely running some sort of con might be important. And it was important to the church that the killer be caught—unless, of course, it was Warren's uncle, in which case his whole family would be devastated.

She sighed. Was there no way out? She wanted to help, but almost anything she said was likely to get somebody in trouble.

"You're not working on the Humphrey case now, right?" she began uncertainly.

Maura finished swallowing a trail of cheese, then answered. "Not officially. The break-in issue is settled—it belongs to homicide now." She studied Leigh's face. "Still, if there are things you don't want to go on record, don't tell them to me. I have obligations."

Leigh nodded. She had expected as much. Maura was the most scrupulously honest person she knew. "I'll be straight with you," she said finally. "I keep hearing and seeing things that might be important, but I don't know that they are for sure, and passing them along could get other people into trouble."

Maura studied her. "Guilty people or innocent people?"

Leigh considered. The fact that Bess was technically guilty of breaking and entering probably didn't matter anymore, now that Humphrey wasn't alive to complain—or to finish setting her up for arson, if in fact that had been his plan. But she had lied to the fire investigator. As for Ted Hugh, Leigh still didn't want to presume what he was guilty of, but she was certain he was guilty of something.

She sighed with exasperation. "I don't even know."

Maura pulled a paper towel off the roll Leigh always kept on the table, wiped her mouth and fingers, and leaned back in her chair.

"Look, Koslow. We're on dangerous ground here. I'm not on this case and I don't want to be on this case, especially if you and your aunt are trying to hide something. You don't want me pestering you to spill your guts, and I don't want you asking me for insider information. So let's not talk about it. Deal?"

Leigh nodded glumly.

"The detectives working on this are good," Maura continued. "They'll find out what went down."

Leigh took a swig of tea and studied her friend's

face. Maura's voice had been unusually edgy as she mentioned the other detectives, and Leigh had a sinking feeling that things on the new job were not going all that well. How much grief had missing the body in the freezer earned her? A good ribbing from the other detectives, at the very least.

Leigh exhaled soberly. She wanted to help but doubted she could. Maura's suggestion was probably for the best. They should stay off the topic of Reginald Humphrey altogether. Furthermore, *she* should stay off the topic of Reginald Humphrey altogether. She could chauffeur Bess around and provide moral support for Warren without getting any more involved. Really, she could.

"So where's Harmon?" Maura asked in a lighter tone. "I figured you'd ask him up too."

Leigh felt a tad guilty. She, Maura, and Warren had been the three musketeers in their college days at Pitt—the Creative Genius, the Wondercop, and the future President of the United States. The threesome still routinely enjoyed pizza feasts together, but the truth was that if Warren had accepted tonight, three would have been a crowd. She had gone to his apartment the minute she got home, but he wasn't there. She had even left a note—but he still hadn't showed. So she had called Maura. Maura who was still blissfully unaware that Warren was also involved in the Humphrey case.

"He's got some family problems," she explained.

"Oh?" Maura asked, sounding surprised. She and Leigh had family problems aplenty, but Warren had always seemed immune. "His parents OK?"

Leigh explained about Warren's father, and decided she might as well explain about his uncle too. She didn't get any further than his name.

"Ted Hugh is Harmon's uncle?" Maura asked, nearly choking. "The guy who—" She stopped herself. "This is not good, Koslow."

Leigh shook her head in agreement. Maura wasn't even working the case, and she had already heard something about Ted Hugh? It did not bode well.

"I'm staying away from this one," Maura resolved. "If the detectives know—" She stopped herself again. "How's Harmon taking all this?"

"As well as could be expected, I suppose."

"Katharine Bower still around?"

Leigh bristled. "They're still dating, I think," she said stiffly, "but I don't know how serious it is."

Maura stared at her for a moment, then stifled a smile. "Actually, I was just asking in case Ted Hugh needed a good attorney."

Leigh's face reddened. "Oh."

Shortly after dinner Maura departed to visit her mother at the assisted-living complex, and before the door had completely closed behind her, Leigh's phone rang. She dove after it anxiously. Warren must be home. Perhaps he would invite her down?

"Hello, Warren?" she said hopefully.

"No, dear," came a voice as flat as death. "Just your mother."

A ten-ton weight settled on Leigh's insides. "Oh. Hi, Mom."

"You'll have to come back to Bess's."

Leigh's voice was thin. "What? Why?"

A long exaggerated sigh flowed over the telephone wire. "I should think you'd be a little bit more concerned about protecting yourself."

Leigh waited for an explanation, but none came.

"You have talked with your lawyer, haven't you?" Frances said accusingly.

Leigh held the phone away from her head. She was tempted to hang up and claim a disconnection, but her mother was wise to that one. She counted to five instead. "Mom," she said finally, trying her best to come up with a soothing tone, "I haven't been accused of anything. I just found the body. He was already dead—he'd been dead for days. This is *not* like what happened before. OK?"

Frances sighed again. It was one of her best—the particularly long, woeful sigh that mourned her fate at having a daughter bent on self-annihilation. "You need your lawyer," she insisted.

Leigh counted to seven. "Mom, Katharine Bower *was* my lawyer. She's not anymore. It's not like I keep a defense attorney on retainer."

Frances didn't miss a beat. "That might not—"

Leigh pulled the phone away from her head and sat on it. After a count of ten and two deep cleansing breaths, she tuned back in.

"—and he said he was going to question you too, so I told him if it would be more convenient for him, you would be happy to come over here—"

"Mom!" Leigh interrupted. "What are you talking about?"

"The detective, dear. He should be here any minute, so you'd better start off now. What are you wearing? You should put on something nice. What about that blue pantsuit that I bought you for—"

Leigh didn't hear any more. She mumbled a good-bye, hung up, grabbed her wallet and keys, and headed out the door.

In jeans.

Detective George Hollandsworth of the Allegheny County Detectives Division had to be pretty close to retirement, and he wasn't wearing a ring. Consequently, it came as no surprise that Leigh found her aunt sitting comfortably next to him on the couch, wearing a fresh, low-cut, lime green suit.

"I just don't know how you do it, Detective," she cooed. "But we're all so glad you do!"

Frances popped out of the kitchen with a cup of tea and a scowl. The tea was for the detective. The scowl was for family members only. "Now that Leigh's here, I think we should let the detective begin," she said with authority. "I'm sure he'd like to get home at a reasonable hour." *And to his significant other, which he probably already has,* her tone implied as she looked sharply at her sister.

Bess, who Leigh suspected would be acting considerably more sober if Frances weren't around to bait, fluffed the back of her beehive and flashed the detective a smile. "I'm sure we'll do whatever we can to help him. Won't we, Leigh?"

Leigh nodded. Hollandsworth was one of the two detectives who had questioned them that morning, then shown up later at the church. Maura had said they were good, and Maura was usually right about such things.

"I know you ladies told us all about the circumstances under which Reginald Humphrey's body appeared at the animal shelter," the detective began. He had a fabulous voice, deep and melodic. Bess seemed almost to sway with the flow of it, her eyes shamelessly adoring.

Frances cleared her throat.

"But we now have reason to believe that Humphrey died elsewhere. Most likely, the First Church of the New Millennium."

"Really?" Bess asked lightly. If she was trying to act surprised, it was a poor effort. Especially for an accomplished amateur actress.

"Since you're a member of the executive board of that church, I'd like to ask you a few more questions," the detective continued.

"Certainly," Bess purred.

"First off, could you give me the names of the other board members?"

Bess complied. Counting Humphrey himself, there were ten. Her, Ted Hugh, the Ed that belonged to

Barbara, Betty Ivey, Sam Schafer (the youth leader), and four others whose names Leigh didn't recognize.

"In general," the detective continued, after he had taken down all the names, "how would you characterize the relationship between Reverend Humphrey and the rest of the board?"

Bess's coy demeanor slipped into recession as she used her brain to think about it. "The board had its disagreements from time to time," she answered. "But they were mostly between the lay members. They all respected Humphrey."

Leigh wondered if the detective had caught Bess's transparent use of "they" instead of "we." From the slight flicker in his eyes, it looked like he had. But he wasn't letting on just yet.

"So you would not say that animosity existed between Humphrey and the board at large?" he asked.

"Absolutely not," Bess answered.

"What about between Humphrey and other members of the board individually?"

There was a moment of silence as Bess hesitated. Leigh felt her blood pressure rising. They both knew that Ted Hugh not only disliked Humphrey, but had been particularly angry with him the evening of the wedding rehearsal. Yet unbeknownst to Bess, saying so could very well be putting nails in the man's coffin. Leigh felt a pang of regret. Why hadn't she warned Bess about Ted Hugh's predicament earlier?

"I really can't answer that, Detective," Bess said sincerely. "I've heard people express negative things about Humphrey now and then, but that doesn't mean any of them hated him enough to kill him. They're all good people, and I won't spread hearsay."

Leigh exhaled. *Good answer.*

The detective tried again. "Let me be a bit more direct. Do you personally know of any reason anyone might have had to end Reginald Humphrey's life?"

Bess breathed a little easier. "No, sir, I don't. I've been wondering that myself."

The detective paused a moment, then changed topics. "Was the First Church of the New Millennium in good shape financially?"

"Very good shape, for a young church," Bess answered proudly. "The members are all quite generous."

"Any volatile issues happening right now? Building improvements? Staff problems?"

Bess shook her head. "It's been smooth sailing, at least since I got on the board a few months ago. And I've been on a boatload of church boards, so I ought to know."

The detective nodded and switched gears again. "Had you ever met Noel Humphrey before yesterday afternoon?"

Bess shook her head. "I'd seen pictures of her. That's all."

"Any idea where she might have gone after she left the church yesterday?"

Bess shook her head again, and Leigh's eyebrows rose. So, the missionary of convenience had still not returned—and the police were looking for her. And why not? She'd be a suspect, of course. Leigh brightened at the thought.

The detective leaned forward and took a sip of the tea Frances had brought, then nodded at her gratefully. Bess watched him with thinly veiled lust, then slipped back into flirt mode. "Is there anything else we can help you with, Detective?" she asked with a smile.

"Actually, there is," he answered, smiling back. "I need to ask both you and Miss Koslow some questions about what you saw Monday night, but I'll need to talk with each of you alone."

Leigh and Bess exchanged nervous glances, but Frances rose immediately. "Of course, Detective. You

can use the study. It's right through there. Let me get
your tea."

Bess looked at Leigh. "You go on first, kiddo. I'm
sure you'd like to get back home." The last statement
was punctuated with a wink.

Frances parked the detective and his tea in the tiny
front room that housed Bess's second husband's pride
and joy—his extensive antique book collection. With
Hollandsworth planted in the comfortable leather recliner, there was no place for Leigh to sit but on the
cushionless window seat. She hoped the inquisition
would be short.

"I understand you attended the wedding rehearsal
that was held at the First Church of the New Millennium this last Monday night?" he began.

Leigh nodded. "My aunt had just had surgery on
her ankle that morning, so I was there to help out."
She told him what time they had arrived and left, how
many people were there, and how many had still been
there when she left. Those questions were easy.

"Did you talk to Reverend Humphrey yourself that
night?" he asked pleasantly.

It took her a moment to remember that she had.
She had tested him out about his boot camp buddies,
and she had almost decided he wasn't the man in
Bess's photograph after all. "Yes, I did," she answered. "Briefly. He asked me if I belonged to another church, and I said yes. He was very cordial."

"Did he seem upset to you? Nervous, edgy?
Depressed?"

Leigh shook her head and answered truthfully. "Not
at all. He seemed quite relaxed." *Considering how
tense everyone else was.*

"What about the mood of the others?" the detective
continued on cue. "Did you notice anyone that night
that seemed upset, angry, anxious?"

She took as deep a breath as she thought she could
take without being too obvious. "I didn't know most

of the people very well," she answered truthfully. "So I don't know what normal was for them. But there seemed to be some general tension in the air, yes."

She exhaled, feeling immediately guilty. She wasn't going to lie, but she hated the prospect of making things worse for Warren's family. Surely there was a way out of this. "I mean, wedding rehearsals are always a little tense, because everyone's nervous. And the bride and groom chose family members for the wedding party, which is never smart."

She was babbling like a ditzoid now, but she decided to go with it. "The bride's father wanted everything to be perfect—like most proud fathers, I suppose. And it was a little confusing, having the host pastor and the guest pastor splitting up the ceremony. But in the end it went well. One of the groomsmen—he's an old friend of mine—gave the bride's father a pep talk, and then everything seemed fine."

She stopped, a little breathless. That had all sounded harmless enough, hadn't it?

The detective scribbled for a moment, then looked up into Leigh's eyes. "Your friend who talked to Ted Hugh, who might that be?"

"Warren Harmon," she gulped, a pit forming immediately in her stomach. She knew that Warren would have to be questioned like everyone else at the rehearsal, but she still felt like a fink.

"A member of the groom's family?"

"No, he's the bride's cousin. Ted Hugh is his uncle by marriage."

"All right," the detective answered pleasantly. He finished scribbling and put away his notebook. "That'll be all for now. Thank you for your cooperation."

Leigh stood up from the hard window seat, her legs feeling like lead as she took a step toward the door. She hated the thought of the detectives grilling Warren about his uncle. He would tell the truth, of course, but it was a horrible position for him to be in. She wheeled around. "Warren Harmon is the register of wills, you know," she burst out. "He's a very honest person."

The corners of the detective's mouth twitched as he tried to suppress a smile. "Thank you, Miss Koslow."

Leigh turned back around. She was such an idiot.

"You told the truth, didn't you?" Frances demanded as soon as the study door had closed behind Bess. Leigh would have liked a word with her aunt before the detective began, but he hadn't just fallen off the turnip truck. He had brought Bess in the moment Leigh went out, keeping within his line of sight any meaningful glance they might exchange.

"Well, didn't you?" Frances repeated, her skepticism increasing.

"Of course I did, Mom," Leigh mumbled. "I just wish I hadn't turned into a babbling nitwit when he asked about Warren."

Frances paused a moment. "Warren Harmon?" Her voice quavered with distress. Frances had been Warren's number-one fan since Leigh had first brought him to a family picnic in their college days. He had been a smart, respectful, stable, and suitably unattractive young man, and Frances had begun the nuptial nudging immediately, much to Leigh's annoyance.

She hadn't ever stopped either. "How have you involved Warren?" Frances asked accusingly.

"I didn't involve anybody!" Leigh protested, then remembered that her mother had no idea who had belonged to the wedding party in question, much less the First Church of the New Millennium in general. She took a deep breath and explained everything, including both the condemning nature of Ted Hugh's erratic behavior Monday night, and Warren's certainty that his uncle wasn't a murderer.

When she had finished, Frances seemed relieved. "If Warren Harmon says his uncle is innocent, he's innocent," she announced. "As for your babbling, you were just being a little overprotective." She smiled condescendingly and patted her daughter's shoulder. "Nothing wrong with that."

Leigh winced, but couldn't help being slightly appreciative. Her mother's unwavering belief that Warren walked on water used to bug the hell out of her. Now it was coming in handy.

"But you'd better get back to your apartment building," Frances added firmly. "You should at least warn Warren that he might be questioned soon."

Leigh got up and headed for the door. *She should go see Warren.* Definitely. Her mother was right.

It was scary.

Chapter 14

When Leigh turned the corner toward Warren Harmon's apartment, her spirits fell. She recognized the man walking away from it immediately. It was the second homicide detective.

"Hello, Miss Koslow," he said cheerfully, then followed her line of sight to Warren's door. "I was just talking with your friend, Mr. Harmon. Has Hollandsworth caught up with you yet?"

"Yes," she said with as much pleasantness as she could muster. "Just now."

"Fine, then. Thanks for your time." The detective nodded to her and walked on past. As soon as he was out of sight, she knocked anxiously on Warren's door. He opened it immediately, perhaps assuming the detective was back. "Leigh, it's you," he said, sounding somewhat relieved. "Come on in."

She hadn't gotten far before she was treated to the sight of Katharine Bower pouring herself a drink in his kitchen—and looking quite at home. Katharine nodded a neutral greeting, which Leigh returned.

"I got your message," Warren explained, "but when I called you weren't home. What's up?"

"I was over at Bess's," Leigh explained, sinking down into an armchair. "Looks like the detectives split up—she and I got Hollandsworth."

Warren sat down on the couch, and Katharine sat down close beside him. Leigh tensed. "I hope you didn't try to hide anything," he told her seriously. "It won't do any good in the long run, and I don't want you or Bess to get in trouble."

Leigh shook her head. "We were truthful, but not effusive." She remembered the babbling incident, and her face reddened. "Did it go OK with you?" she asked quickly.

"Warren did splendidly," Katharine praised, moving still closer on the couch. "I may convince the firm to take him on as a witness coach."

"Thanks, but no thanks," Warren said with a smile. "I'll stick to county government for now."

"State government next week," Katharine teased.

The lawyer was in fine form tonight, Leigh thought ruefully. Ribbing Warren about his political ambitions was supposed to be her job. "Do you think they suspect your uncle?" she asked, breaking the mood. The smile he'd had on his face faded, and she regretted the question.

"I'm certain of it," he said sadly. "All I could do was lend my assurances that Ted Hugh isn't a violent man."

Leigh felt awful. She wanted desperately to help, but all she had managed to do for Warren so far was clue Hollandsworth in on the fact that she was trying to protect him—and remind him of his uncle's plight the second he had gotten pleasantly distracted. She turned to Katharine. The lawyer was doing him a heck of a lot more good than she was, after all. "Did you get the real story out of Ted yesterday?" she asked hopefully.

Katharine and Warren exchanged glances. "Yes, I did," Katharine answered. "And it's a doozie. But it's confidential, I'm afraid."

"Oh, I know that," Leigh said quickly, embarrassed.

"It's all right," Warren interjected. He turned to Leigh. "As for the story my uncle told Katharine in confidence, I don't know either. But after talking with her, he was willing to tell Shannon and I at least most of the truth. The bottom line is, he wants everyone to understand that no matter how bad it looks, he didn't kill Reginald Humphrey.''

Leigh sat quietly, waiting.

"The first part of what he told us at the church earlier was true. He and Humphrey had some sort of disagreement recently, and he was afraid Humphrey would try to sabotage the wedding somehow.''

Leigh raised an eyebrow skeptically. "Do you really think that's true? I mean, why would Humphrey risk doing something that could ruin his public image?''

Warren shook his head. "I can't imagine that he would, but my uncle isn't above irrational paranoia, so from his point of view, I can see it. Anyway, he says he wanted to talk to Humphrey after the rehearsal to clear the air. He wanted to end the animosity.''

"Didn't he say before that he blew his top and yelled? And that Humphrey took off scared?''

Warren nodded. "That was a lie. He made it up to explain why Humphrey's car left first. He really did want to clear the air—after we talked at the rehearsal, he said that's what he was going to do—and I believed him.''

"So what happened?'' Leigh prompted. "What did they say to each other?''

"Nothing,'' Warren answered. "Ted hung around the church until everyone else had left, then went to Humphrey's office, as they had agreed on earlier. When he got there, Humphrey was already dead.''

Leigh swallowed. If Ted Hugh was to be believed, it would mean that Humphrey had been killed earlier in the evening—while any number of church members were still milling about.

"My uncle's first thought was that Humphrey had been strangled,'' Warren continued. "He was lying on the floor, curled up, with his hands at his throat. Then Ted noticed that the insulin kit was out.''

Leigh's eyes widened. "The insulin kit? As in, he'd just given himself a shot?"

Warren nodded. "A bottle of insulin was sitting next to the kit on his desk, and there was a syringe on the floor right beside him."

"But . . ." she stammered, thinking quickly. "That could mean he killed himself! Or that it was some kind of accident. Could he have overdosed?"

"That was my uncle's second thought," Warren confirmed. He paused a moment and sighed. "It's the next part that's hard to follow, but if you knew Ted, it would make sense, believe me.

"He figured that either Humphrey had overdosed accidentally, or that someone had slipped something into his insulin. Ted didn't particularly care how it happened. All he could think about was the fact that when the body was discovered, Joy's wedding would be ruined."

Leigh's eyebrows rose, and Warren raised an apologetic hand. "I know, I know. I'm not trying to argue that Ted's got all his marbles. But that's how he saw it. Humphrey was dead, and there was nothing he could do about that. But he *could* save the wedding, and send Joy off a happy bride.

"He figured all he had to do was move the body— get it out of the church. He also knew that he couldn't possibly carry a big, bulky bundle out to his car without some risk of being seen. Even if the Ivey sisters were asleep, the parking lot was brightly lit and readily visible to passing cars. So he decided he'd take the body out the other door on the back side of the church. He pulled down the curtain, wrapped up the body, and threw in the insulin kit. Then he headed for the animal shelter, hoping to find a dumpster or anywhere else he could safely hide the body for a while. When he couldn't find a good spot outside, he kicked open the basement door. The freezer was right there—and it seemed like a good idea."

"He should have known the body would be found eventually," Leigh commented.

"He didn't care. He just wanted to get it out of the way until the wedding was over. And even if it was found beforehand, as long as it wasn't on church property, the wedding could still happen as planned—without police tape across the aisles.

"After he dumped the body, he went back to the church and fixed up the room to make it look like Humphrey had left voluntarily. He says he cleaned up some food that had been left out and threw the syringe in the waste can with the others. He pulled the remaining curtain across the window so the absence of the first might not be so noticeable. Then he drove Humphrey's car to the park, left everything inside it, and walked back to the church."

Leigh couldn't resist some sense of satisfaction—she had gotten the last part right on the nose, at least. "So why did he leave Humphrey's keys and coat in the car? Was he hoping someone would steal it?"

Warren shrugged. "I don't think he thought that through. He just didn't want to have anything else to dispose of. He had gotten Humphrey's things out of the church and by that point he just wanted to get out of there himself."

Leigh sat silently a moment, thinking. She and Bess had seen syringes in the wastebasket on Tuesday night, right after the wedding. "If someone had tampered with Humphrey's insulin, couldn't the syringe on the floor prove it?" she asked hopefully.

Katharine shook her head. "It's long gone—I checked already. The trash was taken out days ago."

"Oh," Leigh said, deflated.

"But I suspect that the police have the insulin bottle, and they'll certainly test that," the lawyer continued. "If Ted is lucky, they won't find anything. This isn't an official homicide investigation yet, you realize, because the cause of death is still open. The detectives are working it up as a suspected homicide because of the circumstances in which the body was found, but the coroner still hasn't ruled out death by natural causes."

Leigh said nothing for a moment, then a smile spread over her face. "Well, if nobody killed him, then everything will be fine!" she said optimistically, thinking how certain her aunt had been that no one at the First Church of the New Millennium was a murderer.

"Probably," Katharine answered cautiously. "But we can't count on that. My contact at the coroner's office told me that the autopsy showed hypovolemic shock and laryngoedema—which are consistent with some types of poisoning. They'll be running a toxicology screen, and if they find anything, we're in for a fight. Ted has a lot going against him—namely motive, opportunity, a history of emotional instability, and one false story already on record.

"If he's willing to take my advice and confess to moving the body now, he may escape murder charges if the ruling does come back homicide. Otherwise, it's only a matter of time before the detectives match up his prints with those on the freezer and on Humphrey's car. Either way, he could be facing charges of breaking and entering." Katharine laid a hand on Warren's knee and gave it an affectionate squeeze. "I'm sorry your family's having to go through this. But you know I'll do the best I can."

Warren beamed at the lawyer appreciatively, and Leigh made an excuse to leave. She was truly glad he was getting good legal aid, but if Katharine's hand moved any higher up his leg, she was going to do something embarrassing.

Friday morning arrived, and Leigh woke up in a rotten mood. She had tossed and turned all night, which meant that she would be spending the rest of the day groggy and irritable. She didn't even have to go over to Bess's today—Frances was on duty now, and Lydie would take over most of the weekend. But it was the last day of her week off from Hook, Inc., and it was clearly going to be miserable.

She had left Warren's apartment last night feeling like the consummate third wheel. Katharine had fallen all over herself to see her out, and it didn't take a brain surgeon to read between the lines.

She walked over to the window and felt her insides churn. She didn't want to know, but she had to look. Steeling herself for the worst, she scanned the parking spot where Katharine Bower's gold Lexus had—until last check at 2:00 A.M.—been firmly parked.

It was gone. Her heart jumped a little, then settled back. Her clock said 7:13—for all she knew, Katharine could have left fifteen minutes ago.

Leigh scowled her way through two cups of coffee, impervious even to the charms of Mao Tse, who was so happy to have her roaming human in residence again that she started chasing imaginary Martians—her favorite game.

On the third cup of coffee, Leigh started feeling a little queasy and decided to lay off. The current state of things in her life, she reasoned, was just not acceptable. She couldn't keep on suffering in silence while Warren and Katharine got closer. She either had to make up her mind to stay out of it no matter what stage their relationship had reached, or she had to do something. Like level the playing field. Like admitting to Warren that her feelings about him had changed.

She ruminated over the thought for a moment. It was certainly risky. Granted, she had always known that Warren was attracted to her. A woman, even an eighteen-year-old girl, simply doesn't miss these things. But he had never acted on the attraction. Nothing. Why not?

She liked to think it was because he could read her so well. He had known she didn't feel the same way, and if he had ever crossed the line, they wouldn't have enjoyed the easy friendship they'd had for so many years. But if that was the case, why couldn't he see how she felt now?

Feeling particularly frumpy all of a sudden, she got dressed and ran a brush through her hair. If Warren really was in love with Katharine, she thought miserably, what right did she have to mess that up? After all, she had certainly had her chance. Katharine was a great lady, and by all appearances, she treated him well. And right now she was being a lot more help to him than Leigh possibly could.

She exhaled in frustration and collapsed on the couch again. Maybe backing off *was* the right thing to do.

Mao Tse leapt onto her stomach and meowed plaintively. Leigh scooped the cat up and kissed her between the eyes. "What do you say, Mao?" she asked. "Should it just be you and me?"

Mao purred another second, then scrambled out of Leigh's arms and dove onto the floor. "More Martians?" Leigh chuckled. But as Mao took off again, she noticed the cat had something real between her teeth. It was a colorful cat toy, complete with catnip and a feather tail. Leigh had never seen it before.

"Where did you get that, girl?" she asked, but Mao Tse had already dragged her kill off to the bedroom, howling in triumph.

Warren. All she had asked him to do was look in on Mao now and then, make sure her bowls were full. And he had gone out and bought her a toy.

Leigh stood up again, her resolve building. She had to level with him. If she didn't, she would spend the rest of her life kicking herself. What was the worst that could happen, anyway? So he gave her a polite, sympathetic stare and said he was flattered but not interested. So what? She would feel like a idiot, true,

but what did it really matter? She always felt like an
idiot.

She headed straight out of her apartment and down
the stairs, checking her watch when she reached his
door: 7:38. If she was lucky, he wouldn't have left for
work yet. She knocked.

It took a while for the door to open. "Leigh," Warren said, not quite as pleasantly as usual. "Is something wrong?"

"No," she said quickly, looking at his tired face and
wet hair. He had on his standard business slacks and
shirt, but no tie yet. He was obviously trying to get
ready to leave, and her timing, as always, was lousy.
She started to weaken, but bucked herself up. The fact
that he was tired might be construed as a bad sign,
but the fact that he had apparently woke up in just as
foul a mood as she had was quite positive indeed.

"I don't want to make you late for work," she
began, "but I wanted to talk to you about something."

"Can you talk while I get ready?" he asked, walking
into the bedroom. "I may not get in a full day's work
today, but I'd like to start out with an honest effort."

He made it sound as though his uncle's arrest was
imminent, and Leigh felt a tug of sympathy. His
mother would not take the news well. She would be
counting on him to keep the family intact and out of
grief, and, like the loyal son he was, he would do his
best. But he wasn't going to succeed.

"I'm sorry," she said sincerely, following him.

He stopped what he was doing for just a moment
and smiled at her. "Thank you. But I really don't want
to talk about my uncle right now. Was there something else you wanted?" He turned to the closet and
picked out a tie.

The timing was wrong and she knew it. But when
would it be right? She had to start sometime. Somewhere.

"You know how you always say I have lousy taste

in men?" she began uncertainly, suddenly wishing she had scripted things first.

He grinned as he tied on the tie. "Well, it's true, isn't it?"

"For the most part," she confessed. "But I've been thinking about it a lot lately, and I think I've always been attracted to the wrong type because I haven't known what it was I really wanted."

"Oh?" he remarked casually, running a comb through his hair.

Timing again. Was he really in the mood to hear this?

Get a spine, woman!

She took a deep breath. "I want someone who understands me."

The words were not completely out of her mouth before the apartment buzzer sounded. Ignoring it, he turned toward her, his eyes searching her face.

"Your buzzer," she said stupidly, pointing.

He looked at her for another second, then headed for the door. Leigh hesitated in the bedroom for a moment, trying to figure out what to say next. When she heard Katharine's voice coming over the speaker, her heart sank. She walked out into the living room to find Warren looking even more miserable than when she had first arrived.

"Bad news?" she asked quietly.

"She didn't say," he answered. "But she's on her way up."

Leigh swallowed. "You want me to leave?"

"No," he said, looking at her closely again. "What was it you were saying?"

Leigh turned her eyes away. He was looking at her like he knew what she was about to say, but with Katharine Bower due to pop in any second, how could she?

"Leigh?" he encouraged, stepping closer.

"Katharine's coming up," she sputtered, and the

door opened. Leigh felt a sudden rush of annoyance. The woman wasn't even knocking now?

Katharine blew through the door in a single motion, laptop case in hand. Her cheeks were flushed with adrenaline and contrasted strikingly with her crisp yellow suit, making Leigh painfully aware of her own jeans and sweatshirt—and the fact that she hadn't even put makeup on yet.

"No coroner's report yet," the lawyer told Warren briskly. "But your uncle has been called in for more questioning. He was in a serious panic when I talked to him on the phone just now, and I'm afraid I may need your help to calm him down. Can you come with me?"

The familiarity in Katharine's voice made Leigh's whole body tense. It was a few moments before the lawyer even noticed her standing there, and when she did, the look in her eyes wasn't particularly kind. "Hello, Leigh," she said stiffly.

Leigh returned the greeting with equal stiffness, a tide of nausea rolling up in her middle. Katharine had always been the soul of politeness before. *Had* something happened between her and Warren last night? If so, she decided quickly, she didn't want to know. She headed for the door. "Warren," she said, not looking at him, "if there's anything Bess or I can do to help, just let us know, OK?"

She was gone before he could answer.

Chapter 15

Remembering that her original plan for the week had been to do absolutely nothing, Leigh decided to give the idea a shot. She went back to her apartment, gave Mao Tse a few extra cat treats, then headed out to forget her and everyone else's problems for a while.

It was snowing fairly heavily as she pulled out of the parking lot, and she wondered if any accumulation was expected. Not that any self-respecting Pittsburgher would be put off by an inch or two, but since she didn't know where she was going and her gas tank was running low—any more she'd like to know about. She switched on KDKA to catch the weather, then turned north on McKnight Road toward the nearest pay-at-the-pump gas station. Before the commercials had ended, however, her Cavalier had reached Dunkin' Donuts, and given the loud, irresistible call of that institution, she had no choice but to park and go in.

She had finished off two double-chocolate donuts and was halfway through a blueberry muffin when she gave up on the nothing idea. It wasn't going to work. She was dying to fill her aunt in on everything she'd found out last night, especially the fact that Humphrey might have died of natural causes. And she wanted to do it in person.

It was still snowing, albeit more lightly, by the time she reached Franklin Park, but thanks to the hard-working salt trucks, the roads were still clear. For her aunt's sake, Leigh hoped the squall ended soon. Bess was dependent on Frances for her transportation, and though Frances could drive on snow as well as anyone, the fact was she wouldn't. Certainly not with a passenger on crutches.

Leigh pulled up to the farmhouse and was surprised to find no sign of her mother's car. Refusing to believe both women had gone out, Leigh sprinted up to Bess's front door to check. Cold, wet snow clung to her sneakers as she went, and she wished she'd had the sense to wear boots. She knocked on the door loudly, and within a few moments Bess opened the door herself.

"Oh, I'm sorry," Leigh apologized quickly. "I didn't think." She shook the snow off her shoes and stepped inside. "Where's Mom?" she asked. "I can't believe she left you alone!"

"She's out filling a *very important* prescription," Bess said deviously. "I was just enjoying a little solitude."

Leigh felt suitably embarrassed. Her aunt hadn't had a moment's privacy in a week, and when she had finally found a plan to shake off Frances, here came the niece again. Unannounced, no less. Leigh was in the process of apologizing again when a car pulled up behind hers, a car that didn't belong to Frances.

"Well, will you look at that?" Bess exclaimed, ignoring the apology in favor of watching the newcomer emerge from her Monte Carlo. "The mystery woman returns. What do you suppose she wants with me?"

Leigh shrugged. They both watched with interest as Noel Humphrey hugged her short fur-trimmed coat tightly around her upper body and walked briskly up the porch steps. She, at least, was wearing boots.

"Hello," she said with a smile that was friendly yet appropriately sober. "It seems so cold here. I suppose I'm overreacting a bit, but I'm used to a warmer continent, you know."

Leigh and Bess exchanged glances, and thoughts.

Both were tempted to call this bizarre little fraud to task, but under the circumstances, neither dared. They were entirely too curious about what the heck she was doing there.

"Noel," Bess began warmly, "it's so good to see you again. We didn't know where you'd gone. Are you all right? Please, come in. This must have been such a shock for you."

Their guest nodded and walked in boldly, and Leigh took a quick look around for Punkster. Like the other cats, he was nowhere in sight. Frances had apparently locked them all out on the porch again, and it was just as well—a flying attack cat was probably not what Humphrey's widow had come for.

Noel took off her coat and settled uneasily into an armchair, declining the offer of a cup of tea. She was dressed a bit more conservatively than before, with a tight polyester shirt and flared pants instead of a mini-skirt. Nevertheless, it was hard to picture anything in this woman's wardrobe wearing well in equatorial Africa.

"I'm sorry to drop in unannounced," the woman began, her large doe eyes radiating regret—and anxiety. "But I had to talk to you. Reginald always spoke so highly of you, you know."

Bess's eyes flickered with an amusement that Leigh hoped only she could see. "Did he?" her aunt answered evenly. "How sweet. He had nothing but praise for you as well, as I'm sure you know."

Noel Humphrey smiled broadly, bringing some previously disguised crow's feet to the surface. Leigh had thought the woman was around fifty, but on closer examination, she appeared to be not much younger than Bess. "My husband was a wonderful man," she began, tears forming. "But he had his enemies. Everywhere we lived, people always misunderstood him. They feared the kind of emotions he could bring out in people, the heights he was capable of reaching."

She paused a moment to dab her eyes with a handkerchief. "I'll tell you ladies the truth," she continued. "I'm not surprised that someone tried to kill my Reginald. I'm only surprised they succeeded."

She held her trembling chin high, and Bess and Leigh exchanged another covert, skeptical glance. The clothes, the artificially preserved face, the whole persona—everything about this woman was so incredibly surreal, it was as if they had all walked unwittingly onto a stage, and were now in the middle of a very bad performance.

"He was a strong man," Bess soothed, applying a fine amount of thespian polish herself. "And we're all very sorry he's gone. The whole church is devastated, and we feel terrible that you had to find out the way you did. Is there anything we can do to help? Do you have a place to stay?"

"Thank you for your concern," Noel answered sweetly. "But I'll be all right. I'm keeping my location a secret for now—until I find out what happened." She paused a moment, then flashed the full force of her doe eyes at Bess. "I'm here because I thought *you* might know."

Bess's eyed widened. "Me?" she proclaimed innocently. "Oh, no. I'm afraid I'm as much in the dark as anyone. I never even believed that the reverend had enemies! Not till it happened, at least. He was such a good man."

Leigh watched her aunt's nose, certain that it would start to grow any moment. It was unsettling to see just how convincing a liar Bess was. What else had she lied about, anyway?

Noel's eyes, suitably crestfallen, dropped to focus on her boots.

"I'm so sorry," Bess continued. "Why would you think I might know something?" She paused a moment, then spoke with new enthusiasm. "Did Humphrey tell you that I did? Perhaps I know something and don't realize it!"

Noel slowly brought the red-rimmed doe eyes back up to Bess's face. "I talked to him on the phone," she said softly. "After the fire."

"He called you in Africa?" Leigh questioned. She hadn't meant to interrupt, but she couldn't help wanting to catch the woman in an outright lie.

"No, dear," Noel answered tolerantly. "I've been in the country for weeks now, raising funds for the mission in Kananga. I was working my way over from the West Coast. I called him last weekend at the church, and he told me that he feared for his life. I headed straight out here, but I didn't tell him that." Her voice caught. "I wanted to surprise him."

Leigh reminded herself that it was highly unlikely this woman really was a devoted wife. Otherwise it was a sad story, bad acting or no, and the situation was depressing enough already.

"What did he say?" Bess prompted, undistracted from her own agenda.

Noel blotted her eyes again. "He said that someone had thrown a Molotov cocktail through his window, and that you were there. He thought you might, well, *know* something."

Leigh watched in amazement as the eyes of the doe morphed—ever so subtly—into those of a vixen. Her blood chilled a little. *So that was it.*

Bess didn't flinch. She met the woman's eyes evenly, her voice as sugary sweet as ever. "I'm afraid I can't help you. I've told the police all I know about the fire. I'm just happy I was able to reach the dear man in time—though in the end, I suppose we all let him down." Her eyes radiated regret at his death, and Leigh knew that was one emotion her aunt did feel sincerely. "We should have taken him more seriously when he said his life was in danger. But none of us believed him."

Noel listened to this speech with a flat, unflinching stare, but when Bess finished speaking with no trace of guilt or paranoia, the doe eyes returned quickly. "When I left the church the other day, I didn't know where to go, who to talk to. I just found a motel and stared at the ceiling. I didn't think I could go back to the church and face all those people again. But Reginald had told me how you lived right behind the church, so when I felt like I'd gotten myself together enough, I came here."

Leigh hung on Noel's every word, trying not to get lost. A minute ago it seemed the woman was ready to pick up right where Humphrey had left off—with a little hint of extortion. But she had backed off quickly. Perhaps she was just fishing?

"I was hoping that you could tell me—I mean—" Her voice trembled. "I still don't know how my husband actually died."

Bess and Leigh looked at each other. It was still an open question.

"I'm afraid no one really knows yet," Leigh answered. Silence followed as she thought about how to explain, but oddly, Noel nodded her head, not seeming surprised.

"Will there be a memorial service?" she asked, her voice cracking again.

"The church staff has already started planning a funeral," Bess assured her. "But of course, the arrangements will be up to you now."

Noel shook her head, tears dropping freely. "I can't think about that—I'm sorry. The church should do what it thinks best. Reginald would want it that way. He has no other family. Just me." She raised her head a bit to show a rally of strength. "Will the service be soon?"

"As soon as possible," Bess said soothingly. "But I'm afraid we do have to wait until the coroner's office releases the body. There's an investigation going on, you know."

The words were no sooner out of Bess's mouth than it happened. Noel's carefully applied exterior seemed to shatter, her face draining instantly of all color and vim. A guttural sound escaped her lips, followed by a short, sharp intake of breath.

"Noel!" Bess said in alarm, leaning forward on the couch. She reached out and touched the woman's knee, then shook it vigorously. "Noel!"

Leigh reached their guest at the same time. "Mrs. Humphrey? Are you OK?"

It was several seconds before Noel moved. Then she jumped up suddenly, grabbed her coat, and hugged it tightly around her. "I have to get out of here," she announced, and before Leigh or Bess could say another word, she was out the door, into her Monte Carlo, and gone.

"What happened to her?" Leigh asked incredulously, watching the car speed off down the salt-covered road.

Bess, who had managed to rise from the couch by herself and was standing tentatively on one foot, sat back down again. "That was quite a performance," she said thoughtfully, motioning for Leigh to join her. "Right up to the end. Now, *that* was real."

Leigh nodded as she sat back down. "I agree. Something you said gave her quite a shock. I just can't imagine what."

"I said that there was an investigation going on," Bess recounted. "What could possibly be so surprising about that? She said herself she thought he was murdered."

"She certainly did," Leigh said thoughtfully, "right off the bat." She paused. Something hadn't seemed right about that, and now it struck her just what. "Wait a minute. Noel said she hadn't talked to anybody since she left the church yesterday. But nobody told her then what had happened to Humphrey. I just said he had passed away. It could have been a heart attack or a car accident, for all she knew. In fact, I don't think she even asked! I suppose she could have heard about it on the news later, but—" She broke off in mid-sentence as another thought struck her.

"Aunt Bess," she said anxiously, "the last thing you said to her—you mentioned the coroner. You said that the body hadn't been released yet."

Bess stared at her niece in confusion. "So? Don't they always do autopsies in murder cases?"

Leigh was silent for a moment. "You said you thought that Humphrey had been planning a disappearing act all along, and that Noel might have been a part of it, right?"

Her aunt nodded.

"Well, maybe you were right. Maybe Noel Humphrey came to town *expecting* to find her husband missing. Maybe she even *expected* that he would be presumed dead."

Bess's pupil's widened in understanding. "But she wouldn't be expecting a body at the coroner's office, would she?"

Leigh shook her head. "Not if she assumed he was still alive."

Both women sat in silence, digesting the concept, and Leigh felt another wave of guilt. If her theory was right, they had insensitively broken the news of Humphrey's death to his widow not once but twice. And judging from the depth of her reaction just now, she might very well have really cared for him.

Leigh tried not to dwell on the thought, but took a deep breath and launched into a retelling of what she had learned from Warren and Katharine the night before. Not surprisingly, her aunt instantly assumed Humphrey had died of natural causes.

"I knew there had to be a reasonable explanation!"

Bess said with relief. "To think that I even considered that a church member could have—" She stopped herself. "Ridiculous! Now all we have to do is figure out how Noel fits in all this. And try to keep Ted Hugh out of jail, of course. I'm sure I can convince the shelter board not to press charges, if that will help." She looked at her niece with new hope. "The church may just survive after all, as long as the congregation never finds out that Humphrey was a fraud in the first place." Her eyes suddenly turned serious. "And I'll need you to help me keep that secret, kiddo."

A powerful knock gave both women a start. "Good heavens!" Bess said, craning her neck toward the door as a large shadow fell over the stained glass windows. "Who can that be?"

Leigh jumped up, recognizing the silhouette—and the knock, immediately. Her stomach churned uncomfortably. Seeing Maura Polanski at the door was normally a cheerful affair, but not now. Not here. She opened the door and wordlessly invited the detective in.

"I'm glad you're here, Koslow," Maura said, a bit stiffly. "I was hoping to catch you and your aunt together."

Leigh nodded. From the miserable look on the detective's face, she gathered that her wish to stay off the Humphrey case had not been granted. Evidently the department had discovered that one of their own had an "in." Naturally, they'd expect her to use it.

Leigh looked at her friend sympathetically, knowing that being asked to harass her and Bess was probably only half of the requirement. "Have you talked to Warren this morning?" she asked anxiously, showing the detective to the couch.

Maura nodded solemnly. "Ted Hugh's been charged with breaking and entering. He's on his way to the county jail now."

Bad memories washed over Leigh like a backed-

up garbage disposal. She shuddered. "I was hoping
Katharine could avoid his being arrested," she thought
out loud.

"She might have if Hugh hadn't started spouting off
obscenities at Hollandsworth," Maura answered heavily. Then, as if shaking off bad memories herself, she
changed the subject. "I'm here because I'd like to talk
with your aunt for a minute." She turned to the
woman sitting on the couch beside her and nodded in
greeting. "Ms. Cogley, I hope you don't mind."

"Call me Bess. And shoot," the older woman said
with a smile.

Leigh didn't sit. She preferred to fidget.

Maura smiled politely back. "I've been talking to
the homicide detectives assigned to the Humphrey
case, and they're having a bit of a problem."

Bess blinked her eyes innocently. "Oh?"

"They've interviewed the staff and all the members
of the executive board of the First Church of the New
Millennium, as well as several other members of the
congregation who seemed to be particularly close to
Humphrey."

Bess nodded, not appearing in the least anxious.
"And?"

"And," Maura continued in a casual tone, "both
the detectives commented on the same two things.
First, that everyone they talked to seemed genuinely
surprised by his death, even though he told the congregation just last Sunday that he thought his life was
in danger. And second, that everyone seemed to like
Humphrey personally, even though most admitted to
a few things that bugged them about him. Everyone,
that is, except for the people on the executive board."

Bess's eyebrows rose. "The board? You mean, they
didn't like him, or they didn't say anything bad about
him?"

Maura watched Bess closely. "The board members
all said glowing things about Humphrey. But both the

detectives had the same impression, that none of them could stand the man."

Leigh bit a fingernail. The description, she was sure, would describe her aunt's testimony perfectly. Maura probably already knew that. But the other board members too?

Bess seemed equally perplexed. "You—I mean, they—the other detectives—thought the board members didn't like Humphrey?"

Maura nodded. "I was hoping you'd be willing to tell me why that is."

Leigh tried to catch her aunt's eye. This was the perfect moment for her to spill it. It would make everything so much easier. No one was going to press charges against her for being a snoop, and filling the detectives in on the fraud angle could help them find the real killer. If there even was a killer.

But Bess kept her eyes firmly on her splinted ankle, lifting them only to answer Maura in a soft, sincere voice. "I wasn't at all fond of Reginald Humphrey," she admitted. "But that was just a personal thing. He's done a wonderful job of building up the church. And as for why the other board members wouldn't like him, I'm really not sure. I thought they did like him. Or at least respected him." She paused a moment, deep in thought.

Maura sat quietly and waited. Leigh watched her aunt's eyes, and decided her words were sincere, at least about not knowing what the other board members had against Humphrey. She seemed genuinely perplexed.

"Now that I think about it," Bess continued, looking at Maura again, "the dynamics of the board were odd at times. I've been on lots of boards—I know how things go. There are always disputes. But this was the smoothest-running board I've ever been on. Humphrey suggested something, and everybody pretty

much agreed with him, even when I would have
thought they wouldn't."

She was quiet again, and Maura cut in. "Do you
have any idea why that might be?"

"No," Bess answered quickly. "I always assumed it
was because they valued his opinion, or at least because they didn't feel strongly enough to go against
the majority. But now I don't know."

She paused another moment, then started. "Oh, no,
I should have mentioned! His wife was just here. I'm
sure you want to talk to her, don't you?"

"Humphrey's wife?" Maura clarified, pulling out
her notepad. "Do you know where she's staying?"

Bess shook her head. "She said she was staying at
a motel, but she didn't say which one."

Maura scribbled something hastily. "I'll pass that
along," she said gratefully. Then she looked Bess
straight in the eye. "I hope if you think of anything
else that might help, you'll let the detectives know.
More often than not, when people try to hide the
truth—even with good intentions—it only makes more
trouble. We're just trying to figure out whether or not
a crime was committed here, to make things safer for
everybody. If you could pass that on, I'd appreciate
it."

Bess returned Maura's steady gaze, her eyes respectful. "Thank you, Detective. I'll do what I can."

Maura thanked Bess for her time and rose to leave,
and Leigh nervously walked the detective out onto the
front porch. "You're back on the case, aren't you?"
she asked hesitantly, once the door had closed behind them.

"Not officially," Maura answered, her voice pained.
"Hollandsworth sent me out here because it's clear
the board members are hiding something, and he
thought—since I had a personal connection—that
maybe I could help."

Leigh surveyed her friend's slightly slumping shoulders with dismay. This wasn't the old fire-and-brimstone, law-and-order Maura Polanski she knew and loved. That Maura would have reamed out both her and Bess for withholding information, and probably enjoyed it. This Maura had lost something. Her self-confidence.

Overlooking Humphrey's body in the freezer might be understandable, but that didn't mean Maura wasn't catching hell over it. And though she was used to deflecting barbs about everything related to being a stoic, 210-pound policewoman, she wasn't used to making mistakes.

Leigh bit her lip. She herself had plenty of expertise in that area, but unfortunately, it was nontransferable. Maura was just going to have to prove herself.

And this case might be the test.

"Bess really doesn't know what's going on with the other board members," Leigh assured her. She wanted to say more, but she couldn't—not yet anyway. She exhaled in frustration. "Look, Maura. We all want the same things here, including Bess. Warren's uncle didn't kill anybody, and if Humphrey was murdered, we all want to find out who really did do it. So there shouldn't be a problem here. There *won't* be a problem. I promise."

She paused, wondering if it was clear she was trying to convince herself as well as her audience.

Maura looked back at her, her eyes stern. "I just hope whatever it is your aunt *is* covering up isn't something that could clear Ted Hugh."

Leigh had no answer to that. She was hoping the very same thing.

Chapter 16

When Leigh walked back into the farmhouse after seeing Maura off, Bess had already started making phone calls, undoubtedly to spread the still unproven theory that Humphrey had died of natural causes. Hopefully, she was also trying to get the breaking-and-entering charges against Ted Hugh dropped.

Deciding not to disturb her, Leigh walked past into the kitchen, poured herself a drink, and took it to the sun porch. Narrowly sidestepping a paw swipe from Punkster—who was lying in wait behind a potted plant—she made her way carefully to the gliding love seat. She put her drink on the floor, sat down on one end, and promptly fell over on her side, one cheek shmooshed against the vinyl cushion.

Perhaps she could think better horizontally, she reasoned. She needed to think. Covering up suspicions that Humphrey was a fraud was one thing. Covering up the near certainty of it, particularly in the middle of a potential murder investigation, was another. She no longer had any doubts that Reginald "Money" Humphrey had been a con artist. It was irritating that he had passed the test of not recognizing his old army buddies, but there were too many other strikes against him, Noel herself being a big one. The First Church of the New Millennium had undoubtedly been donating money to support her, which meant that Humphrey had been cheating the congregation in at least one way. There were others, she was sure.

But what if Humphrey really had died of natural causes? Wishful thinking aside, it was probably less far-fetched than his being murdered, she reasoned. After all, even if Humphrey had been stealing from the church in any number of creative ways, no one seemed to be aware of it, even now. And even if they were, murder was a rather drastic reaction. Why not just call the police? Of course, the fact that Humphrey had been killed at the church didn't necessarily rule out murder by an outsider. That was another can of worms entirely.

Leigh thought a while longer, then decided she'd thought enough. Likely or unlikely, if there was any chance Humphrey had actually been murdered, covering up information was playing with fire. Now, how could she convince Bess of that?

She walked back into the house, exposing a chunk of calf to Punkster's left hook on the way. Bess was in the middle of a lively conversation, and she couldn't help but eavesdrop as she settled into the recliner.

"Uh-huh," Bess was saying skeptically. "And did he say who killed him?"

Leigh's eyebrows rose.

"Well, JFK never would say either, would he? Maybe they have some sort of code."

Leigh looked at her aunt questioningly, and Bess rolled her eyes. "Of course, Evelyn. But I thought you should know what the coroner suspects. All right, then."

Bess said good-bye and sank the phone in its cradle with a flourish. "Evelyn Ewing," she explained with a grin. "She's ninety-one, and a good egg, even if she is rich as sin and terminally cranky. Likes to amuse herself by pretending to be a medium. She just told me in no uncertain terms that Humphrey couldn't possibly have died of natural causes, because he'd appeared to her in a dream last night and told her to avenge his murder."

"But he didn't say who killed him, of course," Leigh said, playing along.

"Well, naturally not."

Taking note of her aunt's good humor, Leigh decided now was as good a time as any for what she had to say. "Aunt Bess," she began seriously, "I'm certainly hoping that Humphrey did die of natural causes, that the charges against Ted Hugh can be dropped, and that this whole investigation will just go away. But if the autopsy results *do* come back as—"

"Nonsense," Bess interrupted firmly, picking up the phone again. "It won't happen. Nobody killed Humphrey. And nobody ever has to know he was a fraud."

"But if he *was* a fraud," Leigh jumped in determinedly, "it would make a big difference to the murder investigation. Right now the detectives have nothing to go on for motive. But Humphrey the con could have any number of old enemies just waiting to pop him off. The guilty party could be out there right now, roaming around free while Warren's uncle rots in jail."

She sat back and took a breath, proud of her speech. One look at her aunt, however, showed it had not been successful.

Bess said nothing for a moment, choosing instead to look at her niece with wretched, doleful eyes. The expression was familiar; Leigh had seen it just last winter when the Red Barn Theater put on *A Streetcar Named Desire*. It was the Blanche DuBois look, and Bess played it to perfection. "I can't believe you think so little of me," she said pathetically. "How can you think I'd be so selfish? I would never sit idly by and let Ted Hugh—or anyone else—go to jail for something they didn't do. But that's not going to happen, and there's a greater good at stake."

She paused for effect, and Leigh managed to keep quiet till she started again. "When I told you that I was trying to gather evidence to debunk Humphrey, I didn't mean that I would confront the congregation with it. I only meant to confront *him* with it. I figured that with a little clever persuasion, and perhaps a bit of a monetary nudge, I could convince him to resign quietly and never be heard from again.

"You see, losing a pastor isn't so bad in an established, mainstream church. You get used to the bad ones coming and going. But the First Church of the New Millennium is different. Most of the young people have never been in a church before. And if they find out that the only positive religious experience they've ever had was built on the charm of a con artist, they'll never go back to church—anywhere."

Leigh looked back at her aunt with frustration. Blanche had a point.

"Please don't tell anyone, particularly your friend Maura, our suspicions about Humphrey," Bess pleaded. "Not just yet. Think how much harm it could cause, only for us to find out later that he died of a heart attack."

The sound of a car engine—most probably her mother's Taurus—filtered in from the driveway, and Leigh took it as her cue to leave. "I'll think about it, Aunt Bess," she said heavily, rising. "But I can't promise anything."

Leigh felt guilty again. She wasn't sure why she felt guilty—she just did. Maura wanted her to be up front about what she knew; Bess wanted her to keep quiet. She couldn't make both happy.

She sighed and rounded the corner onto Nicholson Road. It was lunchtime already, and her stomach was enthusiastically suggesting a Baja chicken gordita. Deciding to comply, she turned toward Taco Bell. But as she passed the church parking lot, a flash of candy apple red caught her eye. It was Noel Humphrey's Monte Carlo. She had obviously not gotten far.

Leigh swung the Cavalier into the parking lot after

it, a grin forming. She could do Maura one small favor, anyway. Parking quickly, she headed for the side door and slipped in. There were no voices coming from the office, so she crept to the doorway and peered around the corner.

The office was empty except for the youngest secretary, Cindy, who sat at her metal desk staring into space. Her phone was off the hook.

"Hello," Leigh said, not too loudly, but loudly enough to make Cindy jump an inch.

"Oh, hello," the girl said, reddening. "I'm sorry. I didn't see you there. You're Bess Cogley's niece, right?"

Leigh nodded. "I just wondered if Shannon was here. I'd like to talk to her."

Cindy shook her head. "She's, well, you must know about Ted getting arrested."

"Yes," Leigh said with a sad nod, "but I thought she might drop by. I wanted to know if there was anything I could do for her."

Cindy offered to pass along a message, and Leigh proceeded with her real mission. "Is that Noel Humphrey's car in the lot?" she asked innocently.

The secretary nodded, her eyes widening. "She's in the parlor with Barbara and Ed. She came in earlier with tears streaming down her cheeks, saying she wanted to help make the burial arrangements."

Leigh's eyebrows rose. Noel had just told Bess that she wanted nothing to do with the burial arrangements. But then, perhaps that was before she realized he was really dead.

Cindy ignored Leigh's reaction, casting a mournful glance down the hall instead. It was clear she would love to be a fly on the wall in the parlor that very minute, but apparently duty called. Such as it was.

"Could I use your phone?" Leigh asked politely.

Cindy looked down at the receiver that lay on her desk, and promptly reddened. "Sure," she said, plopping it back in place. "I, um . . . the reporters were calling, you know." She excused herself to use the rest room and left Leigh to make her call in private.

Perfect. Leigh scrounged around in her wallet for Maura's latest business card and dialed the number quickly. Detective Polanski was not available. Would she like to speak with someone else?

She would. Cupping a hand around her mouth and talking quietly, just in case anyone at the church was listening, Leigh reported Noel's whereabouts. With any luck, one of the detectives would be able to catch her before she flew the coop again.

She had just hung up the phone when a surprisingly agile elderly woman appeared in the office doorway and headed straight for her.

"You're not Barbara," the woman said accusingly, eyes narrowed.

"No," Leigh agreed. "I'm Bess Cogley's niece, Leigh. I'm just using the phone. Barbara's in the parlor, I believe."

The woman narrowed her eyes. "Well, you need to get off the phone. I've been calling all morning." She turned around sharply. "Your aunt's a nice lady," she muttered as she walked away. "A bit too loose for my tastes, but a nice lady."

Leigh watched the woman's retreating back with a grin. There was at least one thing she looked forward to about getting really old—being able to say whatever the heck she wanted, and not getting called on it. She gave the woman a few seconds' worth of a head start, then walked down the hall toward the parlor after her. The woman opened the door without knocking and burst right in—and Leigh snuck up close enough to listen through the doorway.

"You're his wife, aren't you?" the interloper began accusingly.

Noel's voice, thin and simpering, reached Leigh's ears. "Why, yes, I am."

"Hmmm," the older woman murmured. "You don't look like a missionary to me. You look like something off a hippie wagon."

Leigh stifled a laugh. She really couldn't wait to do that.

Noel's voice had gotten stronger. "This isn't my working wardrobe," she said flatly, not quite succeeding in hiding her defensiveness. "I'm raising funds for the mission, and when I come to a cold climate, I'm afraid I don't have much choice about what to wear. I manage with whatever's donated so that everything else can go straight to the African people. It would be wrong for me to buy nice clothes for myself."

"Hmmph." Leigh couldn't see the older woman's face, but the muttered syllable made it quite evident she wasn't buying. *Good for her.*

"Did you want something, Evelyn? We were discussing funeral arrangements." It was Barbara's voice, overbearing and irritated. Evidently, she *was* buying.

"Yes, I do want something," Evelyn announced. "I wanted to let you know that Reverend Humphrey appeared to me in a dream last night."

There was a moment of silence, then Barbara spoke patronizingly. 'Oh? And what did he say?"

"He said that he was counting on me to avenge his killer. And I plan on doing it."

"But Bess says—"

"I already heard what she said," Evelyn interrupted. "She's wrong. He was murdered."

There was a scuffling sound, as if someone was getting up quickly. "By who?" The voice was Noel's—high and demanding.

Evelyn paused. "He didn't say. But he may next time."

No one else said anything, and Leigh retreated, sensing that Evelyn was about to make a dramatic exit. She slipped around the corner and waited until the older woman had gone, then crept back within earshot of the parlor.

"Don't pay any attention to her, dear," Barbara was saying soothingly.

"She sees Elvis, you know," Ed chimed in with a snicker.

Leigh listened for more, but somebody—probably Barbara—shut the door again. She stepped up closer and tried to keep listening, but the sound was too muffled. She sighed and walked back toward the office. Where were the detectives? They were going to miss Ms. Humphrey again. She could tell Noel they were coming, but something told her that would result in an even more quickly revved-up Monte Carlo.

If only she knew more about cars . . .

Her illegal thoughts were interrupted by Cindy, who caught her at the door to the office and quickly pulled her inside. "I saw you snooping out there," the young secretary said, her tone more respectful than accusatory. "What were they saying?"

Leigh looked into Cindy's vacuous blue eyes and decided she wasn't a threat to anyone, despite the fact that she was darned good at watching people when they didn't know it. "Evelyn saw Humphrey in a dream. She's supposed to find his killer."

The hope in the blue eyes dampened. "Is that all?" she said sulkily. "I was kind of hoping she was here to donate money to the memorial fund."

"The memorial fund?"

Cindy smiled broadly. "It was kind of my idea. Using the money people would spend on flowers and giving it to Noel instead—for her mission."

"I'm sure Noel will be thrilled," Leigh said sincerely. *Very thrilled.* "Does she know about it yet?"

Cindy shook her head. "I think Barbara is telling her now. Everyone thinks it's a great idea." She paused, her round mouth suddenly pouting. "Except for your aunt. I don't know what her problem is."

Leigh had some idea, but since she didn't choose to share it, she changed the subject instead. "Evelyn said Bess was a bit loose for her tastes," she said with a smile.

Cindy smiled back. "Evelyn's a hoot. So's your aunt—usually. I admire a woman who's in charge of her own sexual destiny. That's why I like this church."

Leigh's eyebrows rose. She wasn't sure what "sexual destiny" was, but she couldn't wait to hear what the First Church of the New Millennium had to do with it. "Pardon?"

"You know," Cindy said with a grin. "Reverend Humphrey was a big believer in monogamy, but he never came down hard on the divorce issue. 'When life throws you a curveball,' he'd say, 'you've got to adapt—or get out of the way.'"

Leigh stared blankly. Granted, she wasn't the best person in the world at baseball analogies, but this one seemed to be lacking. "And what did that mean exactly?"

Cindy laughed. "I think it means 'love the one you're with.' But of course, he'd never say that."

Of course. "So what did he say?" Leigh asked, suddenly more interested in Reginald Humphrey's theology.

Cindy looked at her seriously. "There were a lot of issues he was a little vague on, to tell you the truth. But he was wonderful at making people feel good about themselves." She sighed. "He was such a big help to me when I failed out of beauty school. I felt so low, but he convinced me I was worth something. He gave me the job here. Most pastors would have looked at me like I was something out of the gutter, but Humphrey didn't pass judgment. He just wanted me to feel good about myself again."

Leigh considered. "So Humphrey wasn't a fire-and-brimstone type preacher?" she asked.

"Oh, no," Cindy answered, her eyes wide. "I hate

that stuff. I don't think Humphrey even believed there was a hell, though he never came right out and said that either. What he would say is that everyone bears the consequences of their sins while they're here on earth."

Not an uncommon view, Leigh thought. She wasn't even sure she disagreed with it.

"That's why, in order to be completely happy, you need to unburden your soul and deal with your life's baggage head-on."

Stop there. "You mean, like getting counseling?" Leigh asked. A tie-in with a local quack therapist she could see.

"Sometimes," Cindy said speculatively. "But Humphrey did a lot of counseling on his own. Like I said, he worked wonders with me."

Cindy's eyes had turned moist, and Leigh felt bad for the semi-interrogation. This was one person who didn't secretly dislike Humphrey—she was sure of it. "I told him about—well, an unhealthy relationship I'd once had," the girl continued, her voice faltering. "He was so understanding. Not judgmental at all. He helped me see that it wasn't my fault, that I deserved to be happy again."

Leigh grabbed a tissue off Cindy's desk and forwarded it along. Interesting information or no interesting information, she didn't want to be responsible for ruining this poor girl's day.

"Cindy, are you OK?" The soft voice came from behind them, and Leigh turned to see Shannon standing behind her shoulder.

"I'm fine," Cindy said hurriedly, wiping away the rest of her tears and trying to smile. "I just got a little choked up again. But don't worry about me. What's happening with Ted?"

"The arraignment is scheduled for this afternoon," Shannon said with a visible effort to sound brave. "Ted should be out on bail as soon as it's over."

"That's great!" Cindy said with enthusiasm. She went on to babble at length about how certain everyone was that Humphrey had died of natural causes, and how all the unpleasantness would be over with shortly. Some people might be upset about Ted messing with the body, but everyone would understand eventually—really, they would.

Leigh didn't share Cindy's unbridled optimism, but at the moment she was in favor of anything that could make Shannon look healthier. Deep hollows seemed to have formed overnight under the woman's cheeks and eyes, and the modest outfit she wore hung on her body as if she were made of wire.

"Shannon!" Barbara called from the office doorway, "How are you? How is Ted?" She and Ed rushed in, and Shannon explained her situation again. Leigh looked anxiously over the couple's shoulders to see if Noel was with them, but the distant rev of a motor answered her question.

Damn! She slipped out around the others in the office and tore off toward the Cavalier. Maybe she could catch Noel, or at least follow her to where she was staying. The detectives had to talk to her. If they were worth their salt, they'd see through her in a minute, and the whole case would open up—homicide or no homicide. Bess might believe that the church was better off not knowing Humphrey was a con artist, but Leigh wasn't convinced. Especially not with people like Cindy anxious to throw more money Noel's way.

The last flash of red drifted out of sight down the road just as she jammed her keys into the ignition and cranked. But the Cavalier made only a gurgling sound. She looked at the dashboard and cursed fluently.

The car was out of gas.

Chapter 17

Oh, right. The gas station. Cursing the irresistibility of donuts, Leigh slammed her car door and trudged back into the church, where the people she had run out on now stood staring at her.

She was able to explain her automotive woes pretty easily, but explaining why she had taken off after Noel like a bat out of hell was trickier. "It's very important that the detectives speak with Humphrey's wife," she began. "There are legalities that need to be taken care of by the next of kin, you know." She had no idea if that was true, but it sounded plausible, so she kept going. "Besides, they might need her to get personal information on Humphrey—medical history, that sort of thing."

"Of course!" Barbara said dramatically, her hand flying to her mouth. "We should have thought of that! What if the coroner can't figure out what really killed him? The detectives did ask me if I knew who Humphrey's personal physician was, but I didn't, darn it! Do you know, Shannon?"

Shannon shook her head regretfully. "No, he never talked about things like that. If the church had provided insurance, we might have some paperwork. But as you know, Humphrey refused benefits; he preferred to handle his own affairs." Her brow knitted. "I never suspected he might have any health problems—other than the diabetes, of course."

Barbara shook her head in agreement. "The diabetes

is all I ever heard about. He had bronchitis last fall, but otherwise he seemed fit as a fiddle. Still, it wouldn't hurt to call people and see if anyone remembers anything. If we could get into his personal papers, we might find something . . . but I guess they're all gone now."

Barbara was undoubtedly envisioning a pile of ashes, but Leigh was envisioning something else. She had been trying to forget her questionable dealings with Humphrey's mini-storage unit, but what if there was valuable information inside? Information that could point to a natural cause of death?

"Leigh?" Shannon's soft voice interrupted her thoughts.

"I'm sorry," she said, suddenly aware that she'd zoned out of the conversation. "What did you say?"

"I asked if you'd like a lift to a gas station," Shannon repeated. "I have an empty gas can in the back of the Suburban." She smiled pleasantly, almost pleasantly enough to erase the worry lines etched in her pale face.

Leigh smiled back. "That would be great," she said thankfully, "but are you sure you don't need to be somewhere else right now?"

Shannon shook her head. "I came here to pick up some papers that Ted's lawyer wanted, and I do need to get them to her, but this won't take long. Besides, I've been hoping to get a chance to talk with you."

Leigh saw no point in resisting. They said good-bye to the other staffers, climbed into the Suburban (Ted's toy, she was sure), and buckled up. Shannon started the engine, checked every available mirror, looked over her shoulder, and headed out.

"This is a nice car," Leigh began, making chitchat. The truth was, she hated SUVs—mainly because she couldn't afford one.

"It's Ted's," Shannon said tonelessly. "I don't like driving it, but when we left this morning, we didn't know—."

Her voice cracked, and Leigh felt terrible. Why did she always have to ask questions that upset people?

A recovery was needed. "Katharine Bower will have Ted out in no time—and I'm not just saying that," she stated firmly. "I ought to know. She got me out."

Shannon smiled, and her voice steadied. "Warren told us about that. I'm so sorry, it must have been awful for you. I do trust Katharine—she seems very competent. I still can't help worrying, though. I guess it's just my nature."

Leigh would have to agree. The Suburban was trolling along Nicholson Road at five miles an hour below the posted speed limit, and she was starting to fidget in her seat.

"I don't think Katharine is very good for Warren, however. I'm hoping he moves along soon."

Leigh looked up with wide eyes. Where had *that* come from?

Shannon caught her expression and smiled. "I'm sorry. I don't mean to be nebby. But I think you and Warren would make a lovely couple. Katharine's a nice woman, but she's too career driven, and I know Warren wants a family." She cleared her throat. "There, I've said it. Now I can sleep with a clear conscience." She smiled at Leigh again.

Leigh smiled back but didn't say anything. For once she couldn't think of anything to say. She turned her head to look out the window, and wondered if she could run faster than the trees seemed to be going by. The morning's snow was long gone, the salty road slush already having dried to a dull white sheen on the asphalt. She fidgeted some more. "Do you like working at the church?" she managed finally.

"Very much," Shannon answered. "I've always liked office work. I was a medical receptionist for years—that's how I met Ted. I was working for a dermatologist, and he had this nasty rash—" She stopped, her cheeks reddening a little. "Well, never mind about that. Anyway, he encouraged me to go back and get my accounting degree. It's come in very handy."

Leigh saw the opening and jumped. "So do you do all the bookkeeping for the church?"

Shannon smiled a little. "No. Only a little here and there. I offered to do more, but Humphrey was very involved in every aspect of the church, and he liked to do most of the financial management himself. He didn't have any formal training, but he seemed to know what he was doing."

I bet. "Did the church support Noel's mission?" Leigh asked innocently.

"Of course," Shannon answered. "We support a variety of mission projects, but hers is naturally the pet." She approached a green light and slowed down cautiously. The light turned yellow, and the Suburban halted in its tracks. Leigh squeezed her door handle to avoid screaming.

"Do you work part-time or full-time?" she said quickly, trying to distract herself.

"I'm a volunteer, actually," Shannon answered cheerfully. "We don't really need the money, and I like working for a worthy cause. It is only part-time, though. I also do some bookkeeping for the Open Door shelter on the North Side."

Leigh nodded. It sounded like Shannon and Bess had the volunteer bug in common. But the similarity ended there. Bess was flamboyant and vivacious; Shannon was like an obsequious little mouse, dressed up in a larger rodent's clothes. Leigh surveyed her critically—the pretty face hidden behind the poor haircut and cheap glasses, the clothes that hid any trace of a figure. Perhaps she had some sort of self-esteem problem?

Leigh wondered briefly if Shannon could be the victim of spouse abuse, but she dismissed the thought. Warren was adamant that Ted wasn't a violent man, and she herself had noticed the tenderness in Ted's eyes whenever he looked at his wife or daughter.

Shannon was probably just another nonconformist.

She had, after all, married a neurotic widower with a rash.

When the Suburban rolled gently back into the church parking lot a few hundred years later, Leigh thanked Shannon profusely, emptied the gas can into her tank, and returned the vessel as quickly as possible. Her mother's Taurus was also in the church lot, which meant Bess must be visiting again. What was her aunt up to now—and how had she conned Frances into driving her?

Shannon's SUV departed—slowly and cautiously—and Leigh headed back inside the church. She was starving. Promising herself that a Baja chicken gordita would soon be hers, she scouted out the building for her aunt. She needn't have bothered—Bess was waiting for her just inside the door.

"Quickly," Bess said in a hushed voice. "Take this. I don't want Frances to see."

Leigh looked down at the familiar-looking key Bess had pressed into her hand, and a bad feeling rolled up in her stomach. "Aunt Bess—"

An emphatic shooshing gesture cut her off. "I want you to go back there and check it out again," she whispered. "I'd go myself, but I can't get away from Atilla the Hun. I don't know why we didn't think of it earlier, but when Barbara called, it occurred to me that the mini-storage—"

"Aunt Bess," Leigh said again, quietly but firmly, "you should be handing this over to the detectives, not me. Or at the very least to Noel. His stuff is rightfully hers now."

Bess looked at her niece as if she had lost her mind. "Noel is the *last* person who needs to see this stuff! Heaven knows what she would do with it. What you need to do with it is check to see if there's anything that might indicate what Humphrey died of. Doctor's visit receipts, old prescription bottles, that sort of thing. If you find any, we can turn them in and say he left them at the church."

Leigh's appetite had departed. "Aunt Bess," she began once more, trying to stay calm, "I can't do that. We already broke into the place once. Let's just say that we found the key in the church somewhere. If there's evidence that's relevant, the detectives can find it themselves. I'll call Maura—"

"No!" Bess shot back fiercely, then lowered her voice again. "If the detectives even hear that that place exists, they're sure to figure out that he set the fire himself. I bet there are even things in there that he told people had burned! There's no way that mini-storage can become public knowledge without everyone knowing Humphrey was a fraud."

"Maybe they should," Leigh said seriously, looking her aunt squarely in the eye.

Bess returned her gaze, her determination edged with sadness again. "I thought you understood, Leigh. I just can't let that happen. Not unless I have no choice. If the coroner's report comes back homicide, then I'll march right straight to the detectives and tell them everything. I swear. But if Humphrey died on his own, nobody else has to lose here. I can get rid of Noel—I'll buy her off myself if I have to—Ted will be out of danger, and the church can go on with a new pastor. It's the best thing for everyone." Her eyes turned pleading. "*Please*, Leigh. Go back to the mini-storage. No one will ever know you were there."

"Bess!" Frances screeched from somewhere down the hall. "I thought you were resting in the parlor! What are you doing back on your feet? Come sit down, or I'm taking you right back home again."

Bess's hands closed Leigh's firmly over the key, and after one last, beseeching gaze she turned back to Frances. "Coming, Master!"

Leigh offered her mother a cursory wave and quickly retreated. She wanted to drop the key down a storm drain right then and there, but somehow that didn't happen. It burned a hole in the palm of her hand as she walked to the Cavalier, and when she recognized Detective Hollandsworth's car pulling into the lot, she dropped it guiltily into her pocket.

She hopped into the Cavalier and started the engine. Sure, *now* he shows up. It was his sluggishness that was the problem, she reasoned. If he had been a little quicker responding to her report of Noel being at the church, she wouldn't have to go where she was going now.

And that would make everybody happier.

The door of SPE Mini Storage unit #47 slid up easily. Leigh had watched her own gloved hands opening it, wishing desperately that they were someone else's. Maura would kill her if she knew. There was no question about that. It was only a matter of how. And although the detective's behavior on the job was strictly by the book, Leigh feared her friend had a creative streak.

A cold wind had started blowing, and she pulled the door almost closed behind her. After pulling the cord on the single light bulb in the ceiling, she could see well enough to look around. Everything looked the same as the last time she had been there, and no wonder. By then Humphrey had been dead a day already—who else was going to mess with it?

She thumbed through the contents of the open boxes, looking for one that might house old medication containers. She and Bess had looked through many of them, but they hadn't really been looking for medical stuff then, and there were other, sealed boxes they hadn't gotten to at all before Leigh had panicked.

In retrospect, she wished they'd finished the job the first time. At least then they hadn't been interfering with a possible murder investigation. She walked around and surveyed the rest of the sealed boxes, her eyes settling on one whose packing tape had long since yellowed. As she picked it up, her heart jumped. The letters MH were scrawled across its top with a black marker.

She settled the box into position under the light and began working at the tape. MH could mean anything, of course—from "move here" to "Mom's hairdryer." But as far as she was concerned, it meant "Money Humphrey."

The packing tape seemed to have morphed over time into superhumanly strong strips coated with goo, and she was pretty sure the keys she was using to split the tape would never be the same. But eventually her persistence was rewarded. She opened the box and looked down into an unlikely jumble of dusty books, clothes, and games.

She pulled out the clothes first and noticed quickly that they were not typical clothes, but uniforms. One seemed to be an old policeman's uniform; the other was vintage Salvation Army. Decks of cards were everywhere, some pornographic. And aside from an early edition of *Swiss Family Robinson*, the books had a definite theme. *How to Pick Pockets for Fun and Profit*, *Gambling Scams*, *Sleight of Hand*, and a half dozen books on billiards were all well worn. One book protected by a plastic case was undoubtedly the pride of the collection: *Expert at the Card Table, A Treatise on the Science and Art of Manipulating Cards*. It was a first edition, dated 1902.

Leigh replaced the clothes and the books and closed the lid. Let no one ever accuse "Money" Humphrey of not being serious about his craft, she thought grimly.

There were two other boxes labeled "MH," but Leigh ignored them. The last thing she needed now was to find even more evidence to feel guilty about withholding from the police. She was supposed to be proving Humphrey *wasn't* murdered, and on that score she was striking out miserably.

Thinking that perhaps she should concentrate on the boxes that looked more recent, she sat down on the cold concrete and pulled a small lidded one into her lap. As the lid slid up and out of the way, she smiled.

Personal items. *Eureka.* She fingered her way through a plastic container of shoelaces, a half-dozen eyeglass cases, a sewing kit, SPF40+ sunscreen, and an electric razor before her eyes settled on a small, oblong leather carrying case. She fumbled with the zipper, determined not to remove her gloves. When the contents came into view, she sucked in a breath.

Paydirt. She had seen such a gadget only once before, when she was in a restaurant in Station Square and a man fell out of his seat and onto the floor. She had jumped up instinctively, trying to remember the Heimlich maneuver, but by the time she reached the table the man's wife had things firmly under control. He had a peanut allergy, she had explained later. And he might very well have died if she hadn't injected him with the device she had taken out of her purse. The same device Humphrey had stashed away in his travel kit, along with a few clean insulin syringes and some Band-Aids.

It was an epinephrine dispenser. The kind carried by people who have allergies so severe that if a reaction isn't treated immediately, they can go into anaphylactic shock. And die.

"Oh, look. It's already open. That's a bit odd, isn't it?"

The squeaky voice wafting under the garage door made Leigh's body stiffen, and the man's voice that followed did nothing to reassure her.

"I'm, uh, not sure how that could be, Mrs. Humphrey. It was shut tight this morning. We always check, you know. Are you sure he didn't give somebody else his key?"

Noel. She knew about Humphrey's storage unit— and she was coming to get his stuff. Leigh dropped the travel kit back into the box, shoved on the lid, and kicked the whole business as far into the back of the unit as she could. "Noel?" she called out, as cheerfully as she could manage, "is that you?"

When the door rolled up she was standing as if waiting for them, an incredibly fake smile plastered on her face. "I'm so glad you're here! You can be so much help, if you're willing. The women at the church thought that we should go through Humphrey's things as soon as possible—in case there was something that might help the investigation. I suggested we ask you to help, but they were afraid it might be too painful for you, this soon." She tried to turn the fake smile into a fake look of concern. "Are you sure you're up to this?"

Noel's eyes, which had been fixed on Leigh with alternating flashes of surprise, anger, caution, and distrust, floated over to the mini-storage manager. "Evidently my husband did leave his key in the custody of the church. I'm sorry to drag you out here for nothing. Thank you for your trouble."

The man nodded patiently and walked away. Noel's eyes turned back on Leigh with a steady, studying look. It seemed like a year before she spoke. "What are you doing here?" she said simply.

"I told you," Leigh said, her smile muscles fatiguing. "We were hoping to find something that could help the investigation. You know, like medical records."

The doe eyes suddenly seemed more black than brown, their expression cold and blank. "My husband was murdered," she said calmly. "How did you get his key?"

Leigh swallowed. She was doing OK so far, though she already regretted the "women at the church" line. It could too easily be disproven. "Your husband gave it to my aunt Bess," she answered slowly, the wheels in her brain doing overtime. "He told her he was afraid to leave it at the church, under the circumstances. That if anything happened to him, she was to make sure you got it."

Noel's brow furrowed, and Leigh kept talking. "She would have given it to you at the house the other day, but she forgot all about it. Her memory isn't what it used to be, I'm afraid." She smiled again. Bess would kill her for that one, but it didn't matter. Maura would pulverize her long before her aunt got a shot.

She decided to lay it on thicker. "I'm sorry. You look upset. I hope you don't think we were prying. It's just . . . we all want to see things get cleared up with the investigation, so we can move forward with the funeral service."

The doe eyes softened, but only a bit. "I appreciate your concern, but I would rather go through my husband's things myself, if you don't mind."

"Oh, of course!" Leigh said graciously, beginning her retreat. "If you find anything unexpected, anything that might help the detectives, I'm sure you'll let them know."

That'll be the day. Leigh offered an insincere thanks and good-bye and spun on her heel. She had taken only a step and a half when Noel's falsetto voice called her back.

"Um, Leigh? That is your name, isn't it?"

She nodded.

"Could I have it, please?"

She stared blankly for a moment, certain she had carried nothing away with her.

"The key," Noel said firmly, holding out her hand.

Fumbling an apology, Leigh pulled the key from her pocket and dutifully placed it in the other woman's palm. Then she murmured another good-bye, collapsed into the Cavalier, and let out a breath.

Well, fine. Now she could tell Bess both that Humphrey knew how to cheat at cards and that he was deathly allergic to something. Without the key, however, she couldn't prove either one.

Chapter 18

Leigh finished off a dinner of instant rice and soy sauce without enthusiasm. It had been well past noon when she had finally gotten the gordita, and then it had lain in her stomach like lead. She wanted desperately to talk to Bess, but explaining the mini-storage adventure with her mother present was not an option. So she had spent the remainder of her last weekday of vacation doing what she probably should have been doing all along—lying on the couch watching TV with a cat on her stomach.

Warren's familiar knock on the door shook her out of her stupor, and she rushed to answer it. The tie she had watched him put on that morning still hung straight and unrumpled, but other than that, he looked like something Mao Tse might enjoy relocating. Having one relative in the hospital and another in jail was clearly taking its toll. She had a sudden impulse to step up and put her arms around him, but just as she began to follow it, she caught sight of a petite redhead emerging from behind him. Her hands dropped to her sides.

"Hello, Leigh," Katharine said with her usual formal pleasantness. "We'd like to talk with you a moment, if you have the time."

Leigh threw a glance at Warren, who looked back at her hopefully. "Sure," she answered, curious. She invited them in as Mao Tse, true to form, hissed and retreated to the bedroom. "'What's up?" she asked, turning off the television and picking her empty rice bowl up off the floor. "Is Ted back home yet?"

"Thanks to his talented attorney, yes," Warren answered, his voice tired. "But if you ask me, he was darned lucky Hollandsworth only booked him for breaking and entering."

Katharine grinned. "Really, Warren, it wasn't that bad. People often lose their composure when they're being arrested."

Warren shot her a skeptical look, and she put a comforting hand on his arm.

Leigh ground her teeth. "Won't you sit down?" She showed Katharine to a chair and Warren to the couch, where she sat down beside him. "Has the coroner's report come back yet?" she asked.

"No," Katharine answered, jumping in. "I understand they've expanded the toxicology work-up, which explains the holdup. But we should know something by tomorrow."

"I see," Leigh said. "How can I help?"

Katharine's green eyes looked at her intently. "Warren tells me your aunt has expressed doubts that Reginald Humphrey was a legitimate minister."

Before Leigh could respond, Warren put an apologetic hand on her arm. "I'm sorry," he said softly. "I know you didn't want your aunt's suspicions to go any further than me. I only mentioned it to Katharine because I had to know if it could make any difference to Ted's defense, and she seems to think it might."

Leigh looked up into his concerned brown eyes and wanted to tell him that if he would boot Katharine out of the room and put his other hand on her other arm, she would forgive him anything. But that seemed a bit self-serving.

"It's all right," she answered smoothly. "I understand." She did understand. But the coroner's report was due tomorrow. It wouldn't hurt Ted if she and Bess held out just a little bit longer, would it?

"My aunt had many doubts about Reginald Humphrey," she confirmed carefully. "But she doesn't have any idea who might have wanted him dead. In fact, she's convinced he died of natural causes, and she won't say or listen to anything to the contrary." She paused, wanting desperately to help somebody somehow. "I can tell you this," she said sincerely. "If the coroner's report comes back as homicide, my aunt will be more than willing to answer any questions you might have about Humphrey and the church. In fact, she'd be delighted." *I'll see to it.*

Katharine studied her skeptically, but her voice was polite. "Thank you." She glanced at her watch, then rose and looked at Warren. "You'd better be getting ready, hadn't you?"

He nodded and rose also. Leigh's heart sank.

"Going somewhere?" she asked shamelessly, proud of herself for omitting the word "together."

"Fund-raiser," he said simply, offering a weary smile. "I wish I could get out of this one, but I've made promises to people." He started toward the door, and Leigh tried not to look as disappointed as she felt. Would they never get a chance to talk alone?

"Warren," she began, not bothering to disguise her earnestness, "we need to get together soon. There's something I want to talk to you about. It's important."

He studied her curiously. "Sure. I'll be out late tonight, but come by tomorrow."

Katharine's eyes flashed at the exchange, but Leigh wasn't sure whether the lawyer feared losing out on information about the case—or something else. Katharine followed Warren out the door, then turned back to Leigh. "I trust you'll keep the best interests of Ted Hugh at heart," she said heavily.

Leigh looked into the other woman's eyes and nodded, message received. It wasn't Ted Hugh they were talking about.

*   *   *

When Leigh approached her aunt's farmhouse the next morning, she was met by both an exuberant Chester, who had been sunning himself on the front porch, and the steady hum of a power saw, which emanated from somewhere on the second floor. Lydie was at it again.

Leigh patted Chester, then rapped briefly on the door and let herself inside, determined not to make her aunt get up again. "What's the occasion?" she asked Bess, who was sitting in her accustomed location on the couch, her foot propped up on the coffee table. "You getting a new addition?"

Bess smiled and rolled her eyes. "No, just a new guest bathroom. Lydie claims the toilet has a slow leak and the floorboards are rotten, so she's going to replace the fixtures and put down a new floor with ceramic tile. Between you and me, I think it's all a ruse. She's just bored to tears at the prospect of staring at yours truly all weekend."

Leigh smiled back wordlessly, not wanting to acknowledge that her aunt was probably right. For Lydie, doing nothing wasn't a vacation—it was torture.

"Watch out!" Bess commanded as Leigh started to walk toward the bottom of the staircase. "Punkster at eleven o'clock."

Leigh looked up at the top of the antique secretary and could just see two gray-tufted ears poking out above the pediment, while a lashing tail curved briefly around the finial.

"That's his new favorite spot," Bess remarked proudly. "He can swoop down from above just like a jaguar."

Not caring to experience the phenomenon, Leigh backtracked and went the long way around the front of the sofa. "Hello, Aunt Lydie!" she called up the stairs, when the buzzing had ceased for a moment.

"Hello, Leigh!" came the cheery response, which was followed by more humming and buzzing. Leigh walked back toward the couch, and hadn't yet sat down when the interrogation began.

"Well, did you go to the mini-storage?" Bess asked hopefully. "What did you find? I thought you'd call— I could have fooled Frances, you know. She'd have never known who I was talking to."

Leigh had no doubt her aunt would have loved carrying on a completely fictional conversation while listening to her report. "I tried to call you a couple of times," she answered. "But the phone was always busy. Finally I just gave up and went to bed." *But I didn't mean to fall asleep,* she remembered ruefully. The plan had been to watch for the return of Warren's car, but she hadn't made it. At least, she reminded herself optimistically, his car had been parked alone in the lot this morning.

"Not again!" Bess complained, fiddling with the phone on her end table. "Honeysuckle is always sleeping on this table, knocking the handset out of whack. I should have known." She exhaled impatiently, "Well, you're here now. Out with it! What did you find?"

Leigh looked at her aunt and let out a breath. Where to begin? First, she passed on the good news that Ted Hugh had been released on bail. Then she described the damning contents of the box marked M.H.

Bess drunk in every word hungrily. "Gambling, eh? I'm not surprised. He had to start somewhere—he's probably been shaving cards since grade school." Her tone turned serious. "But that doesn't matter now. The important thing is proving he died of natural causes. Did you find any medical evidence?"

"Possibly," Leigh answered, then described the epinephrine dispenser. Bess's eyes gleamed, her voice rising with excitement. "Of course! An allergic reaction. I do believe you've got it, kiddo!"

Leigh accepted the compliment with a smile and continued. "Ted Hugh said that after he moved the body, he cleaned up the office to make it look like Humphrey had left on his own. Apparently that included throwing out some food that was left on the desk. Do you think Humphrey could have been allergic to peanuts?"

Bess thought a moment, then shook her head slowly. "No, not that. I've seen him eat peanut butter and jelly sandwiches. He brought them to work all the time." She sat back, her eyes lost in thought. Then suddenly she snapped back up.

"Bees!" she said triumphantly. "Humphrey was absolutely scared to death of them. Everyone knew that. We had a church picnic at North Park once, and he had some of the kids throw away his paper plate and napkin because he was afraid to go near the trash can. They ribbed him about it pretty good, as I recall. Not that something like that is funny."

"People who are allergic to bees can certainly die from a sting," Leigh confirmed. "But inside? At night? In the middle of winter?"

Bess's brow furrowed. "Shoot. I didn't think of that."

"A food allergy is more likely," Leigh insisted. "Maybe he was allergic to some other kind of nut. Or shellfish?"

Bess shook her head. "He wasn't picky about his food when it came to church potlucks, I can tell you that. In fact, I always thought he ate a bit recklessly, considering he was a diabetic. There must be something else."

An unpleasant image formed in Leigh's brain. She had been a teenager, working at her father's clinic, when someone in the reception area had started screaming. A Maltese had just gotten its yearly vaccinations, and all of a sudden it couldn't breathe. Her father had hauled the dog back to the treatment room immediately and injected it with epinephrine, and it had pulled through with flying colors. But she, the dog's owner, and everyone else except her father had nearly had a heart attack.

"He could have reacted to something in his insulin," she suggested. "I've never heard of that exactly, but I bet it could happen."

Bess waved her hand in the air. "Well, I suppose it doesn't matter really. The point is that he might have died from an allergy. Where is this epinephrine gadget? We've got to get it to the detectives right away—we'll tell them we found it at the church or something. Shannon will be ecstatic!"

Bess stopped suddenly as Leigh's body language portended the bad news. "I don't have it," she admitted.

"Oh," Bess responded lightly. "Well, let's go get it, then. Lydie won't miss me."

Leigh sighed. "You don't understand. I don't have the key anymore."

Bess's eyes widened. "And why not? Did you give it back to SPE?"

She shook her head.

"To who, then?"

"Noel."

Bess stared at her in disbelief.

"I didn't want to!" Leigh defended. "She left me no choice." She explained how she had been caught red-handed, and Bess sighed dramatically. "So Noel knew about the mini-storage already," she said with defeat. "More to the point, now *she* knows that *you* knew about it."

Leigh nodded and repeated the lame cover story she had composed on the spot. "I'm not sure if she bought it. I think it's time we tell Maura Polanksi about the mini-storage. If the detectives can get a warrant to search it—"

"No," Bess said firmly. "Then everyone will know Humphrey was a fraud, and I told you I can't let that happen." She took a deep breath. "Maybe Noel came to get something of his, and maybe now that she has it, she'll leave. That will be one less fly in the ointment. As for the investigation, we can do without the epinephrine dispenser. I'll ask around and see if anybody knew what else Humphrey was allergic to. We can pass that on to the detectives without needing any evidence." She patted Leigh's knee approvingly. "It'll be all right. Thanks for doing the dirty work for me, kiddo. I appreciate it."

The protest forming in Leigh's mind was cut off by the shrill ring of the phone on the end table. Bess swooped down immediately to pick it up. "Yes?"

Leigh watched her aunt's face, idly at first, then with more attention as the color drained from her plump cheeks. "That's not true! Who is this?" Bess demanded. "Hello? Hello?"

She hung up the phone with a bang. "The nerve!" she railed, crossing her arms firmly in front of her chest.

"Who was it?" Leigh insisted. "What did they say?"

Bess didn't answer for a moment. She just sat and looked angry.

"Aunt Bess!" Leigh pleaded, getting worried.

"It was a man," Bess answered finally. "If it was a woman, I'd understand it. But it was a man."

"Saying what?"

"He said, 'I know you killed him—all of you. And you're not getting away with it.' "

Leigh stared. For a moment they just sat quietly, Leigh staring and Bess fuming. "All of who? Why would anyone think you had anything to do with Reginald Humphrey's death?"

"No one would," Bess announced, her tone a weak attempt at lightheartedness. "It was just a prank."

"Well, it's a sick prank," Leigh insisted. Her eyes moved back to the phone. "Wait a minute. What's that code—star 69? We can find out who called!"

She dove for the phone, but before she could reach

it, it rang again. Her hand paused in midair for a moment, then she grabbed it anxiously.

"Hello?" she said, her voice tense.

"Um, hello. Is Bess there?" The voice on the other end of the line was edgy and familiar, and definitely did not belong to a man. Leigh handed the handset over to Bess. "I think it's Barbara," she said with disappointment.

Bess swallowed and took the phone. Leigh didn't bother paying attention at first, but perked up when she heard her aunt mention the name Noel. Her paranoid mind started assuming the worst. Had Noel figured out she had lied about getting the key from Humphrey? Was she going to prosecute Leigh for trespassing? Stealing?

Calm down, she told herself. Noel was the last person who would go to the police for anything. In fact, she seemed to be putting a lot of energy into avoiding them. What was she up to now?

Bess hung up the phone and looked at Leigh worriedly. "Barbara says she's been trying to reach me for hours. It seems Noel contacted her early this morning and asked her to start a phone chain through the entire congregation. She wants to call a church meeting."

Leigh blinked. "She does?"

Bess nodded, and the women stared at each other again.

"What time?" Leigh managed to ask.

Bess looked at the antique clock on her mantel. "About two minutes before we can possibly get there."

By the time Leigh and Bess made it through the front doors of the First Church of the New Millennium, the crowd had already filled most of the seats in the small sanctuary. A chivalrous older gentleman offered Bess his seat on the aisle, and as soon as she was settled, Leigh scanned the room. Shannon was down front, surrounded by a sympathetic throng of younger women. She didn't see Ted anywhere. Nor did she see either of the two homicide detectives.

Leaving Bess with instructions to save her seat on the pew's end rail, Leigh slipped out and across the sanctuary into the parlor. Noel was nowhere to be seen. Was she planning a grand entrance?

She made her way down the hall to the empty church office, picked up the phone on Cindy's desk, and started dialing. She didn't have much time. "Maura?" she said thankfully, glad that her friend had been at her home number for once. "Noel Humphrey has called some kind of meeting at the church, and the homicide detectives aren't here."

"Is she there now?" the detective's husky voice asked immediately.

"She's supposed to be."

"I'm on my way." Maura hung up the phone without ceremony, and Leigh smiled to herself. Somebody from the detective's squad had to catch up with Noel, and if Maura had the edge, so much the better.

She returned to Bess in the sanctuary, and wondered if she should confess her errand. Her aunt didn't want Humphrey exposed as a fraud, but what about Noel? What if the bereaved widow was running some kind of scam herself? If she was, Leigh thought smugly, she would now have to deal with one Maura Polanski.

Leigh's potential confession was cut off short by Ed, who walked slowly to the podium and called the meeting to order. "We're running a little late here," he apologized, "but now I think we're ready. You've all been called here today at the request of the late Reginald Humphrey's widow, Noel, whom we've all heard the reverend speak so highly of. A few of you met her the day of . . ." He paused, sensing the indelicacy he was leading up to. "The day of the gathering after his death. She was a bit out of sorts then, as is understandable. But now she has some important things she'd like to say to us. Noel?"

Ed stepped aside, almost tripping off the top altar platform in the process. Noel jumped quickly to his aid, but he was able to steady himself. She smiled at him warmly, then took over the podium and lowered the microphone.

Leigh and Bess watched her entry, their mouths hanging slightly agape. Marlo/Mary had reentered her time and space machine. The woman with the doe eyes had transformed—from body-hugging polyester all the way to third-world burlap. Noel smiled serenely, her peculiar gray-brown hair hanging limply to her shoulders, and her pale, clean-washed face shining in the altar spotlight.

"Friends," she began, her voice steady, yet with just the right touch of vulnerability, "I'm sure you're wondering why I called you here today. I'm sorry if it's an inconvenience, and I won't keep you long."

She cleared her throat and appeared to be summoning her strength. "I came here this week to surprise my beloved husband, Reginald. We'd been apart for a long time, as I'm sure you know. But I returned to the United States a few weeks ago, and have been doing fund-raising for my mission in Zaire, to which this church has always graciously contributed."

Bess murmured something unpleasant, and this time Leigh was the one to do the rib jabbing.

"I called you all here today," Noel continued, "because I'm concerned about the future of this church, and of my mission. You wonderful people, whether you realize it or not, have been the primary supporters of the Millennium Mission Center in Kananga." She described the work of her mission by making a few vague claims, then moved quickly to the main agenda. "I can only hope, that in the absence of my husband, and as you carry on your charge as the First Church of the New Millennium, that you will continue to support the Kananga mission to whatever extent possible." Her chin trembled on cue, and her eyes began to glisten. "My Reginald cared about you all so deeply. And I know that, if he were here, he would—" Her voice broke off, and she made a show of burying her head in her hands.

Leigh's eyes widened in panic as several women went up to comfort the transparently distraught widow. Couldn't they tell she was acting?

Evidently not. Leigh swallowed painfully. A direct plea for money from Noel wasn't something they'd anticipated, but they should have. Bess looked frantically around the room, her eyes showing the same guilty fear. "I've waited too long!" she whispered harshly. "I should have known this would happen!"

Leigh looked toward the main doors to the sanctuary and sighed in relief. *Yes.* Maura Polanski was there, her large frame flanking the back wall as unobtrusively as possible. "At least this time Noel won't leave the church without being questioned," Leigh told her aunt, nodding in the detective's direction.

Bess shot a glance at Maura and exhaled loudly. "Flower money is one thing, but this is out of control, and I've got to stop it. I won't let the congregation get cheated in perpetuity."

Leigh looked around the room, watching with disappointment as person after person filed down front, offering their condolences—and probably their checkbooks—to the blubbering widow.

Her aunt had her work cut out for her.

Chapter 19

"Excuse me! Excuse me, everyone. I have something to say."

An elderly man, even more frail-looking than Ed, had slowly made his way up to the podium. He took the microphone with a shaky hand and repeated himself until the noise died down.

Leigh leaned over to her aunt's ear. "Who is that? Is he a board member too?"

Bess shook her head. "That's Reuben Colisimo. Old-time Presby man. He's a dear, but I'm afraid he's gone a bit daft the last few years. He absolutely adored Humphrey—they used to play pinochle together."

"Thank you," the man said finally when the room hushed. "There's something I want to say. You all know me. I've been a member of this church—in this building—longer than God." He chuckled at his own joke, then continued. "And you know what a wonderful man I always thought the Reverend Humphrey was. He did what no one else around here could do—he brought the life back into Franklin Presbyterian Church."

Bess fidgeted, then vented into Leigh's ear while Reuben continued to sing the reverend's praises. "He doesn't even realize we're not a Presbyterian church anymore," she sighed.

"Maybe I was closer to the reverend than most," Reuben continued, "and maybe that's why he chose me to speak to. I don't rightly know, but I believe it's my duty to pass his message on to you.''

Leigh and Bess turned their attention quickly back on the speaker. *His message?*

"The reverend appeared to me in a dream last night,'' Reuben said proudly, his voice getting louder. "Maybe I was asleep, and maybe I wasn't, but I know my good friend when I see him. He told me he was preparing to move on to the other side—and frankly, friends, he seemed plum happy about that. But he also told me something else. He said, 'You've got to keep it going, Reuben. You've got to keep the people together. It's all up to you.' ''

He paused and swallowed. "And then he told me this, I'm sure because he knew his dear wife would be talking to you this morning. He said, 'And I want you to make sure my sweet Noel is taken care of. I want you to make sure her mission has everything it needs. It's more important than you know. Because you see, there's a little boy at that mission. A fine little boy named Kunta, and he's been chosen by God for a very important task. But I've also seen that without the help of Noel and her mission, that little boy is going to die. I'm speaking to you tonight because I know *you* won't let that happen, Reuben.' That's what he said.''

The silence that fell over the sanctuary was deafening. It was broken only by a muffled exclamation from Noel, who had sunk into the pastor's chair, surrounded by earnest comforters. "Oh, my Lord!'' she said incredulously. "Kunta! How did you know about Kunta?''

Reuben Colisimo smiled benevolently. "I told you, my dear. Reginald Humphrey spoke to me himself—from the other side.''

The room broke out in a frenzied buzz, and Reuben stepped away from the podium as several church members scrambled to approach him.

Leigh looked at Bess, whose eyes had gone from wide to narrow. "Reuben Colisimo is dreaming," she proclaimed. "It's nonsense."

Leigh watched as Noel pushed her way through the crowd to approach him, and the two embraced. "Do you think he's in on the scam?"

Bess humphed indignantly. "Reuben? Never. He's just losing his marbles."

"But the name," Leigh questioned. "How did he come up with that, you suppose?"

Bess humphed again. "Didn't you watch *Roots,* kiddo? It's probably the only African-sounding name a man like Reuben could think of."

Leigh considered. It *was* a pretty lame name choice. Had Noel only pretended to recognize it? It seemed a bit fortuitous, but it certainly was possible.

People continued to stream forward, a large crowd forming around Noel and Reuben. "This is bad," Bess said, clucking her tongue. "This is very bad."

Leigh watched with interest as Evelyn Ewing, again moving faster than a woman of ninety-one had a right to, pushed up to the podium and grabbed the microphone herself. She held it upside down at first, her lips moving unproductively as she talked into the cords. It took her a moment, but she finally flipped the device around, then proceeded to scream into it as a deafening squeal of feedback rocked the sanctuary.

"Quiet, please," she commanded ironically. "Quiet, everyone. I have something to say as well."

Bess leaned toward Leigh again, smiling. "Now, this should be good," she said hopefully. "Evelyn might claim to have a thing going with Elvis, but underneath all that drama she's as sharp as a tack. She won't let this get out of hand."

"As everyone knows," Evelyn began, "I myself have had many brushes with our brothers and sisters on the other side. And as I told many of you already, the reverend himself also spoke to me—Thursday night." She paused a moment, and Leigh was surprised that she didn't repeat his alleged "avenge my murderer" command for all to hear. Instead she swallowed visibly, then continued in a much more tenuous voice. "But what I need to tell you now is that Reverend Humphrey also appeared to me last night. And this message was a little different."

The room, which had resumed buzzing quietly when Evelyn recited her paranormal qualifications, fell silent again at her change in tone. "This time he told me that it was wrong of him to ask for vengeance against his killer. He said that he had made peace with his murder, and that now he wanted only to ensure that some good came out of his untimely death. He told me that it was his wish that those who cared about him forget about him now—and instead make a commitment to support the Millennium Mission in Kananga."

Leigh stole a sideways glance at her aunt, whose mouth had dropped open. "No," Bess breathed softly. "Evelyn!"

The woman at the podium looked uncomfortable, almost as if she could hear Bess's admonishment. "And then he told me," she continued, her voice shaking, "that although he couldn't explain the situation fully, that the future of our own children could very well depend on a small African boy named Kunta."

Now Leigh's mouth dropped open as well. She wanted to believe her aunt was a decent judge of her own friends' character, but this was ridiculous. She had never seen a more obvious setup in her life. She looked back over her shoulder at the empty spot where Maura had been standing, and noticed that many members of the congregation seemed to agree with her assessment. A sizable number, both young and old, were walking out the back of the church.

Unfortunately, a larger number were pressing forward, eager to further interrogate Reuben and Evelyn. She looked through the growing mass of people milling about the altar, but could not see Noel among them. Wherever the little con artist had crept to, she hoped Maura was close behind.

Leigh was about to excuse herself to help in the chase when a rapidly hobbling Betty Ivey blocked her exit from the pew. "Bess," the older woman gasped, breathing heavily from her efforts, "we have to talk. We've got to stop this. I want you to call the board together—*right away*."

Bess looked into Betty's determined eyes and smiled. "Absolutely."

After checking to make sure that the red Monte Carlo was still parked out front, Leigh began to scour the church. Where would Noel have gone? She couldn't take off completely. Surely the cash that people had in hand wasn't all she was hoping for. She would have to leave an address, probably a post office box. Then she would disappear . . .

No. Not with Maura Polanski on her trail. After all, homicide or no, they were clearly dealing with a case of fraud here. And fraud, thank God, was firmly in Maura's jurisdiction.

She had searched every corner and classroom of the small church building when it occurred to her that there was probably only one place Noel could excuse herself to without rousing suspicion. She pushed opened the door to the ladies' room outside the parlor, and was gratified to see Noel Humphrey repairing her streaked mascara in the mirror. Maura leaned comfortably against the wall behind her.

"So, tell me again, if you don't mind, ma'am," Maura was saying companionably, "the mission in Kananga is supported purely by private contributions from independent churches?"

The detective raised an eyebrow to Leigh as if warning her not to interfere, and Leigh quickly dodged into a stall.

"I raise money wherever I can," Noel answered lightly, unable to completely cover the nervousness in her voice. "My husband was my biggest supporter, but I have other friends on the West Coast who also help out."

Maura tapped her pen on her notebook. "Would you mind giving me their names?"

Noel gave a twittering laugh. "Oh dear, I don't have all that information with me, I'm afraid. Can I call you later?"

When hell freezes over, Leigh thought skeptically, wondering how long she could get by with eavesdropping. Should she flush the toilet for realism?

"I'd like as much information now as you could give me," Maura insisted politely. "It's important that the church members be confident their money is going to a good cause."

"Oh, of course!" Noel agreed brightly. "I have some pamphlets—all about the mission and what it does. I use them in my fund-raising. I don't have any with me at the moment—perhaps I could bring them to you?"

Leigh flushed the toilet and missed Maura's next comment. "The detectives who are investigating your husband's death would very much like to talk to you," the detective was saying as Leigh tuned back in. "In fact, I was hoping you'd come back to the station with me. With your help, I believe they might be able to wrap up the case this weekend."

There was a pause as Noel digested this information. "You know who killed my husband? For sure?"

A hard knock landed on the stall door, and Leigh opened it sheepishly. She didn't need to look at Maura's eyes to read the message they were relaying. *Enough already. Get out.*

Leigh walked to the sink and washed her hands at a leisurely pace. Noel paid little attention—her eyes were fixed on Maura. "Answer me," she demanded. "Do you know who killed him?"

"Possibly no one, ma'am," Maura answered calmly. "But you'll need to ask the homicide detectives about that. Shall we go talk to them?"

Leigh dried her hands on a paper towel and started to arrange her hair in the mirror, but Maura's reflected glare made her change her mind. She sighed and opened the door to leave. She let it swing back slowly, hoping to hear Noel's reply, but none came. The little minx was probably weighing her curiosity against her chances of being arrested for something. And the more they found out about Noel, the more likely "something" seemed to be. What made her so sure that Humphrey had been murdered?

Leigh was halfway back to the sanctuary when an unpleasant thought struck her. In light of everything else that had happened since, she had forgotten about the first phone call Bess had gotten that morning.

I know you killed him. All of you.

Could Noel have disguised her voice to sound like a man? It was the most logical explanation. Noel was the only one—with the possible exception of Evelyn Ewing—who seemed certain that Humphrey had been murdered. She knew that Bess had broken into Humphrey's house the night of the fire. She also knew that Bess and/or Leigh had stolen the key to his ministorage unit. If she had half a brain, she would know they were on to him.

Then there was the bizarre incident with the recyclables bin. It did look as though Humphrey had set that up, probably just to intimidate Bess into not spilling anything she knew or suspected about his role in the fire. If he'd told Noel about that too—and why wouldn't he—it would give her even more reason to suspect that Bess had it in for him.

Leigh digested this theory for another moment, then exhaled in frustration. Surely Noel didn't believe that a woman like Bess would actually kill a man over a lame attempt at extortion. At worst, it would be her word against his, and though the congregation might believe Humphrey's version of events at first, once the police started investigating, they were bound to find skeletons in the pastor's closet—and his credibility would be shot.

So what would make Noel or anyone else so sure that Bess—and whoever the heck "all of you" referred to—had committed murder?

She walked while she thought. And why had Noel come to Pittsburgh in the first place? Was she part of the plan all along? Perhaps Humphrey, having decided the time was right to give up this particular gig, had planned to disappear mysteriously, to be believed dead at the hand of his fictional enemies. Then Noel was to come looking for him. Why? So they could squeeze even more money out of the congregation, of course.

Leigh stopped in her tracks. *Kunta.* The visions. Maybe Evelyn and Reuben weren't in on the game. Maybe they'd been tricked. Tricked into believing they'd really seen Humphrey's ghost. It wouldn't be too difficult, since neither appeared to have all their marbles. Humphrey could show up with some cheap white makeup and a spotlight . . .

She shook her head. It was a brilliant plan, but there was just one problem. Reginald Humphrey was dead.

Wasn't he? A chill crept up her spine, and she started walking quickly. Of course he was dead. She had seen him with her own eyes. Maybe she could be tricked with a wax figure or something—given that the body was frozen stiff—but the coroner certainly couldn't be. And the odds of a switch in the ambulance were too ridiculous to contemplate.

Humphrey was dead. Period. And for whatever reason, Noel—and possibly somebody else—seemed certain that he was murdered. Leigh stopped walking again as a new thought struck her. She might not be able to think of any reason why Bess would want Reginald Humphrey dead, but evidently someone else could. Perhaps Bess *did* have a reason to kill him.

Perhaps she just didn't know it.

Chapter 20

Leigh reached the parlor just as Bess and the other board members were filing in. She didn't wait to be invited, just hustled in and busied herself finding a footrest for her aunt. If she was lucky, no one would notice her.

Bess, for one, didn't seem to mind. "We need to talk," she said heavily as the other board members found seats and pulled them into a tight ring. Leigh slipped out of the circle and sat in a folding chair against the wall. "I'm going to tell you people what I think, and I'm going to tell you now, because it's the only thing that's going to save this congregation from self-destructing."

Leigh took a breath. Bess was finally going to fess up about Humphrey. It was about time.

"Reverend Humphrey may or may not have believed in her," Bess began, "but I'm telling you, I know for a fact that Noel Humphrey is a complete fraud."

Leigh exhaled in frustration. *Noel* Humphrey? *Come on, Aunt Bess. Give it up, already. Please?*

"Well, hell's bells!" began Ed, gesticulating wildly. "Any third grader knows that! We've got to face facts here, people. The time has come. We've got a great church here, with great people. But everyone in this room knows it's built on nothing but a house of cards. Humphrey was rotten to his drawers! For God's sake, the man's dead. Can't we all admit it now?"

Leigh sat frozen in her chair, her mouth dropping open for the fifth time that day. She stole a glance at Bess, whose fillings were equally visible.

"Ed's right," Betty Ivey said firmly, standing up. "We all know what's going on here. Except, perhaps, for you, dear." She nodded sympathetically at Bess. "And I daresay it was only a matter of time."

"Nobody needs to get into specifics," piped up Sam Schafer, the youth leader. "Nobody wants to do that—that's why we let it go this long. But I agree, we can talk about it now. The man's dead."

"How do we know he didn't talk to Noel?" The voice came from a younger woman Leigh didn't recognize, whose face was pale and whose hands were shaking. "If he told her everything he knew—"

"He didn't," Betty Ivey said firmly. She was still standing, as if what she was saying was too important for a chair. "I know he didn't. I talked with Noel earlier. She hinted, all right, she knew what he was doing, but she didn't have the details. If she had, she would have used them."

"Maybe she used it on Reuben and Evelyn," Sam suggested. "I can't imagine why they'd say what they did otherwise."

"Possibly," Betty Ivey said thoughtfully. "But I think Humphrey was reasonably discreet. I think he stuck to board members—and potential board members. Reuben genuinely liked him. You know that, Ed."

Ed's flushed red face made him look ten years younger. "Most everybody did, Dammit."

"*Stuck to board members with what?*" Bess screeched. She was out on the edge of her seat as far as she could get without toppling off, and if she didn't get answered, she undoubtedly would do just that. Leigh was thankful for the outburst. It kept her from making a similar one.

"Oh, dear," Betty Ivey said, deciding to sit down. "You really were in the dark, weren't you?"

Bess's eyes blazed.

"I'll tell you, then," Ed said firmly. He took a deep breath. "Reginald Humphrey was a world-class con artist. Not that he made himself that much money. I don't think the money really drove him. It was the power."

The other board members nodded solemnly. "He was a talented preacher," Ed continued. "He could have been a damn good minister if his heart was really in it. And God help me, I believe he really did like most of it. But something in his mind was twisted. He wanted power over people. He craved it. He had to have control, even if it was just over the little things."

"Every little thing," the younger woman mumbled malevolently.

"He cultivated friendships, built trust. He took his time." Ed paused and looked at Bess. "He would have gotten to you too, eventually, I'm sure." Then he smiled. "Then again, maybe not. Maybe you'd be smart enough to keep your trap closed."

Bess's hand flew to her mouth, and not, Leigh guessed, because of Ed's reference to it. "The confessions!" she cried. "All that nonsense about unburdening your soul. I've never believed in that sort of—" She stopped and looked around the circle. "Oh, my God. He was blackmailing you. All of you."

The board members looked at each other uncomfortably. "I suppose," Betty Ivey said calmly from her seat, "that most people have a few secrets in their past. And there's a part of you that wants to get past them but can't. Humphrey preached constantly about the pitfalls of the encumbered soul. How unresolved guilt can ruin your life. He was very convincing. He was also very patient. I counseled with him for six months before I decided to be honest with him about my past. I thought it would make me feel better. And it did, at first."

"The same thing happened to me," Sam broke in. "I confessed something, and he was very understanding. I felt much better. It was weeks before the suggestions started coming in. My board appointment. The 'understanding.'" His voice cracked with rage. "God, how I hated that man."

Leigh felt her hands start to shake a little. Partly because she hadn't had any lunch, and partly because her blood was running cold. Reginald Humphrey had been blackmailing everyone else on the church board. Any one of them could have killed him to keep their secret safe.

"At first I was sure that Ted had killed him," Ed said after a pause. "Humphrey had just hit him up a while ago, and he nearly went wild. He was so furious—he just couldn't handle it. I'm sure Humphrey himself regretted that move. But I believed Ted's story when I heard it. Somebody else got to him first."

"That's all we need to say, I think," Sam answered firmly. "I don't know who killed the son of a bitch, and I don't care. I assume no one else here does either. If the congregation wants to believe he died of natural causes, then so be it. None of us let on to the detectives about the blackmail. Right?" He looked around the room suspiciously, but everyone in the circle shook their heads. "Fine, then. There's no motive. Maybe the coroner will actually rule the death accidental, and we can all just get on with it."

Bess cleared her throat. Her voice was still a bit thin, but it picked up steam as she went along. "I didn't know about the blackmail," she admitted. "Humphrey tried the confession thing on me lots of times, but I just laughed it off and told him my life was an open book. I never thought anything about it, which was stupid of me. But I did suspect he was a fraud. In fact, I've been trying to prove it." She went on to explain the photograph of the recruit known as Money, her own role in the fire, and Leigh's findings in the mini-storage. The board did not seem surprised.

"He set the fire himself, then," said Ed sulkily. "We should have known. I believed somebody was trying to kill him, frankly."

"So did I, " said Sam. "I was sorry they failed."

Bess spoke up again. "I didn't tell anyone about my suspicions because I didn't want the congregation to know—ever. I was hoping to collect enough evidence to force him out peacefully."

"What matters now," Ed broke in, "is where we go from here. I don't know about the rest of you, but I have no intention of letting that little vixen get her hands on any more of this congregation's money. If we have to come clean with the whole story, so be it."

"No!" the younger woman shouted, jumping to her feet. "I won't go along with that! I'll say you're all lying!" Her panic-stricken face erupted into tears, and Betty Ivey jumped up quickly to soothe her. Whatever Humphrey had on her, Leigh thought sympathetically, it must be a doozy.

"No, Merry, dear," Betty cooed. "No one in this room will allow anyone's secret to get out. We're all in this together. Am I right?"

The other board members nodded eagerly. "That's not what I meant at all," Ed insisted impatiently. "Nobody has to know Humphrey was blackmailing us. We can come up with something else. Hell, all we have to do is prove that Noel's mission is a fraud, and then it'll be clear he was stealing the church's money."

"And it will be clear that the First Church of the New Millennium—and to many of our members, religion in general—is a dishonest, self-serving waste," Bess argued, raising her voice. "The new members will all quit. They'll never go to another church again. Is that what we all want?"

The board members looked at each other guiltily.

"Bess is right," Betty Ivey said finally. "There's got to be a better way."

"There is," Bess said, her eyes shining again. "I know just what we can do. We've got to expose Noel as a fraud, but then we can go a step further. We can convince the congregation that she fooled everybody—including Humphrey himself!"

Sly smiles erupted around the room. "Of course," Betty Ivey said excitedly. "We can say that she was a dishonest little trollop who seduced Humphrey and married him for his money. He believed she was in Africa when she was really off cavorting with other men—and living off the money the church sent her for the mission."

"I could do that," the woman named Merry said optimistically, through a few lingering tears. "I'm in charge of all our outreach funds anyway. I could say that Humphrey sent it dutifully to a post office box in Nevada or somewhere, thinking that it would be forwarded to the mission."

"Perfect," Ed complimented. "Where did it go, anyway? And what about all those other worthy causes we were supposedly supporting?"

Merry's face darkened. "You don't want to know."

"No, we don't," Bess said firmly. "It doesn't matter now. What matters is that we stop the swindling without losing the church. I've already been talking to a pastor friend of mine in Wisconsin. He's looking for a new charge—if we can get him in quick, all this just might work."

"We're going to lose people no matter what," Sam commented. "Some of them just liked Humphrey."

"Of course," Bess responded. "But it's the best we can hope for. Now, are we in this together or are we in this together?"

Leigh looked around the circle. Every head was nodding.

*   *   *

"Absolutely not," Bess said emphatically when she and Leigh were alone in the parlor. "Maura Polanski can't start investigating Noel's 'mission.' The detectives are bound to turn up evidence that Humphrey was a fraud too, and that would ruin everything."

Leigh sighed deeply. Being stuck in the middle was getting old. She was sitting on top of a sizable fraud scandal that she could hand to Maura on a silver platter—and which could probably help boost her friend's temporarily sagging self-confidence, not to mention her reputation with the other detectives. But she could tip Maura off only at the expense of a cause her aunt believed in.

"Maura's not an idiot, Aunt Bess," she argued. "She was at the church earlier. She heard Noel's speech. She's already suspicious."

Bess's lips puckered, and Leigh argued on. "It's only a matter of time before she checks out the mission and finds that it doesn't exist. But that doesn't have to be a problem."

"Not as long as she doesn't start investigating Humphrey too," Bess reasoned. "Which she will if you blab about the mini-storage." She took a breath. "Look, kiddo. I know you want to help your friend out. So go ahead. Tell her anything you want to about Noel. Just don't mention the mini-storage, or the fact that she was trying to blackmail me about breaking into the parsonage. If the police can nail her for soliciting funds under false pretenses, she'll be out of our hair. Whatever she says about Humphrey being in on it, the board can refute. I don't think the congregation will believe Noel over us."

Leigh bit her lip. It was better than nothing. Bess was right—Maura didn't strictly need to uncover Humphrey's fraud, only Noel's. And she could do that without searching the mini-storage.

"Bess Cogley," came a now familiar, crabby falsetto voice. "I need to talk to you." Evelyn Ewing had opened the door to the parlor and was quickly advancing on Leigh and Bess. Despite her steady gait, she looked distinctly uncomfortable. "I don't like to admit such things at my age," she continued, reaching them and taking a seat. "But I don't know what's going on. Do you?"

Bess blinked. "How do you mean?"

Evelyn stared at her, hard. "I distrusted that phony little Jezebel from the beginning. You know I did."

Bess didn't respond, but Leigh nodded. She remembered the older woman's skepticism when she had run into Noel at church the morning before. That attitude hardly fit with the dramatic presentation she had just made to the congregation on the woman's behalf. There was only one possible explanation. Noel had to be blackmailing Evelyn. Perhaps Humphrey had passed a few nuggets along to his wife after all?

"I still don't trust her," Evelyn said with a sigh. "But I saw what I saw."

Bess and Leigh exchanged glances. "Evelyn," Bess began seriously, "don't try to fool me. I know you've got all your marbles and then some, even if you try hard not to act like it. You can tell me the truth. Noel forced you to make that speech. Didn't she?"

The older woman's eyes widened. "Forced me?" she asked with surprise. "Mercy, no. That hussy couldn't force me to do anything. I did it for Reginald."

Bess threw Leigh a puzzled glance, which was returned in kind. "Humphrey told you to lie for him?" she asked.

Evelyn sat up straight, her eyes defensive. "What are you talking about, woman? Nobody makes me do anything—certainly not lie. What I said this morning was the absolute truth, though I was sorely tempted not to say it."

Bess let out a frustrated breath. "Evelyn," she said firmly, "you can go on all you want about communicating with JFK and all that other paranormal nonsense, but we both know it's just a game. Now, can you look me in the eye and tell me that Reginald Humphrey really did appear to you in a dream and tell you to give money to some bogus mission? Can you?"

Evelyn Ewing's proud chin rose. "Yes," she said heavily. "I can."

Chapter 21

Bess and Leigh looked at one another, each hoping the other could make sense out of Evelyn Ewing's claim. Both were disappointed.

Bess tried again. "Can you tell us *exactly* what you saw?"

"I already did," Evelyn said testily. "But I will tell you this. Seeing Reginald, it was different this time."

"Different how?" Bess said hopefully.

The older woman's face tightened with tension. "Different *real*. The other time I saw him, it was like I was having a dream. That's how it always is with the visitors. Sometimes a day dream, sometimes a night dream. But this time I was sure I was awake. Or leastwise, I thought I was. It was night, and I'd been sleeping, but I woke up because I heard a noise. There was a light outside my window, and I could see him there, out in my garden."

Leigh's heart beat faster. "You could hear him? Did he look normal? Did he sound normal?"

Evelyn shook her head. "Not really. But there's usually something a little off kilter about the visitors. He looked just like he was alive, but he was awfully pale. And there was some kind of light around him. His voice wasn't quite right either—loud and a bit fuzzy, like he was using a microphone, only he wasn't. He was just standing there talking to me." She swallowed. "For a minute I really did think it was him. I thought the police were wrong about him being dead."

She turned to Bess, looking uncharacteristically uncertain. "Do you think that could be?"

"Absolutely not," Bess said quickly, with more confidence than Leigh felt. "I saw his body, Evelyn. Trust me, the man is dead. Could it have been someone else pretending to be Humphrey? Maybe in his clothes, with a mask, or lots of makeup?"

Evelyn thought long and hard. "Maybe," she said finally. "I see well enough since my cataract surgery, but the light was funny. And I'd been asleep." She paused a moment, her face darkening. "I shouldn't have said anything."

Leigh agreed with that assessment, but wisely kept her mouth shut. The older woman rose. "I don't like to think I've been tricked," she said, her voice testy again. "But if that woman is a missionary, I'm Florence Nightingale."

Leigh and Bess were on their way back to the sanctuary when they ran into Maura alone in the hallway. Leigh felt a surge of panic. "Where's Noel?" she asked.

Maura shook her head. "Can't hold her, Koslow. It'll take some time to prove the mission doesn't exist. As for her role in Reginald Humphrey's death, it's looking like it doesn't matter."

"But she'll take off!" Leigh protested.

Maura nodded calmly. "Probably. But at least she won't have anybody else's money with her. She hadn't started collecting yet, had she?"

Bess shook her head. "I don't think so. The board just met. We're not recommending that people support her."

Maura nodded. "That's wise."

Leigh's mind flicked back to the detective's earlier statement. "What do you mean about Noel's role in Humphrey's death not mattering?" she asked.

Maura took a deep, official-sounding breath. "I just

talked to Hollandsworth. He's hoping to set up a brief
meeting with the church board later this afternoon.
The coroner's report is in." Leigh immediately opened
her mouth, but Maura held up a hand. "Don't ask
me, Koslow. I don't know any of the details. It's Hollandsworth's bag." She paused a moment, then seemed
to relent somewhat. "I can tell you this. As far as I
know, it sounds like good news for Warren's uncle."

Leigh smiled. Good news? There was a switch.
"Should I call Warren and tell him?" she asked hopefully.

Maura cracked a slight smile. "Knock yourself out.
But his lawyer probably already knows."

She would. Leigh bristled, then felt guilty. She
should be happy that Ted's legal nightmares—and
Warren's associated headaches—were ending. What
difference did it make who gave him the good news?

"Go and see him, kiddo," Bess said with a grin.
"My ample powers of persuasion will be needed here
for a while. And there'll be plenty of folks around to
give me a lift home if I need it. Go."

"Are you—"

"Go."

Leigh went. She drove the Cavalier out of the still
nearly full church parking lot and made a beeline for
her apartment building. She wondered what Warren
was up to. After the scene she had made last night
about wanting to talk to him, would he be expecting
her? She looked at her watch: 1:03. It was later than
she thought. It was a sad state of affairs when she
could miss lunch and almost forget about it.

She knocked on his door for five painful minutes
before giving up. Why couldn't he be home? The
longer she waited to talk to him, the more out of hand
things with Katharine Bower were going to get. She
turned away from his door with a dismal sigh. Where
was he?

Perhaps with Ted and Shannon. They'd probably all

gotten wind of the coroner's report already. Maybe they were having a celebration. Maybe Katharine was with them too. It was a happy thought.

She moped up the two flights of stairs to her apartment, gave Mao Tse a cat treat, and consumed some stale Chee-tos and a orange. Why was there never any food in her apartment? Warren always had food.

Willing herself not to dwell on that topic, she focused her thoughts instead on making sense of Evelyn Ewing's claims. Noel must be behind the "apparitions" somehow. She had to be. No one else profited. But could she really make herself up to look like Humphrey? Leigh's brow furrowed. They were roughly the same height, but it was hard to picture petite little Marlo/Mary passing for a man.

It was much easier to picture her gunning the Monte Carlo toward the state line. There was no doubt she would be long gone by the time Maura had anything concrete on her. Leigh allowed herself a smile. Having Maura corner Noel at the church had been a real coup. Only a complete fool would try and swindle money from a church with a full-fledged fraud detective looking on. Noel would pack up her motel room and—

A picture fought its way into Leigh's mind. There had been some electronic equipment in the ministorage, but not knowing a synthesizer from a boom box, she hadn't paid much attention. Whatever it was, Noel had the key to it. Could it have been audiovisual equipment? Could Noel have created the apparitions with some kind of video projection?

Leigh thought a moment, then shook her head. That would mean Humphrey had arranged the whole thing before he died. Otherwise why use a tape? He could be the apparition himself. That same cold chill started creeping up her spine again, and she fought it back down. *No.* Reginald Humphrey was dead. End of story.

Noel had been responsible. Noel had tried to profit from Humphrey's death by scamming the congregation herself. She had faked the apparitions somehow, and she could have faked a man's voice when she had made the threatening call to Bess. Of course she believed her husband had been murdered! Why wouldn't she? With Humphrey blackmailing everyone on the board, there was plenty of motive to go around. He had nothing strong on Bess, true, but she had clearly been taking action to gather dirt on *him*. It wasn't too much of a stretch for Noel to assume that Bess was aware of everything. The ringleader of a conspiracy.

Leigh looked at her watch again and fidgeted. She couldn't just sit in her apartment all afternoon waiting for Warren to come back. Hollandsworth would be making his announcement at the church soon, and she planned on being there. She patted Mao Tse on the head and picked up her car keys. She would make one extra stop as well.

The odds of finding the same employee on duty as the last time Leigh had visited the S.P.E. Mini-Storage were slim, but for once she got lucky. She recognized the attractive, dark-skinned young manager immediately and offered him her best smile. "Hello. I'm Leigh Koslow. I was here yesterday afternoon, helping Noel Humphrey look through her husband's things."

The man returned her smile, but his eyes glinted in a way that told her he remembered things a little differently. "Yes," he said politely. "What can I do for you?"

"There were some items in the mini-storage that Humphrey wanted to donate to the church, and Noel asked me to come pick them up. She said she would notify you in advance that it was OK." Leigh hoped the nervous twitter in her voice wasn't too obvious. She hated lying, but none of the half-truths she had come up with on the way over had seemed satisfactory.

The man's eyebrows lifted slightly. "I'm sorry, Ms. Koslow. But you two must have your signals crossed." His words were polite, but his eyes were twinkling with amusement. He didn't believe a word she was saying.

Her hopes fell. Why couldn't Humphrey have picked a mini-storage with a dumber manager?

"Ms. Humphrey closed out the unit early this morning," he said cheerfully. "It's open now. Know anybody who needs some space? We're running a special all winter—first month's rent free."

Leigh looked back at the man, who was definitely enjoying toying with her, in surprise. "She moved everything out? Already? How?"

He shrugged. "She had a trailer; she had somebody helping her. There wasn't all that much stuff." He smiled again. "I'm surprised you didn't know."

Somebody helping her? Leigh swallowed. "Could you tell me what the other person looked like?"

He shrugged again. "I never saw him close up. He was short, that's all I know. Might have been a kid. They were both bundled up against the cold, anyway. Ms. Humphrey showed me ID, told me her husband was the man found in that kennel freezer. I read about that in the paper. We're allowed to hand over keys to next of kin, you know." His tone had turned slightly defensive, as if her interrogation was giving him second thoughts.

"You didn't notify the police about the mini-storage unit?" she said, feeding on his fears.

"Of course not," he countered, still defensive. "I didn't realize the dead man had a unit here till she showed up." His face darkened. "What's going on? Was the guy murdered over something he was keeping here?"

Leigh cringed. The last thing she needed was for

this guy to call the police now. Bess would kill her, *if* she had a pulse left when Maura got done. "Oh, no," she said quickly. "Humphrey wasn't murdered. He died of natural causes." Her voice didn't shake as much for that statement, since she was beginning to think it was true. Perhaps the truth wouldn't hurt her at this point. "The thing is, the people at Humphrey's church aren't sure Noel was really his wife."

All trace of jauntiness in the manager's eyes dimmed. "She was listed on the rental agreement as an alternate. I checked," he insisted gravely. "And she had a driver's license that said Noel Humphrey."

Leigh took a deep breath. Honesty was the only way. Otherwise, she had about five more seconds before he kicked her off the premises. "No one is accusing the ministorage of any impropriety," she said, trying to smile. "But we have reason to believe that Noel Humphrey is a fraud. Isn't there anything else you can tell me about the person who was helping her?"

The manager looked at her for a long moment, then shook his head. "Sorry, Ms. Koslow. I told you I didn't get a good look at the man. I just got a glimpse of him—they did most of the unloading before I got here. Anyway, I'm not sure you have a right to that information. Humphrey was our client, this Noel person was listed on the contract, she closed the unit. I can't see where you come into it, and I don't see any reason to invade our ex-clients' privacy." He also made a halfhearted effort to smile. "Again, I'm sorry."

Leigh gritted her teeth, thanked him politely, and left. She climbed into her Cavalier with a new sense of foreboding. She had come hoping to find out whether Humphrey had been storing ghost-making supplies— whatever those might be. She had learned something even more disturbing. Noel had a real flesh-and-blood accomplice. A short one.

*   *   *

The parking lot of the First Church of the New Millennium was so crowded that Leigh ended up walking over from the animal shelter. Evidently, word had spread quickly that Hollandsworth had news on the case, and it was news everyone wanted to hear. By now the board had probably also made it known that Reginald Humphrey had been duped by a dishonest wife, which was bound to bring up a whole new batch of questions and doubts. This was a congregation desperately in need of answers, and she could sympathize. She could use a few herself.

She entered the bustling sanctuary from the back and immediately scanned the crowd. There was no sign of Warren, Shannon, or Ted. Bess was sitting in the first row, however, and Leigh slowly fought her way down front. "What's happening?" she asked eagerly. "Has Hollandsworth said anything yet?"

Bess shook her head. "No, but—"

Her words were cut short by Hollandsworth himself, who strode purposefully into the room and up to the podium without introduction.

"Handsome devil, isn't he?" Bess said with a grin. Leigh didn't respond, but kept her ears craned for the news.

"I didn't really come here prepared to make a speech," Hollandsworth said awkwardly. "But I know all you people care about the late Reverend Humphrey, so I wanted to tell you myself that the investigation into his death has been officially closed."

He paused as a faint murmuring came up from the congregation. "The coroner has ruled Reginald Humphrey's death as accidental. There was no homicide. The deceased's remains can now be remanded to the custody of his next of kin."

A smile spread slowly over Leigh's face, and she exhaled with relief. A louder commotion arose from the congregation, along with a sea of hands. "What

about Ted Hugh? Will the charges be dropped?" a
man on the second row asked accusingly.

"Ted Hugh was not arrested on homicide charges,"
Hollandsworth said tiredly. "He was arrested for
breaking and entering. Those charges have already
been dropped at the request of the animal shelter
board."

Leigh glanced at Bess, who smiled proudly.

Ed approached the podium and whispered something into Hollandsworth's ear. "All right," the detective answered, straightening a piece of paper in front
of him. "I'm not a medical expert, so I'm afraid I
can't answer many questions beyond what the coroner
reported to me. But it looks like Mr. Humphrey died
of anaphylactic shock, a systemic allergic reaction to
his insulin."

Now it was Leigh's turn to be proud. Bess smiled
at her approvingly.

"We were eventually able to locate the physician
who most recently treated Mr. Humphrey's diabetes,"
Hollandsworth continued. "The doctor claims Mr.
Humphrey was poorly compliant with her recommen-
dations. She suspected he was stopping and starting
his insulin therapy on his own, which was especially
dangerous given that he had had previous problems
with local allergic reactions. In her opinion and the
coroner's, he died of an acute, systemic allergic reaction almost immediately after injecting himself. It's
rare, but it happens."

He paused a moment, and Evelyn Ewing's
screeching voice immediately broke in. "How do you
know he wasn't poisoned?"

Hollandsworth nodded. "Poisoning was suspected.
But the coroner's office ran a full battery of toxicology
tests on both the body and the remainder of the bottle
of insulin. All came back negative. There was no
poison."

A sea of hands went up, and Hollandsworth glanced

at his watch before pointing at a young woman on the fifth row. It was Cindy the secretary. "He was allergic to bees, you know," she said importantly. "Could he have been stung by a bee?"

Hollandsworth shook his head again. "No insect bites or stings." He sighed slightly. "The coroner's ruling is official. The death was accidental; the case is closed." He glanced at his watch again. "I'm sorry I can't answer any more questions on the medical side, but again, that's not my area. Thank you all for your cooperation."

He stepped down from the podium and darted away as quickly as he had come. A buzz of conversation swelled in the sanctuary with the intensity of a shuttle launch, and Bess had to raise her voice for her words to reach Leigh's ear.

"Good news, eh?" She was smiling broadly, as broadly as she had ever smiled since the night of the parsonage fire. "Humphrey died because he didn't take good care of himself, Ted is innocent of everything except being a dumbass, and I'm pretty sure our favorite missionary has hit the road. Furthermore, the board is doing an excellent job with our, um, 'assigned task,' if I do say so myself. We've even got Reuben convinced that Noel tricked him with some sort of hologram. Which reminds me, we should really go back to the—"

Leigh shook her head. "I just did. All the stuff's gone."

Bess's eyes widened. "All of it? Overnight?"

She nodded, and Bess's smile broadened even more. "Well, that's good news, isn't it? That means she's gone for good!"

Leigh smiled back superficially, her mind burdened with one loose end that refused to fall into place. No one had killed Humphrey, and his scheming widow was almost certainly gone. So why did it bother her so much that Noel had been at the mini-storage with a man?

A light hand rested briefly on Leigh's shoulder, and she gazed up. It was Katharine Bower, looking particularly slender in a casual electric blue dress. "Hello," the lawyer said in a neutral, professional tone. "I thought you two might like to know that Shannon is at Mercy Hospital. I was meeting with Ted at their house this morning, and she returned home from church, said hello, and collapsed. I drove them both into town."

"Oh, no!" Bess said worriedly. "She wasn't eating, was she? I was worried about that. We all were. Several of the women brought her food— Is she going to be OK?"

Katharine nodded. "They're just going to keep her on an IV overnight, I believe."

"Shannon's always had terrible problems with anorexia," Bess explained to Leigh. "And she's been under so much stress this week."

"I'm sure she'll recover quickly now that her husband is a free man," Katharine said confidently. "Ted was a bit frantic when I left them at the hospital, but Warren agreed to go down and smooth things over. Thank goodness Shannon had him to lean on yesterday. I don't know how she could have handled Ted's arrest otherwise." Her voice had turned more chipper, probably at the thought of the Harmon charm, Leigh considered grimly. "Anyway," Katharine continued, "my job is done. I'm sure Shannon will be feeling better very soon."

"Thank you, Ms. Bower," Bess said in her most gracious tone. "You've done a beautiful job for Ted. The whole church appreciates it."

Katharine smiled back. "You're welcome." She turned to leave, walked about three paces, and whirled around. "Leigh," she said, her tone unusually amiable, "why don't you go find Warren? I think you two need to talk."

Leigh froze. She wanted to make an intelligent response, but none came to mind. She certainly had things to say to Warren, but Katharine didn't know about them. And what could Warren have to say to her? Her heart turned into lead. Anything Katharine would *want* him to tell her couldn't possibly be what she wanted to hear. *Could they have gotten engaged?*

"She'll do just that," Bess answered for her cheerfully, delivering another strategically placed jab to her niece's ribs. "Good-bye, Ms. Bower."

Leigh thawed enough to offer Katharine a half-hearted wave, then sunk back down in her seat. "They're getting married," she said out loud.

"Nonsense," Bess said firmly. "It could be anything. Don't sit there like a zombie. Go find out. Drop my carcass off at home and then hit the road. It's the only thing to do."

"Ouch!" The third jab in the ribs woke Leigh up for good. She was going.

Chapter 22

When Leigh opened the front door of the farmhouse to help her aunt in, Lydie was standing in the living room, the phone to her ear. At least it looked like Lydie. But for a moment Leigh wasn't sure.

Lydie and Leigh's mother were identical twins, and though they looked very similar to the untrained eye, their mannerisms were unlikely to be confused. Lydie was confident, even-tempered, and optimistic. Frances was—well, Frances. But the look on Lydie's face as Leigh and Bess entered the room had to have been borrowed from her twin. It was Frances's classic puckered-brow, tight-jawed worried look. "Worried" with a capital W.

Bess caught it too. "Who is it?" she asked, hobbling forward on her crutches. "Let me have it."

Lydie shook her head and placed the receiver back in its cradle. "Odd," she said thoughtfully. "Very odd."

Bess and Leigh looked at her expectantly. "I haven't been answering the phone," she explained circuitously. "I've been letting the machine pick up. But I came down for a drink and was walking right by it when it rang." She tapped her fingers nervously on the receiver. "I said, hello, and a man's voice said, 'You killed him, all of you. But it was your idea. So you're going to pay.' Then he hung up." She paused, then looked questioningly at Bess. "What do you make of it?"

Leigh threw both her aunts a frightened glance. "It's the same man who called this morning," she said anxiously.

"Whoever it was is out of the loop," Bess said flippantly. "He—or she—must have missed the debriefing. Why don't we do that star sixty-nine thing? I'll tell him to take it up with the insulin manufacturer."

"I tried that," Lydie answered. "Star sixty-nine, I mean. There was no answer."

"I bet they were at a pay phone," Leigh said distantly. Surely Noel and her significant other were on their way out of town by now, she reasoned. They had probably taken off right after Maura had confronted Noel at the church—and before Hollandsworth's meeting had been announced.

"They?" Bess asked suspiciously. "You know something I don't, kiddo?"

Leigh gave a brief summary of her conversation with the mini-storage manager, but Bess was not impressed. "So Noel has a boyfriend. So what?"

"So two are more dangerous than one," Leigh argued. "Noel still thinks you had something to do with Humphrey's death. Maybe she wants to get even."

"Horse feathers," Bess said cynically. "She didn't love Humphrey. She recovered from his death a little too fast for that. Trust me, she's only in it for the money. And she's not getting any of mine."

Leigh decided to try another tack. "Don't you remember how the caller said, 'You killed him—*all* of you?' It was as if he suspected that more than one person wanted Humphrey dead." She looked at Bess meaningfully. "Who could know that besides the board members—and Noel?"

Lydie's lips twisted into a frown. "It sounds like you could be in real trouble, Bess. Francie said—"

"Our loving sister," Bess began heavily, "is a pathological worrywart, and we all know it. I'm fine. The phone call was just a crank. How's that bathroom coming?"

Lydie appeared to be deciding whether or not to allow herself to become distracted when the phone rang again. Leigh dove for it.

"Hello?" she asked huskily, trying to sound like Bess. The effect was more like a pained mule.

"Um, Bess? Is that you?"

Leigh sighed. It was Barbara. Again. She handed the phone to Bess, then walked into the kitchen and picked up the extension.

"It was him," Barbara was saying weakly as Leigh tuned back in. "I swear to God it was him. It was Reginald."

Leigh caught her breath a moment, then exhaled slowly. *Nonsense.* Barbara was falling for the same parlor tricks Noel had used on Reuben and Evelyn.

"That's ridiculous," Bess answered, echoing Leigh's sentiments. "I got a crank call like that myself this morning, and I'll admit it sounded a little like him, but that's it. Your mind's just playing tricks on you."

"But I listened to the message three times," Barbara protested. "He said that the board were all murderers, and that they would all pay. Especially you. What could he mean by that? Ed says he thought maybe you would know."

Way to pass the buck, Ed, Leigh thought grimly.

"But, Barb," Bess said soothingly, "if the man was accusing someone of killing Humphrey, how could it have *been* Humphrey? He didn't say 'you killed *me,*' did he? That doesn't make any sense."

Barbara sniffled. "I know it doesn't. It's just—" She broke off, and the muffled sounds of nose blowing traveled through the phone line. "I guess you're right. It couldn't have been him. I was just thinking about him, so the voice sounded familiar." She paused, then sounded more panicked again. "But, Bess, who on earth could it be? I thought everything was settled!"

"It could be anybody," Bess said, more confidently than she had a right to. "Any nut who's read the papers or watched local news. Everybody who saw the 'body in the freezer' stories knows what church he worked at, and the fact that he died of natural causes probably hasn't been reported yet. It's just a crank."

Barbara exhaled. "I suppose so. Maybe I am just imagining things."

Leigh gently let the extension click back in its wall hanger. Bess was a good comforter, but her theory was not without logical flaws. The "body in the freezer" did receive a fair amount of local coverage, but as far as she knew, there weren't many specifics given out. Her name—mercifully—had never surfaced. Neither had Bess's, much less Ed's. So how could a crackpot with no ties to the church know who was on the executive board?

"You!" Bess said, wagging a finger at Leigh as she reentered the room. "You have better things to do with your time than eavesdrop on my phone conversations. Go find that man of yours. I'm not talking to you any more until you do." She crossed her arms grumpily across her bountiful chest and glared. "Get out of here."

Leigh sighed. She wanted to go, but she didn't like the phone calls. She didn't like them at all. "I think you should report those calls to the police," she said firmly. "Let me call Maura. She'll know what to do." She dug around in her purse for Maura's business card, then pulled it out. The thing was getting frayed already. It was a bad sign.

"Fine," Bess said, a little too easily. She took the card from Leigh's hand. "I'll call her myself. I promise. You go."

Leigh looked at her aunt skeptically. Maybe no one else in the family could lie well, but Bess wasn't like anyone else in the family, and Leigh didn't believe her for a minute.

Neither, apparently, did Lydie, who stepped forward and removed the card from her sister's hand. "I'll call her, Leigh," she said determinedly. "After all, I'm the one who talked to the man."

Leigh smiled. Lydie would come through. She always did. "Try her at home first," Leigh said, taking the card back and scribbling down the second number.

"Now, get!" Bess demanded, and Leigh complied.

The drive back to her apartment seemed to take days, and when it ended, she was more uptight than when she had started. Warren wasn't at home. Could he still be at the hospital with Shannon and Ted? For his sake, she hoped not.

Her head spun as she returned to the Cavalier, her thoughts looping back to the threatening phone calls. Noel had to be involved. But what could she possibly hope to gain?

She began driving just to drive, and as was usually the case in such situations, she ended up in Avalon—in the parking lot of the Koslow Animal Clinic. Seeing her father's car parked in its usual place of honor behind the Dumpster, she smiled. Office hours were over, but he often came in late on Saturdays to catch up on paperwork, which made it the perfect time to catch him *sans* Frances. Randall was always good for an unsettled mind; he had a gift for putting things in perspective, and he never charged a dime.

She parked the Cavalier and took out her key to the back door, but never got a chance to use it. Before she had gotten to the doorstep, Frances emerged—purse and covered casserole dish in hand.

"Leigh, dear," she began in a flustered tone. "I'm so glad you dropped by. You can give me a lift to your aunt Bess's."

Leigh's shoulders sagged. So much for the heart-to-heart with Randall. Wasn't any of the men in her life available today?

"What's Dad doing?" she asked. "I wanted to talk to him."

"C-section," Frances answered gruffly, handing Leigh the casserole dish. She walked to Randall's car and unloaded a grocery bag. "We were on our way to Bess's together—I promised I'd bring dinner for everyone. But your father wanted to check on a patient, and of course as soon as he turned the lights on, that Parks woman showed up with another one of her bitches in trouble."

Leigh looked toward the clinic wistfully. Kelsey Parks had been breeding bulldogs ever since Leigh was a little girl, and every last litter had required a C-section. She had helped bring a few dozen pups into the world herself, and rubbing a few wet little newborns might be just what she needed tonight. "Does he need any help?" she asked hopefully.

Frances waved her concern away. "Christina's there. She can take care of it. We've got to get going. Your aunt Lydie's been working hard all day—she shouldn't have to cook too. And this casserole is getting cold. I had to bring it inside with me, of course. We haven't had much snow this winter, but it's cold enough in the car to chill a casserole, even if it is covered. . . ."

Frances's words melted into a gray slush between Leigh's ears. She helped load the food into the backseat of the Cavalier, then set out for the haul up 279 and back to Bess's. There would be no puppy rubbing for her tonight.

They were almost to Franklin Park again when Frances stopped babbling and looked at her daughter worriedly. "What is it you're so upset about? I thought everything at the church was settled."

Leigh sighed, and wondered if Lydie had gotten in touch with Maura. Could Bess be in any real danger? And what about the other board members? "Tell me what's going on," Frances hounded. "What did you do?"

Leigh sighed again. She had wanted to run all the disturbing thoughts in her head past her father, but that wasn't going to happen. Perhaps laying it all out for her mother wouldn't hurt. It might at least help organize things in her mind.

At first she tried to tell the story without mentioning the mini-storage break-ins, but when that proved impossible, she braced herself for an explosion. None came. Frances sat quietly and listened without a single scandalized gasp. Heartened, Leigh kept talking, though she still looked at her mother periodically to make sure she hadn't fainted. "So, Lydie was going to call Maura and ask if there was anything they should do about the calls," she finished, out of breath.

Frances turned away and gazed out the window for a moment. "You'd better slow down. The driveway's right here," she said dully.

Leigh, who knew perfectly well where her aunt's driveway was, turned in with only a short skid.

"Do you know anything about Humphrey's childhood?" Frances asked thoughtfully.

"No, I don't think so," Leigh answered, not seeing the relevance. She parked the car and took out the grocery bag while her mother claimed the casserole dish. As they walked up to the front porch, they could just hear Chester yapping from somewhere inside the house. "None of it makes any sense," Leigh continued. "I don't understand who's making the calls, and why they're so upset about Humphrey. And that whole business with Noel trying to make the old people see a ghost—and Barbara thinking it was his voice on the phone. I just don't get it."

Frances opened Bess's door without knocking, then stepped aside for her daughter to go in first. "Well, I don't see why not," she said pompously. "I should think the answer would be obvious enough. Particularly to you."

Leigh stared at her mother in confusion, then

stepped inside her aunt's living room. Frances followed, closing the door behind them. They hadn't gone more than a few steps before they stopped in their tracks. Bess was up without her crutches, leaning against the far wall, looking very perturbed indeed.

Behind them in the other corner was Reginald Humphrey.

Chapter 23

At least, she thought it was Reginald Humphrey.

"Well, hello there," he said with a sneer. "Come on in, please. The more the merrier. I was just introducing myself to your friend the murderer here. Why don't you join her? Then we'll all introduce ourselves."

"Leave them out of it!" Bess demanded, her eyes frightened and furious at the same time. "They have nothing to do with the church."

Leigh couldn't move. She just stared. It was Humphrey—but then again, it wasn't. He had the same height, build, coloring, and facial features, true. But this man had a more distinct mask of freckles across his nose, and his green eyes didn't twinkle. They burned instead. Burned with hate.

Leigh let the grocery bag in her hands drift slowly to the floor, but neither she nor her mother moved, despite the most obvious difference between this man and Reginald Humphrey. The pastor had liked to carry a Bible; this man preferred a gun.

Both enjoyed waving them around. "Well, ladies?" he said impatiently, ignoring Bess's protests. "I said *move*."

Leigh was afraid to take her eyes off the man long enough to look at her mother, but her peripheral vision assured her that Frances was at least still standing. Chester, who had apparently been confined to the back porch, yapped fiercely. They hadn't seen Lydie when they came in. Where was she? Was she all right?

Leigh felt a firm tug on her coat sleeve. Frances was backing away from the man with the gun, but she wasn't taking the shortest route to Bess. She was heading straight along the front of the couch, and she was pulling Leigh with her.

"Hurry up," the man said impatiently. "My beef isn't with you dames. Unless you're on the executive board of the First Church of Half-Wit Suckers. Are you?"

Neither Leigh nor Frances responded. They just kept moving, slowly.

Leigh's mind raced. She had no idea why her mother was pulling on her. Had she totally lost her mind? Probably. Leigh should be the one doing the dragging. Frances should just go ahead and pass out. It would be easier on all of them.

"I can't believe you thought you'd get away with it," the man said to Bess, his eyes darting between the three of them. "Just because you're being blackmailed is no reason to kill a man. It's downright cowardly, if you ask me. Reggie was a good guy. He wouldn't have hurt anybody."

"For the thirteenth time," Bess said irritably, "nobody killed anybody. He died of an allergic reaction to his insulin. Call the detectives. They'll tell you." Bess's eyes glinted with anger even as her voice trembled. Two furious people, one gun. And one nutcase mother who was now pulling Leigh even farther away from Bess and toward the kitchen.

"I'm not calling anybody!" the man snarled. "You're lying. You poisoned him or something. And don't tell me that guy they arrested did the killing, because I ain't buying. Reggie said he was a hothead but gutless, and Reggie knew people. His only mistake was squeezing the guy in the first place. It only takes one loose cannon to spoil the show, you know."

Captive in the far corner, Bess stood up to the man's tirade with steely determination. Frances continued to pull her daughter slowly toward the kitchen, and Leigh started to resist. There was no way they could get all the way through the kitchen and to the porch without his noticing, and she didn't care to be shot as she ran away. Besides, they couldn't just leave Bess inside with him. What the heck was her mother thinking? And why couldn't they hear Lydie upstairs? Her car had been in the driveway when they arrived.

"You know what I think?" the man continued, waving the gun as he talked. "I think that loose cannon fired off into that god-awful pile of hair of yours. That's what I think. Bess Cogley is the ringleader of the board—that's what Reggie said. 'I've got to keep an eye on that one,' he said. You went snooping in his house, looking for something to turn the tables, didn't you? And when that didn't work, you decided to kill him. *My brother.*"

He made a noise with the gun that sounded like a click, and Leigh and Frances both froze. "What I want to know is, who helped you? I need to know who else to pay a call to. I'd hate to miss anybody."

Inexplicably, Frances waved her hands in the air. Leigh swatted them down, but it was too late. The man, who had been too wrapped up in his diatribe against Bess to pay much attention to their indirect course, trained the gun back on them. They were far enough away now that one step would bring them around the back corner to the powder room—and out of his line of sight.

A forceful, unexpected shove from Frances struck Leigh suddenly in the shoulder, and she careened sideways around the corner, barely able to keep her feet.

"Get back here!" the man screamed. Seeing no logical alternative, Leigh tried to comply. She had just got her head back around the corner when things started happening.

In retrospect, it was a comedy of errors, played in slow motion. But at the time it was terrifying. Anxious to pull both women back into his line of sight, the man had taken two steps toward Frances—along the wall behind the couch. It was the same wall that held Bess's antique secretary, and at that particular, fortuitous moment in time, it also held Punkster.

It happened with the man's second step. Noting a human form fully within range, the gray ball of fur leapt from his perch like a flying squirrel. His clawless front paws looped around his victim's neck while his fully loaded back feet took purchase in a shoulder and his teeth clamped soundly over an earlobe.

The man shouted, hands flying, and the gun dropped to the floor. Leigh watched it skid away and started forward to retrieve it. But no sooner had the gun hit the floor than Lydie emerged from the doorway to the staircase, bearing an electric sander. She swung it in the air with all her might, bringing it soundly into contact with the back of the man's head.

He fell to his knees, stunned. Annoyed at the unnecessary interference, Punkster leapt from the man's back and scuttled away with a fierce hiss.

Frances rushed to her twin's side, the casserole dish held high. But the man just rocked unsteadily on his knees, and Frances froze in place. Lydie, her own knees visibly shaking, stretched out a leg and kicked the gun under the couch. Leigh and Bess ran forward.

The man's eyes were squinting painfully as he alternated his gaze from Frances to Lydie. "Well, damn," he said dreamily. "There's two of you, too. Howdy, girls! Always nice to meet another set."

And with that, he crumpled.

The women did nothing but stare at him for a good five seconds. But when footsteps pounded on the porch and the front door opened suddenly, they jumped in unison. Maura Polanski moved quickly toward the object of their attention, her gun drawn.

Seeing the man unarmed and unconscious, she put the weapon away and stooped down. She examined him briefly, then stood up and told the uniformed officer behind her to call an ambulance.

Only then did Frances lower the casserole dish. "Is everybody else OK?" Maura asked with concern, looking them over. They nodded mutely in unison. "Did he have a gun with him?"

Lydie was the first to find her voice. "It's under the couch," she croaked.

Maura pushed the heavy piece of furniture to the side and swept up the pistol. Her expression was solemn, but Leigh sensed amusement brimming underneath. "You ladies mind telling me what happened here?"

The four women just looked at each other.

"You don't think I hurt him too badly, do you?" Lydie asked worriedly. They were all seated at the kitchen table, watching as the man they'd knocked cold was loaded onto a stretcher.

"The EMTs don't think anything's broken," Maura said assuringly. "Probably just a concussion. Don't beat yourself up about it. You did a good job getting that gun away from him safely."

"Thanks to Punkster," Bess said affectionately, stroking the contented gray ball on her lap. "And Francie, of course. I never knew you two were so close." She raised the limp cat's head to her sister's chin and rubbed.

"He was functional," Frances said tightly, pushing the cat away and brushing her shoulder. "Really, Bess. This sweater is angora."

Leigh sat mutely, holding Chester with both hands to prevent him from greeting all the uniformed officials milling about the living room. It was a task, but at least the yapping had stopped. Her brow furrowed as she continued to wonder why her mother hadn't fainted. The woman had actually kept her cool and used her head in a dangerous situation. It was spooky. Even more disturbing was the knowledge that she hadn't come up with a better plan herself.

"I wish I'd gotten here sooner," Maura said regretfully. "But Noel made a break for it."

"Noel?" Bess asked. "You arrested her too?"

Maura nodded. "She was sitting in her Monte Carlo a quarter mile down the road, waiting for Martin. When I pulled over, she took off, but the Franklin Park police cut her off up at Carmody's."

"What did you arrest her for?" Leigh asked, feeling like she had missed something. "And who's Martin?"

Maura pulled a notepad from her breast pocket. "An excellent question, Koslow. Who is Martin, indeed? Martin"—she tossed her head in the direction of the departing stretcher—"goes by many names. Most recently Martin Morford. He's also been—depending on the state of your choice—Marvin Rippin, Marcus Hauck, and Martin Shockley, among others. His real name is Martin Henson."

Leigh restated the obvious. "And he's Reginald Humphrey's identical twin," she said with disgust. Her mother had been right, curse it all. She should have at least suspected that Humphrey's stunt double was a twin. A twin switch was a heck of lot easier to pull off than a hologram—or a resurrection.

Maura nodded. "Those two have been pulling scams ever since they were in juvie. Got pretty creative with the twin thing, as you might imagine. Reggie was apparently the brains of the unit, though. Martin was more of a thug—he even did some hard time in the seventies for a botched robbery. He's wanted right now in Minnesota for assault with a deadly weapon. What happened today will make two."

Leigh looked at her friend with respect. "How do you know all this?"

"Databases are a wonderful thing, Koslow," she

smiled. "So is Ma Bell. Plus, we got a lucky break. Right after Noel split from her phony fund drive, I checked her out on the computer. Turns out originality isn't one of her strong points. She was arrested under the same name in Illinois about five years ago."

"Humphrey isn't her real name either, is it?" Bess asked, her eyes dancing. "And I bet she was never married to Reginald."

"She's really married, all right," Maura answered slyly, "but not to Reginald. Noel is Martin's wife."

Leigh's eyes widened. The wedding photo, at least, was explained. All Reginald had to do was prominently display a few of his brother's pics, and presto— he was both faithfully monogamous and taken. "A wife in absentia who was a missionary," she thought out loud, "it was perfect."

Maura nodded. "Reggie was good. I suspect he'd just about perfected the pastor scam. He'd probably been using the name Humphrey for almost a decade, but that alias isn't on the police database because he hasn't been in trouble. Evidently he's got everything worked out where his victims either don't realize they've been taken, or have a good reason not to report it."

Leigh's head snapped up. "You know about . . ." She paused a moment and glanced at Bess. "All that?"

Bess nodded, with just a touch of embarrassment. "I told her about the board's discussion—and their wishes—on the phone just a little while ago," she confessed with a sigh. "She already knew Reginald was a con."

"I only found out about him because I checked out Noel," Maura explained. "She was his biggest liability, as it turned out. She'd used the name Humphrey before—the three of them probably had a storehouse of phony credentials made up. The name was still good for him, and she picked it up whenever she chose to masquerade as his wife. But that was a dumb move, because her alias was still on the computer from the gig in Illinois, plus she's currently up on fraud charges in Florida under the name McKenna. Her real name is Noel Malbasa, and she's got a record a mile long. Mostly petty stuff, but a few felonies, and repeated occurrences of scams involving twin brothers—which is how I tracked down Martin's and Reginald's real names.

"It looks like Reginald's been working mostly by himself the last few years, but in this case he must have called in reinforcements. My guess is he realized that Ted Hugh was going to be a problem, and he needed help putting on some kind of endgame."

Bess sat up straight, looking pleased with herself. "He was going to fake a disappearance, wasn't he? That's what I said all along. The fire was just setting the stage for him to claim someone was trying to kill him, giving him an excuse to take off."

Maura nodded. "Seems likely. The last time Reginald was arrested was in 1987. He had started up an independent church in Sugar Land, Texas, then left claiming that a bunch of satanists had a contract out on him. The congregation contacted the authorities, and a detective tracked him down through the post office box where he'd asked them to send money. Reginald was there, happy as a clam, starting up a new church."

"Clever," Bess interjected. "But not clever enough. He got caught."

"That time he did," Maura continued. "But only because someone in the congregation got suspicious and called the police. From what you told me, Reginald had a lot of your church's most influential people completely under his thumb. They'd be afraid to ask for help for fear he'd make good on the blackmail threats. As long as everyone else still thought he was a saint, he could stage a few incidents, then flee for his life. Depending on how well the departure went—and how deep the police were digging into the supposed threats on his life—he could either cut and run, or continue to bleed the church for support underground. For all we know, he's got five other churches on a string right now."

Bess's eyes shot daggers at the thought. "But why bring Noel into it?" she said irritably. "It's obvious Humphrey was a talented con, but her skills were middling at best."

Maura shrugged. "Maybe her showing up in the flesh wasn't part of the plan. My guess is he needed to stage something that he couldn't be suspected of doing by himself, like having somebody take pot shots at him. Noel and Martin could handle that easily enough without being seen. But he was probably already dead when they got here. Maybe they got worried when he didn't show up where he was supposed to be, and they decided to send Noel in to find out what the problem was."

"That first time she walked into the church," Leigh said, remembering. "I told her he was dead, and she fainted."

"I still think that was all put on," Bess insisted. "She probably just thought he'd gone ahead of plan and faked his death. The next day when we mentioned the body—that's when she knew."

"If that's true, they didn't waste any time capitalizing on it," Maura remarked. "They saw money in the congregation and cooked up a fast scam."

"Complete with posthumous endorsements from the good reverend himself," Bess said sarcastically. "That would never have worked, by the way. The congregation isn't that stupid. No wonder those two chose Reuben and Evelyn as their victims. Reginald probably told them that Reuben was a legitimate ally—and feeble-minded and loaded, to boot."

"And Noel was at the church yesterday when Evelyn stormed in and announced that Reggie's ghost wanted vengeance," Leigh remembered with a sigh. "That's probably what gave them the idea in the first place."

"They could have used some of the lights and other equipment from the mini-storage," Bess postulated.

Leigh nodded. "Noel was aware of the mini-storage already. Reginald even arranged for her to have access to it. Maybe he was storing stuff for them too, as much as they were in and out of jail." An image of the box marked MH floated across her mind, followed closely by the old black-and-white, boot-camp photograph that had started it all. She had been right in her original assessment—Reginald *didn't* recognize the nicknames of those particular recruits at Fort Jackson. But it was a safe bet that the real freckled youth—Martin "Money" Henson—would have.

Maura's eyebrows arched. "Mini-storage?"

Leigh swallowed and threw a glance at her aunt, who widened her eyes meaningfully. Had Bess mentioned the mini-storage fiascos already? Since Leigh did not remember having been strangled to death, she assumed not.

"We . . ." she began tentatively, avoiding Maura's eyes. "We found out Humphrey—I mean, Henson—had been renting a mini-storage unit. But Noel cleaned the place out already. The manager told me."

Bess smiled at Leigh approvingly. Maura just glared at her, as did Frances. Luckily, Lydie was the first to speak. "Well, I'm just glad it's over." She turned to the detective with a grateful smile. "Thank goodness you got here when you did. If Francie had used that casserole dish on Martin, I do think it would have done him in."

"Oh, foot," Frances muttered suddenly, getting up from the table. "I completely forgot about the casserole. It'll have to go back in the oven. . . ."

"How exactly did you know to come?" Lydie continued to Maura. "I dialed 911 when I heard Martin yelling downstairs, but I didn't think to mention your name."

Maura shook her head. "I headed over right after Bess told me she'd been getting threatening calls from a man, because I was worried about Martin's rap sheet. When I spotted Noel's car I called for backup, but the uniformed officers you called were right behind me." She paused, then smiled. "I wish I'd gotten here ten minutes sooner, but then, you ladies seem quite capable of fending for yourselves."

Lydie blushed, and Frances fussed with the oven settings. Bess threw back her shoulders and grinned proudly. Leigh just felt like an idiot.

"Now if you'll excuse me, there are a few things I need to do," Maura said politely, folding up her notebook and rising from the table. Leigh accompanied the detective to the door with trepidation. She expected more questions about the mini-storage, but none came. Maybe it wasn't that important. At least not the part about her having broken into it with a stolen key. Twice.

"The business about Humph—I mean, Henson being a con artist," she asked Maura in a low voice. "I guess Bess told you how strongly she feels about that not getting out."

"She shared that, yes," the detective said with a knowing smile. "I told her that the department isn't in the habit of keeping secrets. But then, we don't have any need to broadcast Reginald Henson's criminal record either. He's dead, and no one's been complaining about his behavior recently. That case is closed."

Leigh exhaled with relief. "What about Noel and Martin?"

"Noel's being extradited—she's not up on any charges here. As for Martin, Bess had better level with her friends about him. He's going to trial for assault."

Leigh wondered briefly if Bess could make up a convincing story about how the wonderful, honest reverend had been duped by both the woman he loved and his own evil twin.

Sure she could.

Maura started to leave, but Leigh stopped her. In addition to feeling worthless in a crisis, she also felt guilty again. "Um, Maura," she began.

"Yes?"

"I haven't told you everything I know, I mean, that I did know, when all this was going on. Bess and I found out things about Reginald—like the ministorage—that we didn't tell anybody. But we really didn't think it would affect Warren's uncle, and Bess was so concerned about the church falling apart—"

Amazingly, Maura waved the apology away. "Don't sweat it, Koslow. All's well that ends well. You tipped me off about Noel's little mission scam, didn't you?"

Leigh noticed the jaunty look that had returned to her friend's eyes, and smiled. It was about time. "The homicide detectives," she began, suddenly understanding. "They've been investigating Reginald Henson's death and the First Church of the New Millennium for days. But they closed the case without ever figuring out they were dealing with a veteran con artist running a blackmail scam. Or that the widow who so easily avoided them was actually a convicted felon on the lam."

"Yep," Maura answered, grinning broadly. "They sure did."

Chapter 24

Leigh didn't stick around for the casserole. Once the official questioning was over, she headed straight for her Cavalier. She needed to clear her head. It was time to go home.

Her brain was mush. She could have sat at Bess's kitchen table all night, staring at the walls and trying to make sense of everything that had happened. But that would mean contemplating the fact that her life might well have been saved by her mother, her aunt, a psycho cat, and an electric sander, and she really wasn't up to that.

Besides, her father had been on his way over, and he had sounded unusually rattled on the phone. Given Frances's bizarre burst of competence, if he showed up as anything less than unflappable, she would be lost in a permanent Twilight Zone.

She pulled the Cavalier into her apartment lot and felt a gush of comfort at the sight of Warren's VW. *Home at last.* She parked, entered the building, and took the two flights of stairs at a run, then stopped suddenly at his door—hand poised.

Katharine's advice of earlier in afternoon drifted back to her. *Why don't you go find Warren? You two need to talk.*

She had suspected the two of them had made some decision about their relationship. They'd seemed so intense lately—maybe that was why. Maybe they had decided to get married.

She thought about it for only a moment, then decided she didn't care. Maybe the fact that her brain was mush had something to do with it, and maybe it didn't. Maybe she had been thinking too much all along.

She knocked on the door.

Maybe he was in love with Katharine. Maybe they were already engaged. But unless they'd already eloped, it didn't matter. Warren was going to know how she really felt, and that was that. If she made a fool out of herself, fine. Today was the perfect day for it.

The door opened, and Warren offered her a tired smile. "Hey, Leigh. Come on in." She didn't think it possible, but he looked even worse than he had last night. His hair was mussed, his shoulders sagged, and his eyes had bags she had never seen before.

"Are you OK?" she asked worriedly, walking in. "Is Shannon all right?"

He looked at her curiously. "I guess you talked to Katharine, then."

"Briefly," Leigh said quickly, not wanting to talk about Katharine. "Did something happen with Ted?"

Warren smiled feebly. "You could say that. He was so sick with worry over Shannon that he totally lost it. Yelling at the doctors and nurses, refusing to let anyone take her blood. At one point I thought I had him calm enough that I could slip out to the cafeteria for a sandwich, but when I got back, security was throwing him out of the building."

Leigh winced. "That must have been awful."

"I've had better Saturday afternoons," he said with another halfhearted smile. "But Shannon's condition isn't serious this time; that's the main thing. She'll probably be released tomorrow, and Ted is home for the night, so I'm clear for at least eight hours." He took a deep breath and looked at her, then seemed concerned.

"Has something been happening with you? I assumed everything would settle down at the church now that everyone knows Humphrey died of natural causes."

Having no desire to rehash the last twelve hours of her life just yet, Leigh changed the subject. "I have a feeling the church will do just fine. As for my day, it's been eventful, but we'll talk about all that later. First, I want to know how your dad is doing."

This time he smiled for real. "He's much better. He went home from the hospital today. As soon as he can travel, my mother is bound and determined to fly back and give Joy and Tim a proper welcome-home party."

"That's good to hear," Leigh said sincerely. She paused a moment. "So does this mean that you're almost off duty as local guardian of the extended Harmon family?"

He grinned tiredly. "I don't mind really, but I have fallen behind on my real job. I need to work tonight, in fact." His eyes rested on a stack of papers on the bar, and he started sorting through them idly. Then he turned around suddenly, as if remembering something. "You said you wanted to talk to me?"

Leigh froze for a moment. She didn't do well head-on. Approaching from the rear was much more preferable. "When I saw Katharine at the church," she began, planning her strategy as she went, "she said she thought we needed to talk about something."

Warren looked mildly annoyed. "She did, did she? What else did she say?"

Leigh blinked, not understanding his reaction. "Nothing. Why?"

He turned back to his papers again. After a moment he spoke softly, still facing away from her. "Leigh, if you really want to know what's been going on between Katharine and me, I'll tell you."

She didn't say anything. She didn't dare, or he might stop talking.

"Despite all the high drama surrounding the wedding, we both had a wonderful time being part of it," he began. "And it started us talking about marriage."

He paused, still not looking at her. She was afraid to breathe.

"Long story short, we have a lot of respect for each other, but the relationship is over."

Her heart made a little leap inside her chest. She should let it go at that. She knew she should. But she couldn't. Her jaws just started flapping.

"Katharine didn't want to raise a family, did she?" she asked breathlessly.

The question was impertinent, to be sure, but Warren seemed more amused than surprised by it. "Well, I guess you read her better than I did. No, she doesn't. But that wasn't the real issue."

He was still facing away from her, fiddling with the stack of papers. Perhaps he didn't want her to see how hurt he really was. "What *was* the real issue?" she asked apprehensively.

He didn't hesitate with his answer, but he didn't turn around either. "I'm not in the habit of marrying women I'm not in love with."

Leigh's last bit of resistance melted at the words, and before she even realized what she was doing, she stepped up behind him and wrapped her arms around his waist.

He turned around quickly, as though she had stung him. They had always been affectionate pals, but her touch this time was different. She looked in his eyes to see if he had noticed, but all they registered was confusion. She took a deep breath. It was now or never—and never wasn't acceptable.

"Warren," she began, "I have to tell you something. I'm sorry it took me so damn long to figure it out, but—" She wavered, but only for a millisecond. "I

love you. And I don't just mean as a friend. I really
do love you.''

He didn't move, but his eyes flooded with a mixture
of emotions she couldn't interpret. "I want you to be
happy," she continued quickly, "and I didn't want to
mess up your relationship with Katharine if that's
what you really wanted, but I couldn't just stand by
anymore and watch you with another woman in your
arms—it was making me crazy."

Warren still said nothing. His eyes remained fixed
on hers, but the only feeling she could identify in them
was shock. In fact, she was pretty sure his arms, which
were resting loosely on her shoulders, were trembling
almost as much as hers were.

"I just thought you should know," she said quickly,
turning her eyes away. "If you don't feel the same
way about me, I'll under—"

She never finished the sentence, because he kissed
her. One arm pulled her in close, the other came up
to cradle her head as their lips touched. Leigh had
been kissed plenty of times, but the feelings that
flowed through her now were indescribable. Warren
loved her, all right. He was saying it in a million ways,
from the softness of his caress to the earnestness of
his kiss, and, as he finally came up for air, with his
beautiful deep voice.

"I've loved you since I was eighteen years old," he
said softly, still holding her close. "But I'd given up
on you. *Repeatedly*."

Leigh smiled, then shook her head. "I've been such
an idiot. I'm sorry." She burrowed her head into his
shoulder. It felt nice. "I wanted to say something
weeks ago, but I was afraid you were falling in love
with Katharine, and I didn't want to mess up your life
any more."

Warren pulled her head back and kissed her again.
"I'll confess, I did notice that you were looking at me
differently. But you were also avoiding me, and you

kept sending mixed signals. I wasn't sure if—well, I thought maybe you just wanted what you thought you couldn't have."

Leigh shook her head vehemently. "I'm not playing games, Warren." She ran her hand over his cheek and through his wavy brown hair, and realized she had been wanting to do that for a long time.

It wasn't the only thing she had been wanting to do for a long time, she thought deviously. "But I should warn you," she continued with a smirk, "a woman like me comes with *serious, major* strings attached. I want kids, dogs, a minivan, retirement—the works. Can you deal with that, Harmon?"

He laughed out loud, then wrapped his arms around her tightly. "Just try me."

Epilogue

Two weeks later

The woman stood at her kitchen window, looking idly out at the blackness beyond. She supposed she should feel better now that the worst was behind her, but she didn't. And she wouldn't.

She was glad that her loved ones were safe, and she was glad that the church would survive. That's all she had wanted. But she herself could never be truly happy. Not when she had taken a life.

She had known, that horrible night so many years ago, that she would never be truly happy again. The memory was as clear now as ever. All she had to do was close her eyes, and there she was—again. Standing on that empty road, looking down at those two lifeless bodies, knowing her life was over.

That day had started off like any other. She had her learner's permit, her father's rusted-up Ford, and an attitude that only adolescence can produce. Her boyfriend had a new apartment, and she had wanted to go there. He was too old for her, but no one in her family was concerned with such things. Her parents were deeply in debt and fighting all the time; her brothers disappeared for days. No one would even notice if the Ford disappeared for a few hours.

She had made it to the apartment just fine. Unfortunately, her boyfriend had not been alone when she had gotten there. She had stumbled back out to the

Ford and taken to the road—and that had been a big mistake. The gas pedal had seemed her only therapy; speed the catharsis for her grief and rage. She had seen the two boys walking along the shoulder, there was no doubt about that. She saw them long before she entered the bend. But she had been going too fast, she had practiced driving too little, and she turned the wheel too late. The car skidded, and she panicked.

It would have been easier to explain if it was night, but it wasn't. If the road was icy or even wet, but it wasn't. There was no good excuse. When the car finally settled to a stop she simply got out, unhurt, and went to look for the boys. They weren't standing anymore. They just lay there, both of them, unmoving. Their eyes open, seeing nothing.

She would never have deserted them. That was one point she didn't torture herself with. She had checked their pulses, but she knew she wouldn't find any. No one else was in sight. No car. No people outside. Just a few houses a half mile or so away.

She had no idea how long she stood there, looking from them to the horizon, wishing for someone else to make a decision for her. She could walk to the nearest house and look for a phone. She could call an ambulance. She could call the police. But then what?

She knew what. She would go to jail. For all of her youth, maybe all of her life. She would rot and die there. There would be nothing left for her, nothing. And it wouldn't help the boys either. It wouldn't bring them back. No good could possibly come of it.

She remembered sitting down then, sinking to her knees beside the older boy. He looked about sixteen. The younger one, maybe thirteen. There had to be something she could do for them. If it took the rest of her life, she was going to try to make it up to them. But she couldn't do that if she died in jail.

So she had left. Walked away from the bodies, into the Ford, and left. Then she had gone quietly home, cleaned up the car with a wash rag, and waited. The horrendous hit-and-run crime was the talk of the county for weeks, but no one ever came to get her. The Ford had so many dents in it already that not even her father noticed the new ones. No one had seen the accident. And no one saw her driving again. Not for years.

Even now she drove only when she absolutely had to. And she never took any chances. Life was just too precious.

No one could accuse her of not keeping her promise to the boys. She had done nothing but work ever since that day, and every scrap of money she could spare went to their parents. Sometimes she sent flowers and gifts, but mostly cash. Always from a different place— she was very careful about that. But she didn't think the families were looking for her anymore. Not since the letters. It had taken her years to get the courage, but she had finally confessed.

Anonymously, of course. She told the families that she would never, ever have left their sons to die if they had still been alive. And she made the promise to them that she had made to herself—that she would spend the rest of her life making up for her horrible mistake. Not that she expected her crime would go unpunished. She knew that someday she would have to deal with God's justice. But she would rather leave her fate in His hands than that of the state. Nothing on the other side could be as bad as going to prison. Shut away from the sun and the flowers, forced to spend idle hours with truly horrible, soulless people. Unable to do anything good for anybody. Unable to atone. No, she couldn't bear it.

And that's why she had to do this too. At first she had been so excited. Reginald Humphrey seemed able to see straight to her soul—and speak right to her heart. He could tell how burdened she was. He could see the weight of guilt that dragged down her every breath. And he seemed to want to help. He did help. He convinced her that sharing her deepest, darkest secret would set her free. That she could start to live again. That God would forgive her if she could learn to forgive herself.

He might have been right about that. From the moment she told him her story, her heart did feel lighter. And she began to truly believe that maybe, just maybe, she wouldn't burn in the Hell her father had told her about. Her whole world seemed brighter.

Then it had all gone dark again. She had volunteered to work in the church office, knowing her bookkeeping skills were sorely needed. She didn't understand how badly until the day she had managed to wrest the books from Reginald Humphrey's care.

It was then that the disillusionment had begun. He was stealing—stealing from everybody. She understood then why he resisted a formal pledging system, why he preferred a collection plate full of cash. He was embezzling. A little here, a little there. But given the relatively small size of the church, not a fortune anywhere.

She couldn't understand it. He took home a decent salary, and the money he stole wasn't making him much richer. But when she confronted him with the evidence, she began to understand that it wasn't money that drove him. It was power.

And power was what he had, in spades. He had respect; he even had hero worship. Ironically enough, he was an excellent preacher. And to members like Reuben, he could even appear to be a good friend. But when the opportunity arose, he couldn't resist taking that next horrible step. She watched helplessly as one by one, people began to fall under his thumb. Betty, Sam, Merry. He targeted the board members, yes, but he was happy to fry any fish that happened into his net. No sooner did a church member lose the sparkle in their eyes than they found themselves recommended for a position on the board. And then he threatened them into playing by his rules, just as he had threatened her.

She was to doctor the books, not noticing how much cash disappeared between the plate and the bank. She wasn't to question the funds that were going out to "missions," or the inflated cost estimates for designated gift projects. She was to do her job with a smile and not ask pesky questions. If she didn't, she would go to jail.

She often wondered if that would be the better hell for her. Better than sitting by and watching all the people she cared about be swindled—or even worse, be blackmailed just like her. But her going to jail wouldn't help the others. He could still ruin them too.

Then the awful day had come. The day her husband had come home from church with the sparkle gone from his own eye. She had wanted to die then. She didn't know what horrible secret he had just confessed, and she didn't want to know. She didn't care. He was the best thing that had ever happened to her, and there was nothing he could have done that she wouldn't forgive. And she couldn't let him suffer the way she had been suffering.

Humphrey had to die. It was the only way. As long as he was alive, none of their secrets were safe. Even if she could somehow force him to leave the church and leave them alone, he would only pull the same scam somewhere else. But if he was dead, the secrets would die with him. And if she was careful, most of her friends would never know they'd been had.

The more she had thought about it, the more sense it made. Murder was a sin—she knew that. And unlike the last time she had killed, this would be premeditated. If there was a Hell, she had no doubt she would burn. But that was a risk she was willing to take. Her soul was damned anyway, better she should shoulder the responsibility than someone else.

She had planned very carefully. And her years in various doctor's offices had proved quite helpful. When she saw the padded brown envelope in the church's mailbox, she knew exactly what it was. Reginald Humphrey had been seeing an allergist. It was her idea, in fact. From back when she had cared. He was terribly afraid of bees—he had almost died once from a sting, he claimed. So she had told him about hyposensitization. When she had worked in the allergist's office she had seen several patients with bee allergies come in for their injections. They started off with a very tiny dose of bee venom, then got a little more each time. Eventually, their bodies were taught not to respond. It would take time, but he could finally beat the curse and get over his fear.

She had talked him into it, and he was pleased. And when she held the envelope with his next vial of bee venom firmly in her hands, she was pleased too.

Because she knew how she could do it. She wouldn't even have to inject the stuff. He would do that himself.

She held onto the envelope and waited. He had to be almost done with his current insulin bottle, and she had to have access to the spare. When the parsonage burned, everything seemed to come together.

She knew the boardinghouse where he was staying. He had left her an address and phone number, and she had been careful not to share it with anyone else. She had even lifted and copied his key. He could die quietly there, and she could cover her tracks before anyone else knew he was dead. The fact that it would happen before Joy's wedding was regrettable. But she didn't feel she had any choice. His insulin bottle had been almost empty, and if he started the new one, her plan wouldn't work. She had to go for the first opportunity she had, because the next one could be a while.

At the rehearsal dinner, she had her chance. Humphrey had excused himself to the men's room before the meal was served, undoubtedly to give himself a shot. After they had eaten, he had gotten up to schmooze and left his kit on his chair. She worked fast. All she needed was his insulin bottle. She slipped it out and excused herself to the rest room. Using a syringe she had filched long ago from the waste can in his office, she carefully suctioned the small amount of remaining insulin out of the bottle and forced it into the vial of powdered bee venom. She had watched the nurses in the allergist's office dilute the venom with a larger, carefully measured volume of solution, but she wanted to concentrate it as much as she possibly could. Death would not only be more likely, but also quicker and less painful. She hated the man, it was true, but she still didn't want him to suffer. Once the powder had dissolved, she transferred the mixture back into the insulin bottle, relieved that the color remained clear. Humphrey would have no idea.

Replacing the bottle in the kit had been no problem. The problem had come later. She had expected him to go home after the rehearsal, to take his last dose of insulin right before bed, or first thing the next morning. But no, the glutton had stayed late in his office. And not only that, but thanks to a donation from the youth in Fellowship Hall, he had had pizza and donuts at his desk. Humphrey had given himself another insulin shot and dropped dead right there at the church. *The night before Joy's wedding.*

She had come close to panicking then. It was sheer luck that she found him first, curled up on the floor, his hands at his throat. She hated herself at that moment, but she knew what she had to do. Pulling on her driving gloves, she switched the insulin bottle on the floor with the extra one he kept in his office refrigerator. The old bottle, the syringe he used, and the new bottle's packaging all went into her purse. Pulling another old syringe from the wastebasket, she drew up a few doses out of the new insulin bottle and squirted them into her purse too. Then she left the syringe on the floor where the other had fallen.

It would ruin the wedding, and she felt badly about that. But there was nothing she could do. She had waited anxiously the rest of the evening for someone else to find Humphrey dead. But no one did.

No one until Ted. She sighed, then turned from the kitchen window to listen to the sounds of ESPN emanating from the family room. Her husband was home safe, and that was all that mattered now.

She wouldn't have let him go to prison. Not ever. She would readily have agreed to spend the rest of her life behind bars in order to spare him, and she had been ready to confess several times. But she had kept her head, because she knew the truth would hurt Ted more than her silence. If she ever confessed to poisoning Humphrey, no jury in the world would believe they hadn't done it together.

But they hadn't, of course. Ted had no idea what had really happened. And now it looked like no one else ever would either. She didn't know that much about forensics, but she did know that bee venom isn't something toxicologists screen for. It wouldn't be found unless they knew to look for it. And why on earth would they—in the middle of a Pittsburgh winter?

Ted would be proven innocent. She had been sure of that. And she was right.

So all was well. Joy and Tim had come back glowing with contentment, learning of Ted's ordeal only when it was safely in the past. The Harmons had thrown a fabulous welcome-home party for the newlyweds, with W. Jim Harmon II looking fit as a fiddle. And she had never seen Warren look happier. He and Bess's niece made such a lovely couple.

It was a happy ending all around. Noel and Humphrey's noxious brother were taken care of, and

Reginald Humphrey himself would never swindle, manipulate, or blackmail anyone ever again. Most of the people in the congregation would never know what an evil person their founder really was, and they'd be better off that way. Bess had convinced the board to hire her pastor friend, and the church would soon be building steam again—this time legitimately. As for herself, she would redouble her efforts with the volunteerism. Maybe even convince Ted to give some money to a real African mission. There were lots of things she wanted to do.

"Honey?" Ted said from the doorway. "You coming back? I'm getting lonely in here."

She smiled, turned out the kitchen light, and walked into his outstretched arms. She had made a promise to those two boys on the road. And she was going to keep it. As for the fate of her soul, she'd just have to wait and see.